ADVENTURES
ON THE ROAD TO ME

K.D. Van Brunt

www.BOROUGHSPUBLISHINGGROUP.com

ADVENTURES ON THE ROAD TO ME
Copyright © 2021 K.D. Van Brunt

ISBN: 978-1-953810-71-7

To those who need a little redemption

ADVENTURES
ON THE ROAD TO ME

CHAPTER ONE

"Go wander around inside the store," Mom tells me. "Stick to the script. Stay visible. I'll be at the jewelry counter at one-fifteen sharp."

"I know the drill, Mom." I roll my eyes, making sure she sees my display, and walk away from our Camaro convertible we parked in a garage at a mall in Beverly Hills. I cover ten yards before she speaks again.

"West."

"What?" The impatience in my voice is obvious.

"*Urmați soare.*"

This makes me smile. It's the Romanian phrase she tells me every time when we separate during a game. It means "follow the sun."

"*Mă duc unde duce,*" I answer, pressing two fingers to my lips before gesturing at her with them. "I go where it leads." It's our traditional response.

As I walk toward the entrance to Macy's, I resist the urge to pull up my saggy jeans. Instead, I let them droop even farther until my butt is basically hanging out in back, way over-exposing my red silk boxers. Fortunately, my oversize LA Lakers hoodie covers a good part of my backside. With a jerk on the strap, I adjust the position of the backpack on my shoulder.

Most days I'm a seventeen-year-old girl named West—Westlyn, actually. A girl you might pass on the street and not even glance twice at. But today, I'm a guy. And I look like a gangsta, with my straight-billed Dodger cap and tattoos on my hands. The words "*abrazar la muerte*"—embrace death—scrawl in green cursive script across my right hand. The head of a *chupacabra* is on my left. I've never seen one, so I had to take the woman's word that this fanged monster head was spot-on. It doesn't matter. The ink is temporary.

Meanwhile, my head itches to the point of distraction, but I force myself to ignore it. Gangstas don't have scalp conditions. At least, not in the movies I've seen. My hair is tucked into a black-haired wig and the locks hang to my shoulders. The thing feels like it's full of bugs trying to burrow into my scalp. I may feel like crap, but I look like a seriously badass member of MS-13.

Cultural appropriation, baby.

The most uncomfortable thing about my get-up, though, isn't the wig. It's the black chest binder squeezing my chest. Under the baggy hoodie, I look as flat as… Well, as a guy with Tarzan pecs.

The moment I enter the store, my movements attract the attention of a man in a navy-blue suit and a crimson tie. He's a store detective, or what they call in the biz a "loss prevention agent." He trails after me as I wander through the menswear section, exactly as I intended. He's supposed to be covert, but Mom and I can spot these dudes a mile away. We call them straws because they suck at what they do.

I begin our game in earnest by browsing through the women's lingerie section, studying the price tags. A sheer baby-doll chemise goes for twelve hundred bucks.

My original straw hands me off to a new straw—he's maybe thirty, lean, blond, and seriously intense. I'm careful not to do anything to trigger a confrontation, but I engage in enough questionable browsing to raise suspicions. The fact that I have a backpack has already raised their alertness level to DEFCON 2, so I have to be careful.

I wander over to the men's cologne area and pick up a bottle with a $375 price tag and inhale a sniff of the strong, musky smell of the sample, unable to stop my nose from crinkling in disgust. It smells like a guy's sweaty armpit with a slathering of menthol—or what I'd imagine the smell to be.

The straw edges closer to me, but I quickly replace the bottle on the shelf and move on, careful to keep my hands away from my pockets and hoodie. I need to play him enough to make him suspicious, but not enough to get frisked and tossed out of the store. By the time the appointed hour arrives, three straws are orbiting around me like satellites around a planet.

Feigning obliviousness to my entourage, I stroll over to the high-end jewelry section of the store, gazing intensely at the watches and gold bracelets. The straws begin to mutter frantically into their palm mics, no doubt spreading the word: Hispanic gang guy has been spotted in the bling section. Prepare for a smash and grab.

Perfect. I need all eyes on me.

The woman behind the jewelry counter scowls in my direction before shooting a surreptitious glance at blond straw guy, making sure he's aware someone like me is defiling her workspace. According to her name tag, she's Beth.

Time to draw Beth into the game.

I make my way over to a display of tennis bracelets where I spend a few minutes studying them.

"Yo, Barbie," I say to Beth in a low, growly voice. "How much is dis one?"

Disgust flits across her face, and she answers in a barely civil voice. "Eight hundred seventy-five dollars."

"All dat for dis little ding?"

She raises one perfect eyebrow. "Yes, all *that* for *this* little *thing*."

"Hmm." Nodding appreciatively, I move on to study the watches for a while, occasionally asking prices, trying to sell myself as a low-life juvenile delinquent capable of anything. I squat to catch a closer look at a watch when Mom arrives. She's dressed in a stunning, green silk Givenchy dress and a cream sunhat. She's wearing an emerald bracelet and three diamond rings on her fingers. The rocks are all fake, of course, but you'd need a jeweler's loupe to know it. She's carrying several Macy's bags, as if she's already spent a ton of cash here, and the blonde wig she's wearing is perfect.

Acting supremely unaware of my presence, Mom places her faux designer handbag on top of the glass display case I'm leaning against.

"I'm interested in a necklace for my mother for her birthday," Mom tells Beth.

I have to hold back the urge to giggle at her fake, elite white woman accent.

Their conversation quickly becomes animated, since it turns out Beth also has a mother with a birthday this month. Gradually, Mom and Beth move away from me toward the necklaces in the display cases, which I have avoided as per the plan. Leaving her bag behind on the counter nearby, Mom has an unending stream of questions about diamonds and garnets, and rose gold versus white gold.

After several minutes of chatter, I pick up Mom's purse from the counter and walk it over to her. Two of the straws flinch, poised to tackle me if I try to run, but I keep my gait slow and casual.

"Here, ma'am," I say, holding her purse out to her. "Shouldn't leave dis lying around."

Mom gazes down her nose at me, and the pungent sweetness of her perfume washes my way. She shoots me a perfect glare of haughty disdain before dismissively grabbing her purse. I back away, smile, and head for the bathroom, weaving my way through the crowds of shoppers clogging the aisles—the store is packed this afternoon. Two of the straws immediately peel off and follow me, taking up a position outside the hallway leading to the restrooms. I figure they'll at least let me pee before giving me a two-man escort out of the store.

Once I'm out of sight in the long corridor, I whip off my wig, letting my hair cascade down. I give it a shake and head into the ladies' room. Inside one of the stalls, I slither out of my jeans, hoodie, and boxers, grateful to unwrap the boa constrictor binder from around my bra. From inside my backpack, I pull out a pair of skinny jeans, a tangerine-colored sleeveless shirt, and a pair of off-white flats. I dress quickly and vigorously scrub off my tattoos. After a minute of primping in front of the mirror, I look the part of a spoiled white girl from one of the nearby swanky neighborhoods.

Cultural appropriation, baby.

On my way out of the bathroom, I deposit my gang gear and cheap backpack in the lavatory trash bin, jamming them down deep under wads of wet paper towels. Disgusting. Eventually, Macy's will figure out what I've done, but by then we'll be long gone and good luck finding us.

The two straws who followed me have advanced down the restroom corridor and are milling about outside the men's room, looking grim and ready to burst through the door after my alter ego. They are totally oblivious as I exit the ladies' room, stroll past them, and disappear into the crowd of shoppers on my way to the jewelry counter.

"Hi, Mom," I say, coming up alongside her. "Are you almost done? I'm really hungry."

"Ten minutes, dear," she replies. "I've narrowed it down to three possibilities." Mom points quickly to several necklaces in the display case, tapping the glass several times with her long fingernail.

"They all look the same," I say with a shrug.

"Beth, would you mind bringing them out again so I can show my daughter."

"Not at all, Mrs. Finnegan."

The necklaces are draped around beige necklace display busts, each piece containing a dazzling array of diamonds. One has a pendant with an emerald the size of a large almond.

Impressive. Mom does have a good eye.

"I'm going to take the middle one." Mom reaches into her purse for her wallet and lets out a spine-tingling shriek. "Someone *stole* my wallet. *It's gone.*"

"That punk stole it," Beth says with a gasp.

The final stage of the game is now under way. There are no time-outs, no do-overs. As always, my belly flutters with a mixture of adrenaline and panic. This is where I do my thing. I'm nervous, but confident. I've been doing this for a really long time.

First, though, I need to make sure Beth completely buys into the scam, so I snatch Mom's purse, paw through it, and shake my head at Mom and then at Beth, thus confirming the missing wallet. This seals the deal.

"That kid swiped her wallet," Beth yells at the straw approaching us.

"The little bastard," Mom cries out, nearly drowning in fake tears. Leaving her purse behind on the counter again, she strides furiously toward the store entrance, as if in pursuit of the pond scum.

The straw guy blurts out, "Hold on, the kid is still in the bathroom," and dashes off in that direction to join his compadres.

"Mrs. Finnegan," Beth cries. "*Wait.*" She grabs Mom's purse and sprints after her, jogging ten steps down the aisle to continue hailing Mom. Beth is totally distracted. Sucker.

Amid this scene of complete chaos, with all eyes now focused on my uber distraught mother and the imaginary thief in the men's bathroom, my fingers reach for the necklaces Beth left on the counter but begin to tremble halfway there.

Stop it, I tell myself. *You can't hesitate.*

Gritting my teeth, I plunge ahead and deftly slip each necklace off its display, slide them into my front pocket, and then calmly walk away.

Just as I push through the rear exit fifteen seconds later, a distant, strangled cry erupts from Beth. "Oh my God."

Walking quickly, but not running, I cross La Cienega and lose myself in the crowd along Beverly Boulevard. It takes only a few minutes to reach the Taco Bell we pinpointed earlier as our meetup spot. I order several burritos to go to give Mom time to get out of her getup, find the car, and meet me out back. Bag of food in hand, I step out the back door, and Mom is already waiting for me in our rental Camaro. I hop inside, and we shoot down Santa Monica Boulevard until we hook up with the Pacific Coast Highway, and then head north to the Bay Area.

"West—" Mom nods approvingly. "—you rock."

I adopt my best Elvis voice and reply, "Thank you. Thank you very much."

Just another day at the office for Mom and me.

CHAPTER TWO

After an hour in the hotel bathroom, I emerge towel-drying my newly dyed, chestnut brown hair. It's my natural color, but I'd dyed it blonde for our two-week tour of Southern California jewelry stores. Tonight, we're holed up in the Four Seasons Hotel in San Francisco before we leave the state tomorrow morning.

We checked in under Diana and Westlyn Banica, our "clean" identities—the ones we use for everything but stealing. They're also the names we use for all of our bank accounts, credit cards, and driver licenses. The key to a long criminal life, Mom says, is to scrupulously keep the "bad you" segregated from the "good you."

"Passable," Mom says, when she sees my wet hair.

"I guess I'm done being a blonde for a while."

"At least six months," she agrees. "Tomorrow, we get your hair cut short. They'll be searching for a blonde girl with long hair."

She hands me a contact lens case, ignoring the scowl erupting on my face. I *hate* these things.

"In case someone noticed your brown eyes, they're going to be blue for the next month."

"Can't I have green eyes again?" We have colored contacts in seven shades. I look phenomenal in green.

"This isn't a negotiation. Just do it."

I nod reluctantly. Pictures of us from surveillance cameras are probably circulating among the police all over the state—the price of success. However, those pictures show two blonde women who look nothing like us, at least not anymore.

Since we blew into LA, we rolled five stores. The only misfire was a Zales in San Diego. We tried to distract the clerk with Mom feigning an asthma attack and needing her inhaler from the car, but she didn't sell it well enough, and the clerk never took her eyes off me.

"Did you get rid of the car?" I ask.

"All gone. We'll get a new one tomorrow." Her voice is a little wistful. Both of us loved tooling around in the Camaro, basking under the occasional May sun with the top down, wearing our designer sunglasses. "Tomorrow we fly to Chicago to meet with Chin."

Yuck. I hate Chicago, and I *really* hate Mr. Chin. He's got skin like a lizard and even speaks with a hissing sound. But he is our best buyer—fence, actually—so I have to shake his hand and let him kiss me on the cheek every time we meet in his swank shop on Jewelers Row off Wabash.

Sucking in a deep breath, I remind myself it's only a couple more months before we knock off for August and head to Florida to chill.

I grab my caramel-colored, leather messenger bag off the bed to get out my laptop. Some of its contents tumble onto the floor at Mom's feet, including my Kindle. A couple beats of silence descend on the room. Mom stares at the device and then at me.

Oopsie. I told her that I got rid of it.

With her face twisted into a frown, she says, "Give me that thing." I hand her the device. "You need to get your head out of the clouds, West."

"Sorry. I get bored watching TV all the time." Then I switch to Romanian, which sometimes works to calm her down, and tell her to leave me alone, "*Lasa-ma in pace.*"

"Sure, as soon as I smash this stupid thing to bits," she replies.

Nice, Mom. Real nice.

"It's not a problem anymore." I hold out my hand.

She tosses it onto the bed beside me with a flip of her hand, like she's throwing a Frisbee. Then she stomps into the bathroom. Her turn.

With a sigh, I let my shoulders slump. Mom doesn't like to read, and she doesn't want me to like it either, but I do. I can't help it. I read everything, even though I have to do it in secret. But this isn't really about Kindles and reading. It's about Atlanta. I messed up there, and Mom can't seem to get over it, no matter how well I've done since.

All I can do is to keep doing what I'm doing. Emily Dickinson, my favorite poet, said, "Action is redemption." I believe it...and I need it.

"I'm going to check on my students," I tell her when she reemerges after a few minutes, and then I flop into the desk chair. In moments, my MacBook Air is out of my backpack and booting up. I have an online "degree program" I run with lots of satisfied "students."

Wordlessly, Mom comes up behind me, places a hand on my shoulder, and squeezes. It's her way of saying "Sorry. I overreacted." My hand reaches up and covers hers, squeezing back. Apology accepted.

Back to business.

Mom spreads out the jewelry we "acquired" this past week on the off-white bedsheets and begins photographing the pieces with her phone to text to Chin. Halfway through, her cell buzzes, and she punches the answer icon.

"Hello. Peter?" Her eyebrows furrow as she listens. "What happened?"

Peter Banica. Uncle Peter. My dead father's brother. He works with us off and on. When I was younger, he teamed up with Mom to train me.

While Mom and I mostly stick to short cons, ones that take an hour or two tops, Peter is a master of the long con. His games may take days or weeks to play out, but the payoff is always huge. I like working with him. His irreverence is a refreshing change from Mom's dour prudishness.

Mom disappears into the bathroom and shuts the door.

My attention refocuses on the laptop screen. A couple mouse clicks brings up the Riesling University home page—yep, just like the wine—and I log in with my administrator's password.

This hustle is a simple one, but simple is often best. I'm the dean of Riesling U. We have a nice website, which I designed, and we give course credit for life experiences. If you fill out our detailed questionnaire and pay $500, I'll issue you a genuine bachelor's degree in business administration, criminal justice, hotel management, or any one of a dozen other majors we offer. For $1,500 and a longer questionnaire, you can have a master's degree. I dutifully save the questionnaires, but never actually read them.

Today, two orders await me: Angela wants a master's degree in business, and Ernest wants a bachelor's degree in computer science.

When we get to Chicago, I'll generate authentic-looking documents with real wax seals—professional and suitable for framing.

As I email my congratulations to Angela and Ernie, the bathroom door bangs open again, and Mom storms out with a grim expression: the one she wears when we're in the middle of a game that's beginning to go south on us. This can't be good.

"Change in plans."

I close my laptop, push back from the desk, and swivel to face her. "What?"

She sighs wearily. "Peter's run into some trouble with his current project. He needs a closer."

Sometimes, at the end of a long con, the mark hesitates to take the bait. The closer's job is to give him the gentle nudge he needs to take the plunge. Mom is one of the best closers around, so it's no surprise Peter called.

"What does he want you to do?" I ask.

She shakes her head. "Not me. You."

My eyes widen as a wave of surprise mixed with panic washes over me. My heart pounds faster with a surge of anxiety.

Mom hasn't let me close out a game since Atlanta.

Am I back?

I hope so.

If she and Peter want me to close out a deal, this would be huge. It could finally shut the door on all the stuff that went wrong last summer and get me back to where I was.

"This is a really big one, West, and we only have a few weeks."

"Who's the mark?"

"He's a high school guy. You need to persuade him to play along."

"Play along?" I'm a little puzzled. What kind of deal are we talking about here that would require the cooperation of a teenage boy? Unless he's a super celebrity and we're trying to hustle him out of his Hollywood millions, who cares about some kid?

"Yeah," Mom replies, letting out a long, shuddering exhale. "It's stupid beyond all belief. Peter will explain when we see him tomorrow. The bottom line is, this kid is holding up the deal, and you have to kick his can out of the way so Peter can finish the game."

"Well, why…." My voice sputters. "I mean, what am I supposed to do?"

"Relax. It's not going to be anything you can't handle."

Gee, that's comforting…and not very informative. "What's our cut?"

"Thirty-five percent of the net. Three million, maybe more."

"Seriously?" I blurt out. "With a haul like that—"

"We could take a year or two off," Mom finishes.

"I could go back to school." I miss my high school in Kissimmee, Florida. I dropped out after my freshman year to work full-time with Mom, but I've always regretted it. Officially, I'm being homeschooled now.

Wink, wink.

I like being on the road with Mom, but it gets lonely and boring. I miss my English Honors class with Mrs. Beal, who was always recommending books to read. I miss having friends. And I miss the illusion of being normal.

"You're seventeen," Mom reminds me. "You're too old for high school."

Fine. Crush my fantasy. "So, when do we leave?"

"Tomorrow afternoon. But first, we shop. We need to find the right look for you."

"Saks?" I suggest. It's not far from the hotel. I love the place.

"Right. In the meantime, Peter is emailing you some intel on the kid. Study it."

Sure enough, waiting in my inbox is an email with no subject and no message—only an attachment.

The boy's name—my mark—is Tanner Cardwell, a seventeen-year-old guy who, only days before, finished his junior year in high school in Stockton, California. He lives with his widowed father, an older sister, and her young daughter.

Peter included some snaps. One is from a soccer game where Tanner is about to kick the ball down the field. He wears his black hair short, not quite a buzz cut, but close, and he's tall and lanky with the lean build of a runner. Okay, even with dirt and sweat on his jersey, he's a bit of a hottie bugatti.

A second picture must be from the school yearbook since it's a headshot with a laser light background. Meh. Typical dead-eyes photo school photographers churn out by the billions.

The third picture is of Tanner and a group of students in a classroom. It triggers a spark of envy, and it's not because he's apparently rich—or why else would we be wasting time on him. It's because he's so normal.

I'm definitely not.

This guy lives in a house. I live on the road. He has friends and he's a jock. I have Mom and… well, I'm a criminal.

But whatevs.

Yet, for a guy that's got it all, Tanner is not smiling like the other kids in the last picture. He has a sober, lost expression as he gazes into the camera lens. I stare back at him, wondering what he was thinking about.

I read through the rest of the info Peter has on this Tanner dude. The only thing that really registers is he is a big-shot star athlete. I still have no idea why this boy is a problem for Peter, but I guess he'll explain soon enough. In the meantime, I study Tanner's face some more.

Okay, here's how I read him: Tanner Cardwell is a rich white boy, probably dating the head cheerleader. Each day he wakes up and goes to sleep in the same bed. He has friends he hangs out with, and in the fall, he'll be applying to college. Since I have none of those things, clearly we have zip in common.

Good. This makes it easier to do what I have to do.

This is not like Atlanta.

He's not like Josi.

CHAPTER THREE

Atlanta
One year ago
Jewelry by Josi & Jem

"What can I help you with, young lady?" the cheery gray-haired woman asked.

"Gold chain," I answered. Then I shrugged and added, "For my boyfriend."

"This way." She waved a hand to follow her to a display case along the right side of the showroom. "Prices range from two hundred to ten thousand dollars, depending on how long and heavy you want."

"Wow. Awesome selection."

"Let me know if you want me to take one out," the woman said before leaving me alone to browse.

I had no plans to handle any items, let alone buy anything. This was simply an exploration expedition. Mom and I were staying in the nearby Intercontinental Hotel in Buckhead for a couple weeks, casing jewelry stores in the Atlanta area. We planned to ID a half a dozen or so promising locations, disappear, rough out the routines we'd use, and then return in a month or so to harvest what we could.

The exterior of the shop dampened my expectations—a blocky storefront, plate-glass windows, and a quaint, but weathered wooden sign hanging above the door. The entire neighborhood was old, but this building appeared almost nineteenth century in design with the store on the first floor and living quarters on top. Then there was the clunky name: *Jewelry by Josi and Jem*. The three Js.

Everything about the shop screamed waste of my time, but the place was fairly well-respected as my internet searches had uncovered. More importantly, these kind of one-off places often were a bit naïve when it came to security and scam artists. The only question was whether these guys had enough high-end pieces to make it worth our while. We didn't have time to bother with cheap crap. So, here I was, assigned to check out their inventory and eyeball what they had on display.

After I'd spent fifteen minutes browsing, my brow slipped into a frown. So far, the pieces only mildly impressed me. Most were overpriced cookie-cutter junk, the kind of stuff you find in abundance at chain jewelry stores in malls.

One display case did intrigue me. It was devoted to estate jewelry, and many of the items were antiques dating from before the twentieth century. There was a good market for this stuff, particularly for the really top-shelf material. And that was exactly what I saw. I blinked, and my breathing slowed at the sight of an eye-popping ruby pendant. My mouth watered. We could easily fence that baby for forty to fifty grand.

My gaze wandered over the other antiques on display. Several were real keepers, but what sealed the deal were six Patek Phillipe pocket watches, which, collectively, might make a run at a million dollars in a retail sale.

Okay, I'd seen enough. Put this store down on the hit list.

"Jenn," an elderly woman cried out. "Where have you been, my child?"

I straightened and glanced about, searching for this Jenn person, but I was the only customer in the store. So, WTF?

The old lady who spoke must've worked here since she was standing behind one of the counters, dressed in a gray floor-length dress with ruffled sleeves. She also had an elaborate blue hat on her head. If this had been October, I'd say she was trying out her *Little House on the Prairie* Halloween costume. But this was May.

Also, she was grinning at me as if we were old friends.

Kind of creeped me out.

"Jenn, you missed my birthday," the old lady continued in a slightly scolding tone. "Your own grandmother." The old woman stared at me as she spoke, clearly directing her accusation straight at me and no one else. My brain needed a couple of moments before it alerted me: this poor lady mistook me for someone else. To personalize my response, I glanced for a moment at her name tag before speaking. Josi Tinsley.

"Sorry, Miss Tinsley," I replied, "but I think you've got me mixed up with—"

"Sister," a sales lady practically shouted from behind the sales register by the door. It was the woman who helped me earlier. "What are you doing out here?" The poor lady shot me an apologetic look while grasping Josi's shoulders to lead her away.

One side of my mouth quirked up in an amused half smile at these two old biddies.

Josi looked confused, while the other woman was flushed with embarrassment. Josi, whom I guessed to be one of the owners of this place, blinked several times and brought one hand up to her cheek for no apparent reason. I decided to jump into this absurd drama. Why not? I could use a fun diversion.

"I'm sorry to miss your party, Grandma," I said, grinning. "Is there any cake left?"

CHAPTER FOUR

An hour after we left San Francisco, Mom guides our new rental car—a red Nissan Maxima—up a long driveway and stops in front of a monstrously large house surrounded on all sides by a vineyard covering the land in all directions. The sign at the turnoff says this is the Kostinen Vineyard.

Never heard of it. No matter. The place is effing amazing.

I stare open-mouthed at the enormous mansion in front of us with its five-car garage, not really sure if this is for real or part of some Disney castle movie. Mom and I do luxury the way most people do laundry, but this house is ultra-extravagant even by our standards. Mom said this place has twenty bedrooms, but the number seems low. The manor appears big enough to house several mega-VIPs and their entourages.

"Diana." My uncle Peter hurries down the front porch steps to greet us as we climb out of the car. Uncle Peter is Mom's brother-in-law. With jet-black hair, a rugged, athletic figure, and a carefully trimmed mustache and beard, he reminds me of Jake Gyllenhaal in *Spider-Man*. He even has the same beady snake eyes, but they radiate happiness at seeing us.

Mom and Peter hug in the driveway and top it off with an air kiss, while I suck in a deep breath of dry warm air and smile. This is an awesome day—mid-seventies and a cloudless blue sky. If only we were surrounded by a sandy beach instead of grapes.

True, the house is impressive, but it's all superficial. This place, this entire situation, is only a costume I'll put on for a week or two before taking it off and moving on to our next gig.

What am I underneath all of this glitz, glam, and glimmer? I'm not really sure, and how sick is that? Never mind. I'll think about it later. That's why tomorrows exist, right?

As soon as Peter is done hugging Mom, it's my turn. He wraps his arms around me, and I squeeze back. The gel in his hair smells like coconuts.

"You playing nice with your mother?" he asks.

"I have my good days."

"Make sure you have a few bad ones too," he replies with a wink.

Peter and I exchange broad grins. Spending time with him again is like taking a really great vacation. Unlike Mom, he's laid-back and doesn't take himself too seriously. I can relax and enjoy myself a little without worrying about what comes next. Peter lives for the now. Mom, on the other hand, is a super-taut cord with one end anchored in the past and the other tied to a stake planted somewhere in the future. In between the two posts, the cord is always tight and inflexible.

Over glasses of iced tea in the kitchen breakfast nook, Peter gets down to the real reason we're here and the specifics of the game he's running. Apparently, he managed to weasel his way into the Kostinen family's trust and good graces, and get himself appointed as the caretaker for their vineyard while they vacation in Europe.

I'm not surprised. This is what Peter does. He's the BFF you never met before. He goes into a restaurant a stranger but comes out on a first-name basis with the waitstaff, who high-five him and call him "bro," "homie," and "boyfriend." I've tried to learn from him over the years and imitate what he does, but I can't fake it with people the same way he does.

Anyway, whoever these Kostinen folks are, they stood absolutely no chance once Peter tagged them as his next marks. As soon as their vacation plane achieved cruising altitude, he began hunting around for the right sucker to sell their place to.

"So, the Kostinens are in France for another month," Peter begins. "I've managed to locate a buyer for the place, someone who is willing to do an all-cash deal."

"So where do I fit in?" I ask.

"Getting there, niece."

Undeterred, I toss out a second question: "Don't the Kostinens have to be here or sign something for you to sell their vineyard?"

"Not at all," he replies. "They gave me a full power of attorney to do anything I want on their behalf, including selling their property."

How did Peter get a power of attorney? I should know better than to ask. How does he do any of the stuff that's made him a legend? Magic? It's as good an answer as any.

My favorite scam of his, the one that made his reputation, was when he stole the identity of the governor of Illinois for a day, sold a $500 million interest in Millennium Park to the Saudi Arabia sovereign wealth fund, and then disappeared the next day with their $10 million earnest money. The FBI is still scratching its head over that one.

"Okay, so what's the real deal here?" I ask.

Always go to the bottom line first and work up from there, Mom says.

"I have a buyer lined up," Peter says. "He's visiting tomorrow afternoon with his son, which is where you come in. This guy came into a large sum of money a few years back. His father left him a bucket of cash and he can't wait to spend it."

"A fool and his money," I remark.

"A fool, yes," Peter says. "But it's greed that makes him a fool. It's greed that keeps me in business. Anyway, as I told your mother over the phone, Hal Cardwell is dying to hand me his money, but he won't close the deal unless his entire family is on board with moving here. The holdout is his son."

"That doesn't make sense." Since when does anyone care what their kid wants? A guy sees a good investment, he invests. No one asks permission of their child. At least not in the *take-it-and-shut-up* reality I live in.

"Maybe not, but that's what he's telling me," Peter says. "That's part of your job. Find out what's really going on here."

"So, bottom line, persuade this Tanner guy to get with the program?"

"That's it," Peter states. "All you have to do is show him how nice this place is and nudge him in the right direction."

After a deep sigh, I give Peter a whatever shrug.

This doesn't feel right. The key to closing a deal is understanding what's motivating the players. Why are they doing what they're doing? Where are they coming from? Only when you truly understand this can you do what a closer does—pull the right strings.

Peter seems to think all we need to do is dazzle the boy a little and point him in the right direction. I think there's more to it. If it's as easy as Peter says, he wouldn't need me. He'd do it himself.

After fetching my luggage from the car and rolling it into the marble foyer, I ask Mom, "Where am I staying?" This place has many empty bedrooms to choose from.

"Where do you want to stay?" Mom answers.

Glad she asked.

"Someplace where I can play my music, watch embarrassing videos, and never be interrupted by anyone—ever—at least, not without twenty-four hours advanced notice."

Mom gives me the finger and then slowly rotates it around until it's pointing at the floor. Yes, my own mother flips me off sometimes. I often return the gesture, but not when she's looking.

"Basement," she says with a tight smile and a raised, challenging eyebrow.

"Basement's cool. Is there a wet bar down there?"

"Ha, ha," Mom replies, but she's not amused. "I'm going to mark the bottles, so don't even think about it."

I raise my hands in the air in an *I surrender* gesture and say, "Who needs booze when I got an entire kilo of marijuana. Peter gave it to me."

Mom's mouth drops open as she swivels her head to stare death rays at Peter, who blinks rapidly in total confusion. His wide-eyed expression is all the denial necessary. Then he rolls his eyes and says, "When did my niece become such a—"

"Saucebox?" Mom offers acidly.

"Stormy petrel," Peter counters. "It's British."

"I think she was born this way," Mom says with a weary shake of her head. "She doesn't get it from me."

"Gotcha." I grin and wink. Then I finger-gun them, then mock blow smoke from both barrels before re-holstering my faux guns. No one returns my triumphant expression.

"Guys, I'm practicing," I plead. "I gotta hone my skills. Catch me a break here."

Mom and Peter proceed to haul her bags upstairs to the VIP rooms that have balconies overlooking the vineyard, walk-in closets you could park a Ford F-150 in, and bathrooms with spa tubs.

Me? I got the basement, but more to the point, I got space. *Lots* of space.

I can do what I want without Mom hovering over me, and that's all I care about. We tend to stay in swank hotels, but no amount of luxury can alter the basic fact: I spend the entire night in a room with my mother never more than ten feet away from me. It gets old. Real old, real fast. So, keep your turn-down service chocolates, copious toiletry freebies, and decadently stocked minibars, and give me a generous, Mom-free zone. Anything. I don't care if it means sleeping under an overpass.

When I make my way downstairs to the lower level and flip on the light switch, I'm instantly blown away. Look at this place. It's a giant playroom with a dozen or so arcade games, overstuffed leather couches, a pool table, and a flat-screen big enough to land airplanes on.

What Mom so derisively called a "basement" has a couple of massive bedrooms, a home theater room, a spa, and a massive, windows-on-three-sides room with a modest indoor pool.

"Gods and dogs," I say as I explore the downstairs. This mansion is so sweet my teeth hurt.

In mere minutes, I select the bedroom I'll be staying in, heave my suitcase onto the bed, and break it open.

I need to move my stuff into the antique highboy dresser positioned against one wall. No problem, except the drawers are already filled with someone else's clothes. Rifling through the top drawer, I find old lady control-panties and double-D bras. The next drawer down contains compression socks and a bag of butterscotch hard candies.

An image of Josi floats into my mind from the depths of memories I'm trying to forget. With clenched teeth, I force the image to dissipate like smoke in the wind.

So this must be Grandma Kostinen's room.

Mine now.

After emptying all the drawers and stacking the contents onto the floor of one of the closets, I quickly move my clothes in.

A couple hours later, as the smell of someone cooking dinner—probably Mom—wafts down the stairs, I'm sitting cross-legged on one of the chocolate-colored leather couches with my laptop resting on the coffee table in front of me. I've spent the last hour or so searching for anything I can find about this Tanner dude, anything that might give me some insight into who I'll be dealing with. There isn't much, but I find a few tidbits. He doesn't have a Facebook page and his Twitter feed is unenlightening. My Google searches turn up some stuff about the high school soccer team, but not much else.

"*Salut, nepoata.*" Peter.

"Hey," I reply, glancing up and returning his greeting as he steps into the game room.

As usual, he simply calls me niece rather than my name. With a sigh, I close my laptop and gaze up at him. He lowers himself carefully into one of the leather chairs a few yards away, wiggling around for a second to find the most comfortable position.

He's not here for small talk, that's obvious. I unfold my legs and sit up straight. I'm slightly annoyed at the interruption, since, hey, I said no interruptions without advance notice. The twenty-four-hour thing may have been tongue-in-cheek, but the basic point I wanted to be left alone wasn't.

But I'm also curious.

"Let me guess," I say, "we're out of toilet paper and you want me to drive to the store."

He lifts an eyebrow. "I want to see how you're doing."

"All limbs in place and accounted for. Internal organs present and functioning. I'm having slight cramps, but let's not go there. My amygdala is trending toward pissed off."

"Well, we can't have that."

"The amygdala is the part of the brain that controls emotions," I say.

"You *do* read a lot," he replies. "Diana warned me."

"You have a problem with that too?"

I wonder how much Mom has talked to Peter about me. He's family, of course, but he and Mom are not what I would call super close and feel genetically compelled to talk at least once a week. They're more like holiday close. They see each other at Thanksgiving, Christmas, etc., and have great reunion chats, but in between those big family gatherings, they don't have much contact unless somebody died and funeral planning is necessary.

Teaming up for a job is different. This is different. It's not about family. It's business and it's professional. Watching him fumble with his hands, clearly wrestling with how to begin an awkward conversation, leads me to wonder whether he knows about last summer.

"No," he finally answers. "Not at all. I only wanted to see if you're ready for tomorrow. See if you have any questions."

"Nope, I'm good." I don't think this is exactly what he wants to hear from me. So I try a different response. "Any words of advice?"

He grins, and I can tell I hit the nail on the head. Peter wants to tell me how to do my job. Well, this is his Halloween party, and if he wants to pick out what costume I wear, then I'm all ears.

"Ever smoke ribs?" he asks.

Excuse me? It takes me a couple of beats for my brain to process his question and understand he's talking about a cooking method, not something you might do with a bong.

"Uh, no."

"Of course not."

"It's going on my bucket list, though," I hastily add.

"When you ever do," he says, "you should remember that the key is low and slow—keep the heat low and cook 'em damn slow."

"Hell yeah." I raise my fist, and then ask, "What does smoking meat have to do with tomorrow?"

He hesitates for an instant to suck in a deep breath, which he releases in a rush. "We probably have only one shot at this. Think of yourself as playing a chess match. Your moves need to be careful, thought out, and deliberate. You can't shoot from the hip. There's no leeway for rash or impetuous."

He said impetuous. This is Mom's magic word for the year. She must've told him all about the three Js last July. I'm not surprised, and I'm not mad, but I'm disappointed. In her and in me. She still doesn't completely trust me yet. We've been on a roll this spring, but it's not enough. I don't think I'll ever escape the Js. Not in Mom's eyes.

"I wasn't impetuous," I say.

He nods, as if he accepts my correction. "Whatever you call it, it can't happen on this job. Promise?"

I cross my arms and glare at him in a combination of frustration and annoyance. "I didn't ask for this, you know. If you don't think I can handle it, go find someone else."

"There is no one else. At least, no one I could get in the short time I have."

"You know, I don't need this—"

"West, I'm not trying to be a dick. The last thing I want is to make you angry. We're what we are with everyone else in the world, but you and I have to be honest with each other. I trust you or you wouldn't be here. I don't know what all happened in Buckhead last year, and I don't need to know. But I *do* need to know it's not going to happen here."

"We're not in Buckhead," I whisper, and then add sulkily, "It wasn't my fault."

"You were running the show. From what I hear, you could have salvaged the situation."

"I tried…" Sigh. "It won't happen again."

"Then we're good. Come on, I'll show you around the place. It has a few toys you might enjoy." He places his hands on his knees, pushes off to stand, and waves to follow him upstairs.

While I would enjoy time alone, I am intrigued by this place. I've never visited a vineyard before. A grand tour might be interesting. I follow Peter, surprised at how eager I am to see what marvels the property holds.

Once we're outside, Peter asks, "What do you want to see first? The wine barrel caves or the vineyard?"

"I want to see the grapes."

He nods. "Good choice. Let me show you how we get around outside."

CHAPTER FIVE

"Buck up, West," Peter says the next morning as I emerge from my downstairs lair, where I've spent the morning reading. "They should be here any minute."

"I don't know," Mom says when she strolls into the living room and sees my outfit. She studies me from head to toe. "It's too casual."

"Because the event is casual," I reply. "This isn't the prom."

"Your skirt is too short," Mom says, undeterred.

"Oh my effing God," I mutter under my breath. I'm wearing a basic denim skirt. It's supposed to be short.

"You can't even bend over in that," Mom persists.

"I'm not gonna be hiking the ball in a flag football game, okay?"

She frowns. It's clear she also doesn't like the orange polo shirt I chose. It's simple, but it fits me well and complements the reddish tint of my hair.

"At least let me fix your hair," Mom says with a resigned sigh. "It will look better parted on the side."

"Whatever," I grouse, mostly to myself.

My hair is fine, considering how many times I've dyed it the last two months, but I have to throw Mom some kind of bone or she'll squabble with me until the Second Coming. I let her have at it with my hair. I haven't parted it on the side since I was six years old, but if this is what floats her boat and gets her to leave me alone, then it's worth giving in to her.

Minutes later, hair brushed and Mom still scowling, I head for the kitchen. I'm starved.

"Don't eat anything," Mom half yells at my retreating back. "Or you'll have to brush your teeth again."

Jesus H. When this job is over, Mom and I need a serious vacation from each other.

"Only getting a glass of water," I holler back over my shoulder. When I return to the living room minutes later with a tumbler of nice red, ultra-shirt-staining cranberry juice, Mom glares at me. I shouldn't twist her tail like this, but passive aggression is really the only weapon I have when she shifts into boot camp drill instructor mode.

"Remember," Mom says, "the plan today is for you to introduce yourself to the boy. Maybe talk a little if the opportunity presents itself. That's all. Today is a meet and greet."

"I'm going to speak to Hal about setting up an outing later," Peter adds. "Some kind of get-together when you and his son can spend some time together. Maybe a barbecue or something. So—"

"So, don't get out over your skis," Mom interrupts and shakes a finger at me.

While I sip my drink, Peter paces around the living room, pausing occasionally to stare out at the driveway. He gnaws his thumbnail and glances anxiously out the window.

Me? I'm not nervous. It's not like I'm meeting the king of England. Tanner's just a guy.

"Ah, here they are," he says.

Mom clears her throat and rubs her hands together. Jesus, she's nervous too.

Grinning to myself, I tug on her elbow.

"Huh?" she asks absentmindedly, her eyes glued on the scene outside the window.

"I took my bra off," I whisper. "Is that okay?"

"What?" She whirls to face me, eyes wide.

"Just kidding. Chill a little."

"Not funny, West."

A silver Mercedes-Benz S-Class rolls to a stop at the end of the asphalt lane directly behind our puny little Maxima. Three figures emerge from the car—a man and two kids. The man is a squat, gray-haired gentleman with a paunch and a scraggly beard. Hal Cardwell, I presume. One of the kids is Tanner Cardwell. Has to be. The other is a girl with long, champagne blonde hair. She's about my age, I'd say. Is this the sister with the baby? Can't be.

Peter glances sideways at Mom, and then at me, and we all nod to one another in unison. It's game time.

With Peter in the lead, we march out the front door and spill onto the porch. Our visitors lift their gaze up to study us, and that's when Tanner and I make eye contact. I recognize him, but of course he doesn't have any idea who I am. Nevertheless, when our eyes meet, he matches my smile with one of his own.

However, the girl next to him glares at me as if I'm an evil succubus. Then she places an arm protectively on Tanner's shoulder. Girlfriend? Yep.

Well, this is unexpected. Worse, some sixth sense has alerted her I'm a threat. Not fair. I haven't even done anything yet.

A sigh of annoyance escapes me. I'm not going to accomplish anything with her glommed onto his body like mold on bread. So, what to do?

While I'm turning this over in my mind, I check her out. She must be an athlete like him, since she's wearing baggy, unflattering athletic shorts and a rather ratty-looking gray t-shirt with the logo *Property of Stanford Athletics.*

I need to interact with Tanner one-on-one, something glare girl is not going to allow. Peter would say, "Don't sweat it. Take what the situation gives you." Mom would echo that advice by reminding me this is only a meet and greet.

Does it have to be, though?

Tanner is studying me with an inviting look on his face, as though he would welcome talking to me. If I could only have ten minutes alone with him, we might really connect. But how do I separate him from girlfriend?

A wild idea flames up in my mind. It might work. Why wouldn't it work? It's worked before. Except it's berserker crazy and possibly reckless, and Mom would scream I'm going way out over my skis, but I think I can pull this off. Correction...*will* pull this off.

"I'll be right back," I whisper to Mom.

"What?" she replies, half panicked.

"Follow my lead and try to keep up," I mutter.

"West, wait."

Nope. Time and tide wait for no man. I read that somewhere.

Anyway, as inconspicuously as possible, I pivot and dart back into the house, ignoring Mom's wide-as-saucer eyes, and head straight for her makeup chest upstairs. After I lift out several trays so I can reach the bottom, my fingers grope among the sponges and tubes of concealer searching for the special squirt bottle I need. Found it.

When I make it back outside moments later, the porch is empty. Peter and Mom have wandered out onto the lawn to welcome our guests, although both cast furtive glances over their shoulders searching for *moi*. With a carefree wave, I jog over to meet the group and come up alongside Mom just as Peter is introducing her.

"Hal, this is my sister-in-law Diana. Diana Rowen." He blinks a couple of times when he notices I'm back, and says, "And this is my niece, West. They're here for the summer to help with the vineyard. If you decide to buy the place, all of us would be happy to stay on as long as needed to assist with the transition."

We go by Rowen when we're on the road, a name Mom says she got from a pub she and Dad used to visit. Peter is using the surname Glassman for this game. No idea where he came up with that.

"This is my son, Tanner," Hal says, "and Leah, a close friend of the family."

I shake hands with everybody. Tanner's grip is firm and confident, and he returns my gaze with a relaxed, inviting expression. The first feature of his I notice, which I missed in his pictures, are his eyes—a dazzling hazel color. He's wearing khaki cargo shorts, sandals, and a blue shirt with black short sleeves. The shirt is a kind of sports jersey, but since I know less about sports than I do about the geological composition of the planet Venus, I don't even try to guess the team.

Leah extends her hand to clasp mine, but her greeting is mechanical and insincere, and her eyes seem to sparkle with suspicion.

Her hand is almost limp in mine, but I grip it firmly and squeeze. This distracts her and her eyes focus on mine as if they have laser sighting. She doesn't see my other hand nonchalantly swing toward her waist, and she doesn't notice the squirt bottle clutched in my fingers. The bottle needs only a slight pinch from me to send a stream of liquid squirting onto Leah's shirt above the hem. In a half a second, her shirt displays a wet, red stain the size of a half dollar.

"Oh shit, you're bleeding," Mom cries out, pointing to Leah's side.

Mom has picked up on my ruse. If she hadn't seen the spill, somebody else would have soon enough.

"What?" Leah yanks her shirt around to gaze down at a crimson smear.

Sharp intakes of breath come from Tanner and his father. Leah stares down in shock, her mouth falling open. She's probably wondering where all the freaking blood came from since she's not experiencing any pain. The last thing she'd guess is it's special effects gore, aka stage blood.

I should feel guilty flimflamming her like this, but I don't. I have a job to do and she's in the way. Plus, she gave me the stink eye, and no one gets away with that.

"Let's get you inside and get that shirt off," Mom fusses, acting all concerned and compassionate. "I'm a nurse. I can fix you up," Mom adds.

Mom is no more a nurse than I am an MMA fighter, but since Leah isn't really injured, it doesn't matter.

Tanner watches the two of them hurry toward the house. Peter gapes at Mom. He's as confused as the others. He silently mouths WTF at me, and I return his bewildered expression with a smile. Then he realizes I'm up to something, but he has no idea what.

"Uh, West," Peter stammers, "since Tanner is the only one who hasn't seen this place yet, why don't you give him the grand tour while Diana is seeing to Leah?"

Hal and Tanner ignore him and continue to gawk at each other in shock.

"I should go with—" Tanner starts to say, but I interrupt him.

"You'll only be in the way. By the time I show you around, Leah will be right as rain."

Tanner starts to protest again, but Hal swallows hard and cuts off his pending objection in a firm voice. "Go on, Tanner. Leah will be fine. I'll stay with her. Can't have too many cooks in the kitchen."

Tanner glances over at me, mouth open to lodge a further protest. With a tug on his arm, I lead his reluctant body over to the garage doors and the next step of my insane, but lit plan. Inside is a nice ATV, a Honda four-wheeler—red with black trim and a black seat. During our summers in Florida, I practically live on my four-wheeler, so I'm pretty fluent in driving these puppies.

Now this is what I call a meet and greet. Why only swap small talk when we can do something that's actually fun?

"Nice," Tanner says, adding a soft whistle, Leah apparently forgotten for the moment. "A Honda Fourtrax."

"Exactly." I'm impressed. "Do you ride?"

Strangely, his presence causes me to struggle with my control. I should be calm, detached, and professional in dealing with him, but there's an intensity about him that makes my self-confidence waver.

He doesn't glance away, and his hazel eyes seize my attention like the talons of an eagle gripping its prey. A voice in my subconscious tells me not to lie to him, but I stuff a rag in it and shove it back down the hole inside me where it came from.

Everything about me is a lie. It's who I am. What I am. I *have* to lie to him.

He shrugs, unaware of my inner battle. "Yeah, mostly motorcycles, but I do some four-wheeling."

"I always wanted a motorcycle, but my mom thinks I'll crash and die."

Tanner rolls his eyes. Cool. My thoughts exactly.

After hopping on the ATV and squishing my head into a helmet, I toss one to him. "Get on. I'll show you around." He pauses, a hesitant expression on his face. "Come on," I add. "It'll only take a few minutes. Promise."

Relenting, he slides onto the seat behind me, softly putting his fingertips on my hips. My shirt has ridden up a little so his fingers on one side are touching skin. An unexpected shiver makes my body tremble slightly. He withdraws his hands for a second, as if he felt the jolt from our touch, but then places his palms flat against my sides and grips me delicately. I think he's afraid I'll break. My breath hitches, and I momentarily forget what I'm supposed to do next. Oh yeah, put the key in the ignition.

My plan is a simple one. Get him alone for a little while and gain his trust. Or at least as much of his trust as I can. Then I need to find out what is going on with this guy. What's his problem with this place? Once I get inside his head, we can figure out what to do about shoving him out of the way.

The ATV lurches forward, and we accelerate out of the garage. The sudden movement forces him to slide his hands across my belly to keep his balance. We roar down the dirt road leading through the center of the vineyard. I'm following the route Peter showed me yesterday.

Our first stop is the top of a small hill in the center of the vineyard where lines of grapes radiate out on both sides. If knowledge is peanut butter, what I knew of grapes and winemaking twenty-four hours ago was so slight you couldn't spread it across a saltine cracker. That was then. Now, after Peter's crash course, I'm able to banter about words like noble rot, chardonnay, oaking, tannin, and esters like a pro.

Grifting is like acting. We work off a script. I memorize my lines and put on a show.

After dismounting from the ATV, I remove my helmet and gesture toward rows of trellises. "This is where it all starts," I say. "These are cabernet sauvignon grapes."

He gives me a polite nod, but obviously couldn't care less. Okay, we'll skip grapes 101 and move on to something more interesting. I'm not here to be a tour guide anyway. I want him to open up to me a little.

"Your dad seems to know quite a bit about wine," I note, trying to sound casual.

"Well, he thinks he does. Anything else except grapes on this land?"

He's bored. Damn, I'm losing him. I need to get some adrenaline pumping in his veins and wake him up. Apparently, holding on to my body while I lumber along on the ATV isn't doing it for him. Sighing heavily, I decide on a slightly different tack.

"My secret getaway spot," I reply. "Come on, I'll show you."

Back on the Honda, I gun it over the top of the hill and race down the other side, accelerating to a reckless speed. The road takes an abrupt left turn at the bottom, but I purposely don't slow down until the last moment.

Let's see if this wakes him up.

By the time we reach the bottom, Tanner's grip on me has gone from firm to crushing. Smiling deviously, I brake hard at the dead-man's curve at the bottom of the hill, and the front of his helmet bangs against the back of mine. Once I've negotiated the turn, I bring the ATV to a stop in front of a grass-edged pond, roughly the size of a football field.

"Man," Tanner says, quickly dismounting and ripping off his helmet. "For a second there, I thought we were Ethan and Mattie about to crash into a tree."

A silly grin erupts on my face at his literary reference. "*Ethan Frome*," I say.

He smiles back. "It's a classic. Although my favorite Edith Wharton story is *House of Mirth*."

I shake my head in disagreement. "I'd have to go with *The Age of Innocence*."

"That would be my runner-up," he says.

Wow, Tanner reads Edith Wharton? I thought I was the only Gen Z reader of women authors who never had a Twitter account. Maybe we *do* have something in common.

"You read some heavy-duty books for a jock."

"I got it from my mother. She was a librarian. But hey, how'd you know I'm an athlete?"

"You got the bod for it," I reply. "Let me guess. Cross-country or lacrosse." I'm deliberately guessing wrong.

"Soccer. What about you? What do you do?"

"Not a jock. A book nerd who loves nineteenth-century women writers. I'm going to major in English in college." There's a grain of truth to this. If I ever found a way to not steal for a living, I would study English literature.

"Why nineteenth century?"

"They were the best ever," I reply. "They had to be or no one would've listened."

Tanner stoops, picks up a rock and, while crouching, tosses it across the surface of the water. The rock skips five times before sinking out of sight. He turns and gives me a brief bow. It's cute.

I pick up a rock and attempt to match his toss. My rock immediately sinks, so I try again, but with the same result.

"You're not doing it right," he says. "Grip it between your thumb and forefinger and get as low to the ground as you can." I purposely flub another toss. "Here, let me show you."

He selects a flat stone and takes my hand. My idiot body shivers again at his touch, but one side of my mouth curves up in a half-grin as he manipulates my fingers with his. Once I have the appropriate grip, I make a half-hearted attempt to bend over.

"No, you have to get lower. Like this." He places one hand on my stomach and the other on my shoulder, gently pushing me toward the ground. Then his mouth is next to my ear. With his next instructions, his breath stirs my hair. More shivers. "That's it," he whispers. "Now let it fly." He straightens but keeps one hand resting on the small of my back. My arm snaps forward, and with a perfect flick of the wrist, the rock skips across the water several times.

Like I don't know how to skip a rock?

He reaches a hand up for a high five, and I give it an enthusiastic slap. "Under my expert tutelage, West, you could be a gold medal contender if rock skipping ever becomes an Olympic sport. So, what's this place called?" He jerks his square chin at the water.

"Condon Pool."

Tanner glances over at me with a questioning look. "Why do they call a pond a pool?"

I shake my head. "Listen, if your father buys this place, you can call it a lake."

His expression collapses into a grim scowl as if he's caught a whiff of a foul odor. "He won't be buying it if I can help it."

Now we're cooking with gas. I need to find out what his big problem is before I can help him get past it.

I blink several times at him, trying to appear shocked. "You have a problem with living in a mansion in wine country, surrounded by some of the finest grapes on the planet? Most people would kill for this. *I* would kill for this. What's not to like about living here?"

He rubs his temples with his palms as if to fend off a migraine.

"Sure, it's nice and all… I guess," he says. "But my life is ninety miles away. Besides, what does my dad know about running a vineyard? This is some bullshit fantasy of his. There's another place not far from our house he's also looking at. I want him to buy that place instead. Then I could finish my senior year at my high school. Once I leave for college, he can buy a shrimp boat in Louisiana for all I care."

My mind is quickly sorting through what he said. Hal is looking at our vineyard and another property somewhere else, and Tanner is lobbying for site B.

What's site B?

Running a long con is all about manipulation, but you have to know how far you can push a mark. Push too hard, too fast, and you'll lose him for good. Still, I have to find out what this other property is.

"So, is this other place as nice as ours?"

"It's called the Bel Canto Ranch. It has orchards, and they raise walnuts and almonds. The house isn't as fancy and big as here, but it's still sweet. Plus, we'd have full-time caretakers to run the place."

"My uncle is willing to stay on here full-time as long as needed. Your dad would never have to get his fingers dirty."

"Still, this place is hell and gone from Stockton."

I decide to back off about the other property and shift over to his girlfriend. "So, how long have you and Leah been together?"

"We're not together. She's a friend, maybe my best friend. We were a couple for a month two years back, but it didn't take. We're better as friends. Now, she's more like a sister."

Interesting. *He* may see her as only a friend, but I'm not sure she sees him that way. She acted overly protective and in a *I'm in love with the guy* kind of way.

"When my mom died a few years ago," he continues, "Leah practically moved in with us. She cleaned, cooked, did the laundry. I don't know how we would've survived without her."

Interesting. Time to reel in my line and hang up the fishing pole for now. It's our first meeting and I don't want to press too hard. "We should get back before they send out a search party," I say. "What's your number?"

"What?"

"Your cell. So you can text me."

He silently mouths *oh* and gives me the number.

I tap it into a text and send him a message saying, "Hi."

"Call me sometime if you get bored," I say. "You want to drive this beast back?"

He nods enthusiastically. With a hop, I slide into the four-wheeler behind Tanner, but unlike him, I slide my arms around his hard, muscular stomach and grip tightly, molding my body flush against his. There's definitely an unexpected tingling sensation shooting up my spine as I cling to him.

We roar off the dirt road we came down, but I note that Tanner is making it a point to go much faster than I did. I can't help but smile at his showing off.

When we come to an abrupt stop on the lawn in front of the house, Mom, Hal, and Leah are standing on the porch, talking and sipping iced tea. Leah never takes her eyes off me, not even when Tanner is asking her a question. Her gaze follows me as I move over to stand next to Mom.

Leah's suspicious, all right. This girl could be a problem…or a challenge.

With as pleasant a smile as I can muster, I stand by silently and listen to Peter's small talk with Hal as the visit winds down. Tanner watches me the whole time, and my cheeks flush warm when we shake hands good-bye.

"Well, how did it go?" Mom asks, once the Cardwells have left.

"Tanner is not the only problem," I reply. "We have competition."

After I explain about Tanner pushing his father to buy a different piece of property, Peter nods slowly.

"Well, that explains a few things," he says. "Keep working on him as originally planned. We still need him on board. I'm going to find this other ranch and see if there's a way to take it off the market, at least temporarily."

"I may have an idea about that," I tell them.

CHAPTER SIX

Atlanta
One year ago

"How are the orders coming?" Jemadine Tinsley, or Jem, asked.

Like her sister Josinia—Josi, Jem wore clothes that were in fashion when Eisenhower was president. This morning, she wore a vivid blue, figure-hugging dress with a white belt around the waist— what I later learned was called a sheath dress—with a matching hat pinned to her graying hair. She looked quite sophisticated. Fifty years ago, when she was my age, she must have been stunningly beautiful.

"All boxed up and ready to go," I answered as I affixed the last mailing label. "We only had seven sales today. Five tennis bracelets, a set of pearl earrings, and the Jaeger-LeCoultre watch."

"Excellent. How much did we get for the watch?"

I cleared my throat and said, "Forty-three hundred dollars."

"That much? Good heavens," Jem said.

I nodded and confessed, "You had a price tag on it in the shop of twenty-one fifty, but that was way too low, so I doubled it when I listed it on the website."

"Good girl." Jem smiled approvingly at me and retreated into the backroom.

I sat at a desk behind the display counters at the three Js staring at my laptop screen. Jem and Josi had a desktop computer, but it wasn't internet capable, so I used my burner laptop. Theirs had a floppy disc drive for God's sake, and was so old, it may well have come to America on the *Mayflower*. No wonder they squinted at me in bewilderment when I suggested they let me create a website to sell their pieces.

"Internet?" Josi asked, when I broached the idea.

"Yeah, it's a—" I started to explain. "Never mind. Trust me on this one."

The three Js had thousands of estate jewelry pieces crammed into various safes and cabinets in the back of their shop. The few display cases out front were too small to display even a sliver of their inventory, so most of it sat in boxes waiting for someone to rediscover them.

That someone was me.

"Jenn," Josi said, wandering out from the back. "Give your grandmother a hug."

"Sister, she's working," Jem protested from the back office.

I rose from my seat and stepped over to Josi, who was nearly as tall as me. She drew me into her arms. At eighty-one, she was thin, frail, and bony, and always smelled of lavender.

Josi was convinced I was her long-lost granddaughter, Jenn, so that's what she called me. Yeah, she had a six-pack upstairs, but lost the little plastic thingie that holds it together. Early Alzheimer's maybe. But her confusion seemed harmless, so I let her call me Jenn.

Jem, on the other hand, didn't know what to call me. In Josi's presence, she addressed me as Jenn, though always with a pained expression, but when Josi wasn't around, I was back to being West.

"I'm so glad you came back from that wretched Boston College," Josi murmured into my hair and clutched me tighter. "This is where you belong. The three Js will be yours to carry on when we're gone."

The three Js would be mine, all right, but I had no intention of waiting until Josi and Jem ascended to the great jewelry store in the sky. I needed a couple weeks to comb through their vast holdings.

Ten days earlier, when I first came into the shop, I'd stayed to talk with Josi and Jem for two hours while eating a generous slice of red velvet birthday cake. It may be overstating it to say "we" talked: Josi rambled on with hardly a break about stuff that happened twenty, thirty years ago.

"You remember the necklace we sold to Rosalyn Carter last week for the inauguration?" Josi asked. "We need to stock up on it. Women are going to want it."

My mouth twisted up in a crooked grin. I liked these old gals. I didn't have to fake that. And they liked me. When I rose to leave at the end of our first meeting, having stuffed myself silly on cake and apple cider, Jem offered me a job.

Shop girl.

"We'll pay top wages," Jem said. "One hundred dollars a week. But you'll have to earn it, mind you."

"Cool," I replied. "I'll take it."

A hundred dollars a week might've been top wages during World War II, but not today. Still, I wasn't complaining. As a trusted employee, and the mysterious granddaughter, Jenn, I'd have unfettered access to all their diamonds, emeralds, and rubies. My initial plan was to spend a few weeks cataloguing their inventory and selecting the best pieces. Then I'd steal them and disappear. Since Jem and Josi had only a tenuous grasp on what they had, it would be some time before they ever missed any of the stolen items…if ever.

"Come with me," Josi said when I accepted the job. "You can stay in your old room upstairs. It's just the way you left it."

I was going to live upstairs above rooms filled with gems like Smaug sitting on all those mounds of dwarf treasure.

Talk about letting the fox in the henhouse.

"I would love that," I answered.

CHAPTER SEVEN

"That is the *stupidest* idea I've ever heard," Mom says, after I roughed out a possible way to take the competing property out of the game. "*Isus*."

"Don't Jesus me," I shoot back. "This can work. Peter, talk to her. You know the more outrageous the scam, the better the chances of success."

Peter purses his lips. "Where do you come up with this stuff, West? Is it from one of your books?"

"No." My head slumps forward in annoyance and I sigh. Convincing Peter and Mom is going to be harder than the sting itself for eff's sake.

Be calm. Take a deep breath.

"What do we have to lose?" I ask Peter in as serene a voice as I can muster. "I'll know in the first twenty minutes if he's going to bite. If he doesn't, I back off and we try your idea. But if he goes for it, we could eliminate the competition in twenty-four hours at a fraction of the time and cost of doing it your way."

Peter's idea is to put in an offer on the other ranch and tie it up for thirty days, long enough for Hal Cardwell to give up on it and turn his eyes exclusively to our vineyard. The big downside to this? No way does his offer get accepted without us putting down at least $50,000 earnest money, money that we will lose when we don't follow through with the sale. If we do it my way, we'll have to ante up a few thou at most.

Where's the downside?

"It's a waste of time," Mom says. "Besides, we need West to focus on the Tanner kid, not go galivanting around all of San Joaquin County."

"I can do both." Except I *can't* do both. Not really. But I'm not worried. I met Tanner Cardwell yesterday. The plan is for me to leave him alone for a couple of days and then call or text him. I haven't decided which yet. The point is I have a two-day waiting period, which is all I need to deal with this Bel Canto ranch.

"Bullshit," Mom snaps, causing me to blink rapidly. "You're not ready."

My shoulders slump dramatically, and my eyes gaze up at the ceiling in annoyed frustration. She's hung up about Atlanta again.

"Oh, what the hell," Peter says, rubbing the back of his neck. "Let her try. Like she said, it costs us nothing, and she'll know right off if it's going to work."

Mom exhales wearily and then locks her gaze with mine. "West, I swear to god if you fuck things up again, I'll—"

"I won't. Trust me."

"Right," Mom mutters. "I made that mistake last summer."

An hour later, I slow our rental car to nearly a crawl and struggle to read the signs. Cars immediately back up behind me and begin to honk as I bite my lower lip in concentration. I don't want to miss my exit, which is entirely possible since I have never driven through Oakland before.

I can't get the GPS to work, which leaves flirting with disaster. One wrong turn and I'd end up heading west over the Bay Bridge. I might be lost for days. Fortunately, I find the sign I want and exit I-880 at the right spot.

My first glimpse of the Alameda Antiques Fair is heaven. Hundreds and hundreds of dealer tents are lined up row after row, while thousands of people throng the lanes in between. I gaze out at the crowd of eager buyers and sellers and smirk. This is grifter heaven, or in shark terms—blood in the water. I can smell the greed in this place, and where there's greed, there's grift. My mind races at the possibilities.

Mom and I could set up a tent and sell cheap imitations as the real deal.

Or we could scam the dealers since most don't know jack.

When I was sixteen, we cased an auction house in St. Louis. I came back the next day in a brown wig, passing myself off as twenty-one—okay, a rather baby-faced twenty-one. I offered $5,000 for an antique gold necklace with rubies. The dealer—an old dude named Erskine—laughed haughtily at me, saying it was at least $100,000. His attitude changed when Mom came in hours later as a government agent, asking to see the necklace, asserting it was illegally looted from an ancient Greek tomb. Her government ID was laughable, since we didn't know what government agency deals with illegal looting.

It didn't matter. Mom played the part so well she could have been flashing a membership card in the Mickey Mouse Club. Erskine almost had a stroke. After Mom left, promising to return with a federal warrant and seizure order, he was only too glad to sell me the necklace for $5,000. Two weeks later, we fenced it to Chen for $125,000. Sweet as pink Easter Peeps.

My new burner phone I got for the vineyard game dings. It's Mom. Of course it is.

Jesus god, Mom, could you not hover over me like bad body odor? "What?" I growl, not bothering to hide my hostility.

"Where are you?"

"Flea market, getting my props, which I explained like an hour ago?"

"Your plan for the ranch simply isn't going to work," she announces. "This is a waste of time."

"Yes it will. It's brilliant. I can do this."

"We may get only one shot."

"Which is all I need," I state. "Can of corn," I add, using my dead father's old boast. It's one of the few things I remember about him.

After a couple moments of silence, she says, "Be back in time for dinner."

"*Eu voi,*" I reply in Romanian, meaning, "I will."

Once inside the grounds, I waste a few hours strolling through the dealer tables, taking in the smells of food cooking, incense, and bodies. I pause at one stand for almost a half hour, gazing at the old coins under glass, and in the end, I buy a few Morgan silver dollars and assorted gold pieces. Nothing rare. The coin dude almost salivated when I pulled out my wad of cash and began peeling off twenties.

Next up is finding a dealer selling antique farm equipment, but so far I haven't found one.

My phone buzzes again. I don't even have to glance at the number on my screen to know it's Mom again.

"Now what?" My voice is curt and annoyed.

"Uh, sorry," Tanner Cardwell says.

Not Mother. It's him. I didn't expect him to call me first.

A tsunami of surprise prevents the use of my vocal cords for several beats.

"Hello?" he says.

I'm stunned, but pleased. A tiny thrill surges up inside me.

"Oh, hey," I manage to fumble out. "I thought you were my mother calling to nag me."

"Wait, your mother nags you?" Then he pauses, as if to catch his breath. "So, what are you doing? Out frolicking among the grapes or skinny dipping at Condom Pond?"

A bark of laughter escapes me. I so don't frolic.

"It's *Condon*," I correct. "And it's a pool not a pond. Remember?"

"What about skinny-dipping?"

"I cop the Fifth."

"Ah, the plot thickens," he replies. "So, you're not communing with the grapes or doing the…the naked body thing. What are you up to?"

"Well, right now I'm strolling through a flea market in Alameda."

"By yourself?"

I nod. "Yep."

"You should've invited me."

"What, you would've come?"

"Of course," he replies. "Alameda is only, what, eighty miles away?"

Interesting. I think he may be into me. A little, anyway, but a little is all I need. "Well, stay on the phone. You can virtual shop with me."

I'm expecting him to decline, but he doesn't. So we talk for the next hour as I move from table to table, telling him about some of the items and listening to his constant commentary on the stuff I describe. Tanner categorizes the items as crap, complete crap, or possibly not crap.

Pausing to browse at a dealer selling vintage clothes from the sixties, I spend ten minutes relaying what I'm seeing. He urges me to buy the dress with puffy sleeves circa 1967 I described to him.

"But it's pink polka dots on purple," I protest. "It's federal law those two colors cannot appear on the same girl at the same time. And polka dots? They scream LSD."

"The sixties *was* the decade of love…or something like that. Come on, you'll make a statement."

"Oh, I would, a three-word one. I'm an idiot. You know, there's a reason why it's hanging on the two-for-five-dollars rack."

"You can wear it the next time I see you."

The next time I see him? My pulse quickens and my ears are getting hot.

Calm down.

I expected three or four calls before we'd have another meetup. This is awesome. I'm about to say something flirty when I see the sign. "*That's* it."

"What is what?"

"Book seller."

Directly in front of me is a light blue sign with green lettering—*Dee's Books and Baubles*. My lips twitch into a smile. I can spare a few minutes for this. The Dee on the sign is an old, white-haired lady sitting on a folding chair behind tables mounded with old books. Beneath her bifocals, her brown eyes sparkle with life, but her clothes—a natty shift dress—look like she bought them at a thrift store.

And can we talk? She smells like something the dog dug up in the backyard.

"Any first editions?" I ask, more out of curiosity than genuine buyer interest.

"A few," she replies. "What do you like to read?"

"Everything. But mostly I love American literature."

"Me too," Tanner agrees over the phone.

I do almost all my reading on a Kindle to minimize issues with Mom, but there's nothing like the feel of an old-fashioned hardback book.

Wordlessly, Dee stands, walks over to a box under one of the tables, and rummages through it. With a satisfied grin, she withdraws a book with a faded, light green dust jacket inside a protective Mylar sleeve.

"Willa Cather," Dee says. "*A Lost Lady*." She hands me the book.

My smile morphs into a silly grin. "I've read it. I love this story."

I turn the volume over, examining the back, the side, and then I study the front cover, gently tracing my finger over the elegant script of the title. Delicately, I open the book and stare down at a random yellowed page. This is so beautiful.

"I could let you have it for seven hundred fifty dollars," Dee says.

Tanner whistles sharply. "For one book?" he asks. "My God, for that, I could buy six months of large pepperoni pizzas with extra jalapenos."

"You're such a guy."

Dee shoots me a puzzling gaze, thinking I'm talking to her. Gulping sheepishly, I hand the volume back to her and say, "Out of my league, but thank you for showing it to me."

"What about manga?" Tanner asks.

"Uh, *One Piece*?"

"That's it? That's all you've read? What about *Beserk*? *Fullmetal Alchemist*? *Akira*?"

"Sorry, but they're comics. You get that, right?" I try not to sound condescending, but I can't quite pull it off. "They're not real literature."

"Yes, they are."

When I don't respond, he says, "I'm going to give you some of the classics. Take a couple days and binge read them. You'll see. I'm going to turn you around on this one."

I can't stop my laughter. "Are you like *otaku*, dude?"

"Only on Saturdays."

"I do like anime," I offer. "Does that earn me some redemption?"

"Like what?"

"*Sailor Moon*. Well, when I was eleven anyway."

"You're hopeless."

I shrug. "Sorry."

"You should be."

Dee interrupts us. "Why don't you check out our vintage necklaces, dear. They're quite reasonable."

"Boring," Tanner says in a singsong voice. I think he's annoyed I disrespected manga.

Trying to carry on two conversations at once is confusing, but oddly kind of fun. Dee points toward the end of one of the tables, where boxes and boxes of necklaces sit. These I can afford. It's all costume jewelry.

Maybe I'll buy one for me and one for Mom. My fingers shuffle through dozens of pieces, some simply awful and others quite lovely, but my hand stops and then grips tightly one in particular. What catches my attention is the silver-colored chain. It's too nice for cheap stuff.

"Can I look at this?" I ask.

She nods, and I gently extract it from the others and lift it out of the box. My breathing stops at the sight of the vivid green stone hanging on the chain.

"That's a pretty one," Dee confirms. "It's just cut glass, of course. I'd let you have it for ten dollars."

"That's more like it," Tanner comments. "Make sure it goes with purple and pink, though."

His remark makes me smile. Maybe I should go back and get that dress. I can model it for him when we see each other again.

Yeah, right. I'd probably be arrested for indecent fashion exposure.

"This is way too nice for ten bucks," I murmur to Tanner.

I heft the necklace in my hand to get a sense of the weight. Heavy. Twisting the chain around, I study the lobster clasp and suck in a sharp breath when I spot the mark—P 950.

"The chain is platinum," I whisper to him.

Dee tilts her head to catch what I'm burbling into my air pods.

"Buy it. It's a steal," he hisses back.

"Nobody hangs cut glass from platinum," I tell him, studying the luminous green stone.

After reaching into my pocket, I tug out the jeweler's loupe I always carry with me—don't ask—and flick it open. I'm not as good as Mom when it comes to appraising rocks, but I'm not bad. In our biz, we need to be. Dee gawks at me with furrowed brows, apparently torn between stopping me and begging me to go on.

With one eye closed, I study the square, emerald-cut, green stone under 10x magnification, noting the fractures and imperfections, including a tiny air bubble. I've seen enough. I lock eyes with Dee and hand her the necklace. On any other day I would buy it and revel in my find, but not today.

"Where did you get it?" I ask.

"Estate sale. It was in a box of junk jewelry."

"This isn't junk," I tell her. "The chain is platinum, and the stone is an emerald, which means all of the small stones surrounding it must be diamonds. I'd say the emerald is three carats at least."

"Are you sure?" Dee asks.

"Why did you tell her?" Tanner groans in my ear. "So much for buying it for ten bucks."

"Absolutely," I confirm to Dee.

"Lord." She clutches one hand over her chest.

Nah, just call me West.

"A necklace like this would retail for at least ten thousand dollars," I add, before pausing to watch her jaw drop. "It's your lucky day, Miss Dee."

With that, I turn and leave, letting the momentum of the surrounding crowds drag me forward.

I still need to find a rusty antique that looks like it was buried in the dirt for a hundred and fifty years.

"You should have bought it," Tanner says, sounding flabbergasted. "I mean, it *is* a flea market. People come to these places to find great steals."

Sure, I could've bought her stupid necklace for a single Hamilton, but this wasn't my game. It doesn't take Sherlock Holmes to see that Grandma Dee is living hand-to-mouth. The necklace could turn everything around for her.

"It would've been stealing," I reply.

What a strange thing for me to say, given my profession. Yes, I lie and I steal, but *only* from marks, and today Dee isn't my mark.

"I'm hungry," Tanner says. "Let's get something to eat. I'm heading down to the kitchen."

"I'm heading to the food trucks."

Tanner's food is easy. He walks me through the preparation of his sandwich—tuna fish, mayo, American cheese, and jalapeno slices. Yuck to the third power. As a general rule, I don't eat anything that breathes under water, and mixing fish with jalapenos is just plain wrong.

"Okay, I got a decision to make," I tell him as I study several menu boards. "I'm staring at three trucks—falafel, Indian, or cheesesteak."

"Cheesesteak," he immediately replies.

"Okey doke. I'm stepping into line at Vinnie's Phat Philly. Only I've never had a cheesesteak before. Lots of options."

"You've never had a cheesesteak? How is that even possible?"

"They look so messy and out of control."

"Part of why they taste good," Tanner says. "Here, let me walk you through it."

With a shrug and a sigh, I nod as if he can see me. "Right then. Transferring helm control over to you, Ensign Cardwell."

At the counter, the guy inside fires questions at me machine-gun fast, as if shooting bullets, and Tanner makes my choices.

"Beef or chicken?" the man asks.

"Beef," Tanner answers, and I relay his decision.

"Cheese?" the guy immediately shoots back.

"Provolone," Tanner answers equally as fast. He also insists on grilled onions and bacon.

When Vinnie hands me a greasy mess piled high on a sub roll, my stomach squirms at the prospect of the imminent heartburn I'll be suffering. Setting my food down on a nearby picnic table, Tanner and I slow down our conversation to eat.

"This is really good," I say after several bites, "but it's too much. I can't finish. How's yours?"

"I'd rather have a cheesesteak, but as tuna fish goes, it's not bad. So what's next on your shopping list?"

Glancing down at my phone, I frown. "Shit, I only have ten percent juice left on my phone." I don't want to hang up, but I'm a victim of battery betrayal.

"That sounds like my cue." He pauses, but I can tell he has more to say. "Maybe I can come by and see you tomorrow."

Grinning stupidly, I reply, "No need. I'm going to be in your neck of the woods in the morning. We can have lunch."

"It's a date. Meet me at one o'clock." He gives me the name and address of a coffee house in downtown Stockton.

On the drive back to Petaluma, I call Mother to report in. I've missed three of her calls during the time I was talking with Tanner.

"Where the hell have you been?" she shouts.

Ah yes, my loving mother. Queen of the blunt people.

"Hello to you too," I reply. "Let me explain. I—"

"You can't go dark on me. We are a *team*. We work *together*. Got it?"

"I've been on the phone with Tanner for three hours," I blurt out. "He called me."

No response. A couple beats of silence follow.

"Oh," she finally says in a much quieter and clearly startled voice. "How'd it go?" she continues, her tone much more civil.

"He called me," I say. "Things are moving fast. Phase one is over. We move on to phase two tomorrow. I have a date."

More silence. Then she says in a raspy voice, "It hasn't even been twenty-four hours."

"Yeah, well sometimes I get lucky, and sometimes I really am that good."

CHAPTER EIGHT

"Are you listening? Pay attention, West," Mom demands.

A growl rises in my throat, and I readjust my chopsticks to take another stab at my plate of shrimp lo mein. We're enjoying Chinese takeout outside on the patio and taking in a gorgeous sunset. It would be so beautiful and relaxing if only my mother wasn't talking.

"West?"

I toss my chopsticks down and lean back in my chair. "Mom, we've been through this a hundred times. I got it. Back off, parental unit, and let me finish my dinner."

Mom's flogging me with the obvious. She never used to be this way, but I guess I earned it after last year. Still, I have to clench my teeth to keep from lashing out.

"She's right," Peter says. "You're straying into browbeating territory. At least wait until after dessert."

"This is important," Mom shoots back. "Phase two is the most crucial part of the game for a closer. You know that, Peter."

Right. Phase one—attract interest. Phase two—gain trust. Phase three—lower the boom. No one expected me to blow past phase one with Tanner so quickly. Heck, I'm already well into phase two if I'm reading the signs correctly.

"She'll be fine," Peter replies with an irritated scoff before lifting a dumpling to his mouth. "She's a natural."

Mom ignores him and continues preaching. "You have to figure him out and push the right buttons. Be honest and immerse yourself in the role. Remember, this is where most closers fail. Marks may be marks, but they can smell fake and phony a mile away."

"Again, I got this. I actually *like* talking to him. He's funny. I'm not faking it."

Mom eyes me suspiciously at first but gives me an approving nod. "Good. But at the end of the day, he's your mark. Never forget that again. Like is good. Anything more is bad. Right?"

"Yeah, yeah, yeah." I shake my head at her and make sure she sees it. But I get it. I didn't just like Josi and Jem. I adored them and they adored me. That didn't work out so well.

"Don't worry," I say, standing to head back inside. "He's so not my type. Romantically, that is."

The problem is I don't really have a type. Or, if I do, I have no idea what it is.

***

The next morning, I'm up with the sun, packing my backpack with what I'll need. The weather lady on the 6:00 am news said in a way too chirpy voice to expect temps in the nineties, so I'm bringing several bottles of water. Decked out in olive-colored chino shorts and a simple t-shirt, I should be comfortable if I stay in the shade.

I spent most of last night staring up at the ceiling and thinking about my date with Tanner. Before I can focus on him, though, I have to deal with the Bel Canto Ranch—the *other* property—and I have the most kicked-up, kick-ass plan in the world for that. If it works, that is.

"Breakfast?" Peter asks when I enter the kitchen. He's sitting in the breakfast nook, drinking coffee.

"I'll grab something on the road. I want to be there by nine."

"I haven't had a chance to thank you for helping out," he says.

"It's not a freebie, Uncle. We're getting paid pretty well."

"Yes, you are," he says. "Still, you could have gotten paid doing something far less risky."

"And far less fun." I shoot him a wink.

He sighs as if I'm too young to know what I'm talking about.

Then his expression turns serious. "We don't have a lot of time. My window of opportunity ends in four weeks when the Kostinens return from Europe. The deal has to close well before then, and I need at least twenty-four hours to move the money and disappear. I've invested a lot of time putting together this deal with Hal."

"We'll be done in a week," I proclaim.

"So confident. You remind me of Lucian."

Lucian. My father. The man Mom almost never speaks of.

"I don't remember much about him anymore," I answer softly, almost speaking to myself. I used to, but the memories are mostly gone. He died when I was five. What I do remember is his beard and shoulder-length black hair, and the way he would toss me in the air as if I weighed no more than a beach ball.

Gulping down the last of his coffee, Peter stands and walks over to the counter by the sink. After grabbing a set of keys, he says, "Catch."

Cool. He's letting me drive his Tahoe. Much better than Mom's Lame Mobile. Time to get this show on the road. As I turn to head to the front door, a thump on the stairs causes me to turn toward the sound. Wearing one of her silk robes and with a hand covering a yawn, Mom is coming down the steps.

"You'll do fine," she says.

"I know."

"Follow the sun, West."

I kiss two fingers, hold them aloft as always, and reply, "I go where it leads."

***

An hour later, in the middle of a beautiful morning, I'm driving toward Stockton, dutifully following the GPS directions. Although I've had my Florida driver's license since the day after I turned sixteen, I've been driving regularly since I was fourteen. Mom taught me young, saying in our line of work it was essential both of us be able to handle a getaway car.

Shortly after ten, after getting lost for an hour—GPS notwithstanding—I locate the Bel Canto Ranch and officially begin this sub-game. Mom and Peter have small roles to play, but I'm doing most of the acting since this is my idea.

I so can't wait.

After sucking in a deep breath and mouthing a silent prayer to no particular deity, I emerge from the car with my backpack looped over one shoulder. Showtime.

I chose high-waisted shorts because they make me look like a mousy librarian who inherited too much dweeb DNA. Earlier, I slipped on a pair of thick, black-framed glasses and clipped my hair back with a couple of tortoiseshell barrettes. Poorly applied lipstick completes the look. I've aged at least five years and I look like Mrs. Polly Poindexter.

Perfect.

A stoop-shouldered bald guy answers the front door several seconds after I ring the doorbell. With his smooth head and bushy eyebrows, he could pass for an elderly Jean-Luc Picard.

"I'm here to see Mr. Thomas Dellesandro. I understand he's the owner of this property."

"That's me. Who the hell are you?"

Ah, refreshingly brusque.

"Sir, I'm Melissa Terry. I'm a graduate student at UCLA. I wanted to ask permission to examine part of your property and take some pictures. I won't disturb anything."

"Why?" he asks suspiciously.

"I'm researching my dissertation on Charles Earl Bowles and the culture of banditry in nineteenth-century California. I believe he has a connection with the northwestern corner of your land. I'd like to see if any trace of his cabin remains."

"Bowles?"

"Aka Black Bart. He was a bandit who roamed northern California in the mid-to-late eighteen hundreds. Might be some good publicity in it for you if I find anything."

He rubs his chin for several seconds, weighing how to respond. I have a couple of backup lines to trot out if he balks.

"Knock yourself out, miss. But stay out of the crops."

"Thank you, sir. I'll only be a couple hours. You—"

He shuts the door in my face, thereby dismissing me from his porch.

What a fricking tool.

Laughing at what I'm going to do to this guy, I bound down the stairs and begin walking toward the part of his property I've selected. I chose the northwest corner because, according to Google Maps Earth View, a dirt road conveniently leads straight to it and there's nothing there but a small hill with a copse of trees on top.

Once on-site, I go through the motions of taking pictures with my phone, but it's for show in case anyone is watching. Then I kick the dirt around as if I spent time excavating a little. After twenty minutes, I collapse on the ground, hidden from sight, lean against a tree in the shade, and pull out my Kindle. I have time to kill and I'm already sweating from every pore.

When the alarm on my phone goes off at the end of two hours, I stand, brush the dirt and grass from my shorts, and march back to the house, but not before carefully extracting an old, no longer functioning, black powder pistol from my backpack. After Tanner hung up during my flea market trip, I bought the rusted piece of junk for fifty bucks on my way out. The guy assured me the almost unrecognizable lump of metal was actually present at the Battle of Gettysburg and insisted on a price of $500.

Right, buddy. You can't scam a scammer.

"Fifty bucks," I told him. "The offer expires in forty-five seconds."

"This was General Pickett's personal sidearm."

"Yeah, and you're wearing General Lee's underwear," I countered. "Twenty seconds, then I walk."

"You'll get a certificate of authenticity," the guy blurted out, as if whatever meaningless piece of paper he generates is worth anything.

"Ten seconds," I replied. After more than that amount of time passes, I continued, "I'm sorry we can't do business."

I turned to leave, and then he caved. "Wait. Fifty, it is."

When I approach my car, Mr. Dellesandro is in the front yard, crouched over to adjust the position of a lawn sprinkler. He straightens when he sees me coming, his eyebrows drawn down in a squint or possibly a glower.

Time to dangle the bait in front of Mr. Crabby Crab Apple.

"Get your pictures, Miss Terry?"

I nod. "I think I also found the remains of part of a foundation. It could be his cabin. This would confirm what I've read in several of his letters we recently discovered."

"Really?" he exclaims, his surprise evident.

"I also found this." I hold up the blob of metal. "I think it's a Colt Army Model eighteen-sixty pistol. Normally, something like this wouldn't be worth anything in this shape, but it could have tremendous archaeological significance. With your permission, I'd like to send it back to the university lab for testing. It's yours, of course. I'll be sure to return it."

"Is it Black Bart's?"

"I think so," I say with a bob of the head. "But we need to run some tests. Also, I'd like to come back tomorrow morning and scrape away some soil near the cornerstone, if that's all right with you."

"Sure."

Bait taken.

Tomorrow, I set the hook and reel in my mark.

CHAPTER NINE

Atlanta
One year ago

Several days after I moved in with the J sisters, I ambled down the stairs of the living quarters over the shop, ready to make breakfast for the old gals and then get back to work sorting through inventory. Since they weren't charging me rent, and I got free board, maybe $100 a week wasn't so bad after all.

Josi sat at the kitchen dinette table when I entered, sipping her regular morning Earl Grey tea from a chipped cup. She wore a black two-piece dress suit that looked good on her very thin frame. Her face showed wisps of makeup and her eyes sparkled with amusement when she took me in.

I hoped I look as elegant and alive in my eighties as Josi did that morning.

"Good morning," I said cheerily.

She clicked her tongue in a sound of disapproval. Uh-oh, what did I do?

"Oh Jenn, whatever are you wearing?" she half muttered while dragging her teacup to her mouth.

I gulped and glanced down at my blue and yellow leggings. "Uh, pants?" Then I considered my blouse: a gray, V-necked shirt. I looked rather plain IMO. Maybe my white running shoes were what caught her attention.

"It won't do," Josi continued. "You simply must wear a dress if you're going to interact with customers."

"A dress?"

I hate dresses. I decided to change the subject. "So what would you like for breakfast? I'm cooking."

When Mom and I weren't eating out or ordering in, I did all the cooking. Mom sucked at it. I was a pretty decent chef, if I say so myself, having learned everything I knew from watching food shows on TV.

"Since you volunteer, give us goo and the moo," Jem answered, as she walked in to join Josi at the table.

"Sorry?" I asked, scrunching my eyebrows together.

"Pancakes, syrup, and milk," Josi answered. "That's what we called it when I was a young girl."

"There were combinations too, remember?" Jem added. "Goo, the moo, and an oink. That meant add bacon."

"Gee, I can't understand why that expression ever faded from use," I said with a teasing smile.

"If you think that's a killer diller," Jem replied with a grin, "guess what we called a tin of canned milk?"

Thinking this might be a *who's buried in Grant's tomb* kind of question, I ventured, "Milk in a can?"

"An armored heifer," Josi answered.

"And eggs were hen fruit," Jem said, and then sighed. "So long ago."

I made them pancakes, sans oink, and by nine o'clock I skipped downstairs to unlock the front door and flip the Closed sign over to Open. I didn't need to hurry. We never had any foot traffic in the morning and usually only a few browsers in the afternoon. I had yet to meet a customer under the age of forty.

My plan for the day was simple: work the counter, continue inventorying the estate pieces, and update the website I created for them. On my lunch break tomorrow, I would check in with Mom and give her an updated list of jewelry I identified as keepers.

So far, I'd found several items we absolutely had to have: the ruby pendant worth at least forty grand, a nineteenth-century pearl necklace I pegged at twenty grand, an old mine-cut diamond ring at seventy-five grand, and a couple emerald brooches we'd get at least fifteen grand for. Not a bad haul. But I had made my way through only a quarter or so of what the Js had in storage. I'd need at least a couple more weeks to comb through the rest. Once I finished, then it would be time to work out a plan with Mom to appropriate the pieces we wanted.

Scamming Josi and Jem should be a piece of cake. They trusted me as family, and I had full access to everything they owned. We wouldn't take everything, of course, only the really good stuff. By the time I finished fleecing them, they'd never know what hit them.

Easy peasy, lemon squeezy.

CHAPTER TEN

After leaving the Bel Canto Ranch, the gas light on the Tahoe blinks on, so I stop at a filling station off the freeway, where I use the bathroom to change into something more interesting than my current loser costume. I slide on a pair of jean shorts, wiggle into a sleeveless blouse, and adjust my bra. Next, I wipe off the flame red lipstick and replace it with tangerine lip gloss before brushing out my hair.

Voilà! I've shape-shifted back to West Rowan. I'm officially ready to go on stage for my next scene. *A Midsummer Night's Scam*, Act II.

The remaining drive takes twenty minutes up the I-5 over tabletop-flat land virtually devoid of trees. But for irrigation, this area might be Death Valley North.

The GPS directs me to the coffeehouse, which Tanner said was his favorite hangout. Inside where it's air conditioned, I spot him sitting at a table near the door.

"West." He gestures me over. "I'm buying. What do you want?"

"Vanilla latte and a fruit cup."

"That's it? I'm taking you out to lunch here."

"Fine. Get me a sandwich."

He stares at me, waiting for specifics. "I need a *little* more guidance," he says, pinching his thumb and forefinger almost to the point of touching.

"Surprise me. Get me something exotic I'm unlikely to have tried before."

He laughs. "I know just the thing."

When he returns a few minutes later, I'm presented with an unidentifiable bread concoction. It has thick slices of toasted white bread hiding something weird in between. Lifting one edge, I stare at the inside and then raise my eyes. "What is it?" I ask when he doesn't speak.

"Nutella, banana slices, and Canadian bacon." He pauses to study me. "They call it a Canuck Elvis."

"What a combination."

"Hey, you said exotic. I got a doughnut for us to split for dessert."

And there it is. Sitting on a plate is a giant doughnut nearly big enough to double as an emergency flotation device. It's smeared with a thick layer of strawberry icing and covered with multicolored sprinkles. At a loss for words, all I can do is shake my head.

"What? You don't like doughnuts?"

"Not when they're the size of an inner tube. Besides, sprinkles are for little kids."

He chuckles softly. "Are you sprinkle shaming me?"

"Maybe a little." I laugh and point at the folder resting on the table next to his food. "What's that?"

He flips it open, withdraws several sheets of paper stapled together, and slides them across the table.

"It's my AP English reading list," he says. "I'm trying to figure out what to read next."

His reading list is totally irrelevant to this game, but I'm curious to compare what he's being asked to read with what I've read. I shouldn't wander off on this tangent, but reading and stories are what I have instead of a normal life.

He's quiet while I flip pages and methodically scan down the list of titles with my index finger. I've read at least two-thirds of the hundred and fifty or so books listed. Most of the ones I haven't read are relatively recent, although when I see several titles by Henry James, I wince inwardly at not having read anything of his yet.

"Pretty thorough list, huh?" he asks.

"Some curious choices. They include Walt Whitman, but leave out Emily Dickinson. These are mostly guy authors. It sounds like the people who made this list all had penises."

Tanner snickers and starts picking sprinkles off the doughnut and tossing them at me. Some land in my hair. I try to pick one up from the table to toss back, but it's not working.

"*Stop*," I yell.

"You're bad."

"To. The. Bone."

Okay, I've gone off script here. I'm supposed to talk about the vineyard and hint at how fun it would be for us to spend the summer together there. But he's knocked me off my stride with books. He wasn't supposed to be a reader dude. That's *my* secret life.

I push the paper back at him. "So, what's the most recent book you've read off the list?"

"*Sister Carrie.*"

"Impressive," I say. "One of my favorites. What one word comes to your mind when you think of Carrie Meeber?"

"Floozy," he shoots back. "You?"

"Strong."

"Strong? You're kidding."

I shake my head. "She knew what she wanted and did what she had to do to get it, and she didn't let artificial morality hold her back."

"She slept her way to the top," he retorts. "What about poor Hurstwood? He dies a miserable death. She used him, and when he had nothing left to give, she tossed him aside."

"Poor Hurstwood?" I counter, slightly incredulous. "He seduced her while he was married. Where's your indignation over that? You don't think he was using her too?"

"You're right. They're both skuzz monkeys."

I decide to change subjects. "How's Leah?"

"Okay, I guess. She must have bumped up against something when we visited you. She wasn't cut at all."

"You got a girlfriend?"

"Whoa, slow down, West. I'm getting whiplash over these sudden changes in topics."

"Sorry. I'm not much for segues."

"To answer your question, I *sort of* have a girlfriend."

"How do you *sort of* have a girlfriend?"

He shrugs. "We broke up a few months back, but I can't tell if we ever got back together. Weird, huh?"

"Yeah," I stretch out the word. "Wow, real soul mates."

He shrugs. "I'm in it for the—"

"*Stop.*" I thrust my hand out in the universal "halt" gesture. I don't want to hear the next word about to come out of his mouth.

"Free car washes," he continues, after a couple beats of silence. "Her father owns an auto detail business."

"Liar." I'm smiling as I say this.

"Gospel truth," He offers a two-finger, Boy Scouts' salute. "What about you? Boyfriend?"

"Nope. Never."

"That's a little hard to believe," he says.

"We move around a lot."

Yes, that's one answer. The truth is I don't have the luxury of falling for any guy I like. It doesn't work that way. My universe of potential boyfriends is pinpoint small. Mom would never let me hook up with somebody who wasn't in the biz. You know how many guys are in the biz, intelligent and attractive, and my age? It's pretty much a null set.

"So, go out with me again," he says out of the blue.

I sputter in surprise in the middle of a sip of my drink. Okay. Going out again is a good idea. I didn't think we'd click so well, so fast. I'm hardly working at this. My emotions want me to yell "yes" and pump my fist, but the logic center in my brain cautions restraint. So I tilt my head to one side as if weighing the pros and cons.

"All right. It *might* be fun," I eventually reply.

"Cool. I'll buy you breakfast tomorrow and introduce you to the best waffles ever. Then I can show you around town a bit, and you can help me decide what book to read next."

"Make it a late breakfast. I've got an errand I have to run first thing in the morning."

The errand would be scamming the socks off Thomas Dellesandro.

Our conversation goes quiet as we eat our food. Oddly, my sandwich tastes excellent. I would eat this again. Tanner's sandwich, on the other hand, is a different story. It consists of a thick mound of roast turkey with a generous layer of jalapeno peppers on top. Watching him eat it makes my stomach churn with incipient indigestion.

"Do you put jalapenos on everything?"

He nods. "Pretty much. With the exception of Cocoa Puffs and ice cream."

"You know, ten years from now scientists will probably discover a causal link between jalapenos and baldness. Or possibly even erectile dysfunction."

He snorts a quick laugh. "I'll take my chances." Then he makes a show of taking a big bite and chewing slowly before rolling his eyes skyward as if the taste is heavenly.

"You're an idiot."

"Maybe."

***

During the drive back to Petaluma, I twist up the volume on the radio to loss-of-hearing levels when Adam Lambert starts singing "We Are the Champions." Sorry Mom, I like it so much better than the original. The song sums up my emotions right now. I start singing at the top of my lungs and then momentarily take my hands off the steering wheel to play a riff or two on my air guitar, strumming quickly before the car wanders over the center line.

Tanner Cardwell is going *down*.

CHAPTER ELEVEN

The next day I'm back at Bel Canto by eight in the morning. Mr. Dellesandro is waiting for me when I bring the Tahoe to a stop in his driveway. He has a strangely hopeful expression on his face.

I like it. Hope is good. Hope is a gap in the defenses I can squeeze through and take what I want.

"So, Black Bart, eh?" he asks once I've stepped out of the car and slammed the door shut.

"I'm ninety percent positive," I reply. "Historians have long known he had a secret cabin where he would hide out after robbing stagecoaches. Until now, no one was sure where it was, but in the lost letters we recently discovered, he talks about it. Based on his references to the Middle River, it must be in this general area."

"Well, have at it, young lady."

He doesn't say anything further, but I feel his eyes on me as I troop up the road back to the same spot. Before I left yesterday, I stacked a couple of big rocks on top of each other to serve as the cornerstone of this mythical cabin. After kneeling in front of these stones, I remove a garden trowel from my backpack and proceed to dig a square hole two feet across and a foot deep. In the center of the excavated area, I bury an old, rusty tin can I found on the property, positioning it so only the top lip protrudes. With a glance around to make sure no one is watching, I dump the coins I bought at the flea market into the can and cover them with dirt. Then haphazardly, I toss a corroded horseshoe I also bought at the flea market onto the dirt near the can.

With the stage now set, I sit down to wait. It shouldn't take long.

This is a variation of an ancient game called salting, which involves planting valuables in an area in order to induce someone to pay more for the property than it's worth. Only the goal today isn't to jack up the price, but to entice Dellesandro to reconsider selling his ranch.

Sitting cross-legged on the cheat grass near my freshly dug hole, I return to reading my Kindle, careful to keep it hidden from view with a map draped around it. Once again, the morning heat causes my pores to pop with sweat. I should get freaking hazard pay for this.

After an hour, I catch sight of Mr. Dellesandro stomping up the road toward me, looking agitated. Hastily, I stand and act like I'm carefully studying the map.

Crap. I'm holding the map upside down. Quickly, I flip it around.

"Miss Terry," he huffs, once he's come to a stop three feet in front of me. "Who are you?"

I lower the map. "I told you. A graduate student at UCLA."

He squints at me with a grumpy face. "I checked. No one in the history department has heard of you."

I deftly parry his thrust. "I'm not with the history department. I'm with the anthropology department."

He opens his mouth to say "Oh," but no sound emerges. Instead, he drags his fingers over his bald head as if to comb phantom hair.

"Well, I want to know what's going on here. I've been trying to sell this place for over two years, and no one has come close to meeting my asking price."

I shrug. "Sorry. Maybe you're asking too much."

He points an accusing finger at me. "This morning, all in the same hour, two different people called and offered to pay more than the asking price in cash, sight unseen. That's too bizarre to be a coincidence."

Inwardly, I smile. The two prospective buyers would be Mom and Peter.

"Those greedy bastards," I burst out, acting alarmed and angry. I need to sound shocked, but avoid chewing the scenery too much.

"What?"

"Last night I told my faculty advisor I found Black Bart's cabin. He must have let word slip out, and now the sharks are circling."

"What does that have to do with people suddenly clamoring to buy my ranch?"

Hesitantly, I reply, "Black Bart supposedly buried over a hundred thousand dollars of stolen loot at this cabin." I point behind me at the hole. "Some think it's only a legend, but I believe it's true."

"Give me a fucking break."

Ooh, listen to baldy drop an F-bomb. His face positively radiates skepticism.

"According to the stories," I continue, "he placed a horseshoe over the spot to mark the site."

I step aside and gesture for him to look into the hole. He leans his head down to gawk at the horseshoe I randomly tossed in the dirt. He twists his head to stare at me with OMG face.

"What's that thing in the center?" he asks, returning his gaze to the pit.

"I don't know. I was getting ready to check it out when you came. Why don't you pull it out carefully and we'll have a look?"

With a nimble hop, he jumps down into the hole and carefully extracts the blackened tin can from out of the dirt. Then he gently dumps out its contents on the grass at my feet, and his eyes widen at the sight of the dirt-covered gold and silver coins.

He's now ready to believe any line I feed him.

"If Black Bart really buried one hundred thousand dollars here," I tell him, "the cache could be worth fifty or sixty million in today's dollars. It's why people are suddenly trying to buy your property. Whoever owns the land owns the loot."

"What should I do?"

"I would like to assemble a team of archaeologists to excavate this entire area." I pause and bite my lip, squelching the sudden urge to guffaw at the utter absurdity of what I'm saying. "It wouldn't cost you a dime," I go on. "Anything that comes out of the ground would belong to you, but these people could authenticate the site. If we can prove the loot really is Black Bart's, that would increase its value even more."

"What's in it for you?" he asks, half scowling.

He's a bit of a skeptic. Good for you, old man. Fortunately, I anticipated it and have an answer.

"I'm not interested in money, sir. I want the fame and glory. A find like this would put me right up there with Schliemann and Lewis Leakey."

He looks confused. "Who?"

"Never mind. The point is this is a win-win for both of us."

"Okay. Let's do it. How long will it take?"

"Probably a month to get the permits in order. In the meantime, I'd keep a sharp lookout on this area, if I were you. Trespassers might try illegal digging. I wouldn't trust anyone." Well, other than me, of course.

"Damn straight," he says. "I've been hoping to sell the place and move to Phoenix to be closer to the grandkids. The ranch is too much work and there's not enough money in it. But if that treasure is really down there…?" He strokes his chin in thought.

"You could do a lot with the money," I prompt, in a not-so-subtle appeal to his avarice.

"My son has been itching to go into business for himself." He points at the hole in the ground. "This could finally give him the stake he needs. Might smooth over a lot of the potholes between us."

"It could," I agree, not really sure what he's talking about.

"I've lived on this ranch for fifty years," he says with a sigh. "What's another year, eh?"

"The wait will be worth it, sir. Your land will triple in value."

He glances over at me with a hint of a smile. He believes me. He trusts me. And I'm going to hurt him because of it. Except I can't think that way. *This* is who I am. *This* is what I do.

I'm expecting to see greedy, lustful eyes, but he's blinking back tears. For an instant, I feel sorry for him and whatever is going on with his son. It's not about the money for him. It's about reconciling with his boy. I struggle to push away the emotion.

Thomas Dellesandro is a mark. You can't feel sorry. You can't care. You can't regret.

Yet, I do.

When he rubs at his eyes with the palm of his hand, I hesitate for a moment and question whether I should screw him over or not.

It's Atlanta all over again.

But it can't be.

I can't let that happen again.

CHAPTER TWELVE

Atlanta
One year ago

"This is insane," I murmured as I used a letter opener to slice open another envelope.

"What?" Josi asked. "Jenn, don't burble. Speak plainly."

"Your bills are all way past due," I said loud enough for Josi's hard-of-hearing ears to register.

"Pshaw." Josi waved her hand dismissively.

I shook my head, took a deep breath, and went back to sorting through their piles of mail. Josi and I were in the sitting room of the upstairs residence. Me at an antique rolltop desk and Josi lounging on a burgundy settee. The only light in the room came from two lamps with off-white shades ringed with long fringes. Their yellow glow struggled to keep the shadows at bay. They looked like cast-offs from Victorian England.

I held up a utility bill with Urgent stamped on top in bold red letters. "They're going to turn off our power if we don't pay this by last Monday."

"What?" Josi huffed in indignation. "Horse feathers."

I placed the power bill on top of the stack of the notices of overdue debts, which had to be paid immediately. I had another pile going for overdue bills that could slide another month, and a third smaller pile for bills they were current on.

Jem had complained over a lunch of Cobb salads that their creditors were overwhelming her with demands and threats. I volunteered to sort through their bills and organize them. I figured it was simply a case of the Js being disorganized, forgetful, and dismissive of their many debts.

Boy was I wrong. With Jem's help, I registered for online access to their bank accounts.

Oh my god. They barely had enough money for groceries, let alone a mortgage payment and all the other expenses of running a business and owning a home. Their only real source of income was jewelry sales, but these had tailed off significantly in the last couple years. Yes, they picked up somewhat in the last month since I'd been here, thanks to the online store I set up, but it wasn't nearly enough.

I rose to leave Josi, who had drifted off to sleep with her head tilted back. I needed to talk to Jem, whom I found downstairs in the shop, dusting display cases.

"Well, how bad is it?" Jem said when she saw me.

"I'd say we have sixty days before you lose your business and your home."

"Oh my."

"We need to sell *everything*," I said. "And sell it *now*."

"How? You've seen how we operate. We don't have the customers coming in like we once did."

I began shaking my head halfway into her remark. "You can't rely on business as usual. It's not working. First thing we do is launch a special sale on the entire inventory. Then we advertise, advertise, advertise. Newspapers, Twitter, Facebook…everywhere."

"Sale?" she mouthed with an incredulous expression. "We're not peddling used cars here, my dear."

"All of the cheap stuff we sell at cost plus, say, six percent. But once we got them in the door, we try to upsell them our more expensive items. The point is, we need buzz. We need people *wanting*, no *begging*, to visit the store."

"Oh lord," she said, placing one hand over her heart. "What would Father say?"

She was upset, her face flushed. I instantly felt sorry for her and Josi. Still, I didn't think she grasped the full gravity of the situation.

"Ma'am," I said, "you're six months behind on your mortgage. The bank is going to foreclose any day. We have to feed the monster now." Oh Jesus. I might as well have slapped her in the face.

Jem brought her hand up to her mouth as her face crumpled. Then she started to cry. I felt absolutely horrible. I crossed the space between us in a couple steps and wrapped my arms around her frail body. She cried on my shoulder as I hugged her. What Hank Williams would call my "Cold, Cold Heart"…well, it broke a little.

The world around us can be so cruel, unrelenting, and unforgiving. In my brief sixteen-plus years on the planet, I'd certainly figured that out. These women hadn't. They were no longer able to cope with the world and hadn't been for years and years, but they couldn't understand why the universe was no longer on their side.

It was never on your side, I wanted to scream at them.

Life isn't a pleasant stroll to be enjoyed, it's a battle to be fought. Didn't they get that? No, they didn't. Josi and Jem were old spinsters with no family. They had each other and they had their store. That was it. They were two pieces of old driftwood hitched together and tossed mindlessly about by an angry surf.

Except now they had me. I would anchor them. I would take care of them.

Only what the hell was I thinking? What was going on with me? With one hand, I was reaching out to help them get back on their feet, while my other hand was slipping into their back pockets to take away their only means of staying on their feet. How could I do both at once? How could matter and antimatter exist inside a person at the same time?

No fucking clue.

In retrospect I shouldn't've gotten involved in their domestic affairs. The best I can do in rationalizing my actions is that somewhere in the back of my brain I thought helping them might offset hurting them.

"You have enough inventory to get current on your bills," I said soothingly while stroking her hair. "You have enough to live comfortably for the rest of your lives. We need to get it out of your back room and in front of people."

"How?" she asked in between sobs. "You've seen our display cases. They're already packed full."

"We list as much of it as we can on your new online store," I replied. "Then we take our show on the road."

My use of the word "our" didn't escape me. This was a mistake. I knew it at the time, but I said it anyway.

So, that was how I found myself signing the three Js up for an exhibition table at the National Jem and Jewelry Show the following month in Nashville, Tennessee.

CHAPTER THIRTEEN

Once the Bel Canto Ranch is out of sight in the rearview mirror, I speed dial Mom.

"Well?" she asks.

"It worked. He's taking the place off the market."

She lets out what can only be described as a long, shuddering sigh of relief. "Okay, I'm impressed, but don't get cocky."

"I'm going to meet Tanner for brunch. I'll be back before dinner. Hal Cardwell should go ahead with buying Uncle's vineyard now, irrespective of what his son thinks, but just in case, I need to keep working my angles with him."

"Understood," she replies curtly. "Don't discuss the Bel Canto Ranch with him, even if he brings it up, okay?"

***

Brunch with Tanner is sublime, and I don't mean the conversation or his company. No, the pecan and cinnamon Belgian waffles are amazing. Both of us are so focused on the food we've managed to only exchange trifling small talk. We agree the wildfires this year suck. I'm a Miami Dolphins fan, he's a 49ers nut. I'm a bagel girl, he's a doughnut guy.

"How's your father?" I ask, before stuffing the last forkful of waffle and whipped cream in my mouth. It melts on my tongue, sending spasms of pleasure through my tastebuds.

He pauses to swallow a bite of his western omelet. "Kind of bummed. We both are. You remember that ranch I told you about?"

I raise an eyebrow in question and shoot him my best "ranch, what ranch?" expression.

"Anyway, the guy called an hour ago and said it wasn't for sale anymore."

"Sorry." I adopt a consoling tone. "That sucks. What's your father going to do?"

"Search around for another place near Stockton."

Another place near Stockton? I want to remind him about the vineyard, but I need to be subtle lest I betray any bias. As far as Tanner knows, my family and I work there and shouldn't care less who the owners sell it to.

"Another ranch?" I venture.

He shrugs. "Maybe. Of course, Dad is still pushing for the vineyard, but I'm not sure about it."

"Wow, it's great that your father wants your approval before buying something. My mother never seeks my input for anything."

He scratches his jaw and chuckles. "It's not my approval he wants, actually. It's my money."

I struggle to keep my jaw from falling open. What is he talking about? This situation is far more involved than Peter thought or cared to tell me about. In a long con, you have to know your mark as well or better than he knows himself. Acting on half-ass information is damn sloppy. I didn't sign up for this. I'm supposed to help steal money from the old man, not Tanner. A subtle distinction, maybe, but this is a Slurpee of a different flavor.

Before I realize it, I'm grinding my teeth in frustration. I need to know what exactly is going on here. Mom would want me to sound a retreat and huddle with her and Peter to decide what to do next. But I'm going to do what Mom hates—fix bayonet and charge. Or, as Mom describes it, I'm going off script and ad-libbing by the seat of my pants.

I clear my throat and try to sound nonchalant. "Money?"

He scrutinizes me for several moments as if I've raised his suspicions. Immediately, I search for some remark to diffuse the awkward silence, but he speaks first. "When my grandfather passed, he left a quarter of his estate to Dad and the rest he left in trust to Tonya and me. Dad wants us to invest in a place along with him. He doesn't have enough money on his own."

Tonya? Who in Middle-earth is Tonya? Great, another freaking complication. "Tonya?"

"My older sister. She and her daughter live with us."

Oh yeah. That was in the file. I toss subtlety out the window. I need answers. "So, both you and Tonya have to sign off on any place your father wants to buy?"

"If he wants our money."

Oh sweet Jesus. Not only do we have to get Tanner on board, but we have to swing this Tonya person too. I can't believe Peter wasn't able to ferret out what's really going on here. If we'd had solid intel, we could have come up with a better plan than the current *stupid* plan: send West in to flirt.

"So, what's your story? I mean, where are you from?"

Still reeling a little from the new information, I forget to lie and end up telling him the truth. "I grew up in Kissimmee, Florida."

He bobs his head as if he already knew this. "You're staying the summer with your uncle?"

"Until mid-August. Then Mom and I will move into an apartment in Petaluma. I start my senior year in the fall."

"Where?"

Where? How the hell would I know? I didn't dig into my fake backstory that far. I'm going to have to wing this and make an educated guess.

"Petaluma High School," I reply, trying to keep my voice from shaking with uncertainty.

"Yeah, I know some guys there."

The air deflates from my lungs in a slow exhale of relief. Apparently, there really is a Petaluma High School. Note to file— don't make up shit if you're not prepared to answer questions about it.

"You know they filmed parts of *American Graffiti* in Petaluma."

"I did *not* know that," I reply, genuinely surprised.

He's about to say more when his phone buzzes with an annoying ringtone that sounds like clanging pots and pans. He yanks it out of his pocket, stares at the screen, and a scowl spreads across his face.

"One second," he says, before answering the call. "Tonya, what's up?" His scowl deepens, and he rolls his eyes and exhales deeply while shaking his head. "I can't. I have plans this morning *and* this afternoon." After several more seconds of silent listening, Tanner mutters, "It's always an emergency with you. Fine, but you owe me for this." He ends the call. "My sister has a damn ass crisis," he tells me, putting air quotes around "crisis." "I have to go home and babysit my eight-year-old niece for a few hours. Can you take a rain check on me showing you around town?"

An idea blossoms in my brain. Mom wouldn't like this.

"You want some help?"

Not only can I hang with Tanner, but I can take a run at Tonya by helping take care of her kid.

"You don't understand," he whispers as if Tonya might be listening to his next words. "Janey isn't your typical cute kid. She hardly speaks to anyone and doesn't like strangers."

"It'll be fine. I'm great with kids." This from the girl who has never babysat anyone in her life, and who is certainly not above stealing candy from the kid if Mom told me I had to.

"Well, I could definitely use all the help I can get."

Perfect. This will give me a chance to meet Tonya and start earning trust points. In grifting, earning a mark's undying acceptance and allegiance is our gold standard. Win that and game over. The mark will hand over everything to me voluntarily, never realizing until it's too late, and I'm a douchebag liar. Hard to pull off, but it's the grifter version of baseball's perfect game.

And it's what I'm going to do. I'm not just going to win this game—I'm going to smoke it.

As soon as I'm in my car, about to follow Tanner to his house, I call Mom to report. "It's me." Actually, there's no need for me to identify myself. A call from my cell triggers the distinctive ringtone she picked for me: "Hot Child in the City," a moldy-oldie seventies tune. Mom considers it our personal theme song. I still remember dancing to it in the kitchen with her when I was ten while she replayed the song over and over again.

"How'd it go?" Mom asks.

"We got problems. Peter totally missed the boat about what is going down here."

"How so?"

I sigh deeply and plunge into a detailed report.

"So, most of the inheritance money belongs to Hal's two kids, Tanner and Tonya," I say. "Our buddy Hal needs *both* of them on board. Unless they *both* want the vineyard, there isn't going to be a sale."

"God bless America," Mom practically shouts. "So we have to win the hearts and minds of *both* Hal's kids?"

"Correctamundo."

Mom lets out a low growl of frustration. "Any ideas how to deal with this Tonya?" "Maybe I can get to her through her eight-year-old daughter. It's all I got at this point."

Mom yells Peter's name, but her voice is muffled. She must have placed her hand over the speaker. I'm glad I won't be back for a while. She's probably going to rip Peter's arm out of its socket and club him over the head with it.

Everybody makes mistakes, but Mom and I have never screwed up this bad. How could Peter not know where his money would be coming from?

This is one of the main proverbs in the grifter bible: know thy source of funds.

CHAPTER FOURTEEN

With Billie Eilish blasting away inside the Tahoe, I trail Tanner back to his house on a quiet, tree-lined lane in the northern part of Stockton. Across the street, a middle-aged man in a bathrobe and slippers stoops to pick up the paper from his driveway, eying me suspiciously when I emerge from the Tahoe. The Cardwell house is large and quite nice for the neighborhood, but it's not a full-blown mansion. Let's call it a starter castle.

"Hold on to your butt," Tanner says, emerging from his car. "We're going behind enemy lines."

Sure enough, the instant we enter the house, I'm enveloped in complete chaos. The TV in the living room is blaring the show *Dinosaur Train* at full volume. A young girl—Janey, I presume—is sitting on the floor, bawling her lungs out about something, surrounded by at least a dozen dolls in various stages of undress. She's wearing a cute pink romper that sets off her long, silky black hair. The whiff of something burnt lingers in the air.

The noise level causes my muscles to immediately tense. This isn't a home: it's a war zone. Sighing heavily, I follow Tanner into the living room. Time to jump into the deep end.

With a super fake smile pasted on my face, I walk over to the little girl and sit cross-legged on the floor in front of her. She jerks her head up to stare at me, momentarily too surprised to keep crying. She has Tanner's bewitching hazel eyes.

"Hi," I say. "My name's West."

Janey leaps up from the carpet and tears off down the hallway. A door slams shut loudly. Not exactly the reaction I was aiming for, but at least she's not crying anymore.

"She's really shy around strangers," Tanner explains. "She won't come out until you're gone."

We'll see about that. "Let me see if she'll talk to me."

"Knock yourself out." Tanner points down the hallway. I march to a room at the end of it.

"Hey, Janey," I whisper at her closed door. "Can I come in?"

Silence.

Next comes the sound of a chair being dragged across a hardwood floor and shoved against the door.

I think this means *piss off.*

Sorry, Janey, you're not getting rid of me that easily. "You want to see a magic trick? I can show you how it's done." More silence. "Darn it, Tanner and I wanted to take you out on a great adventure today, but I guess we'll have to go alone."

More silence.

Wonderful. So much for my childcare skills. "Good-bye, then," I say. "You really are a pretty girl."

When I return to the living room, a woman in her late twenties storms out of the nearby kitchen and comes to a dead stop when she sees me. Tonya. Tanner follows close behind her. She's dressed in a dark gray pantsuit with a ruffled white blouse.

"This is West Rowen." Tanner gestures toward me.

"A new girlfriend?" Tonya asks, wearing a puzzled expression. "What happened to what's her name?"

"No, it's not like that," he hastens to clarify. "I'm—"

Tonya grimaces, grabs him by the bicep, and forcibly yanks him back to the kitchen. She's trying to whisper, but her voice is so loud I hear every word. "Tan, you can't ignore Janey to go make out with your new girlfriend."

"She's not my girlfriend. She—"

"Whatever. Keep your eyes on Janey and positively no junk food, got it?"

"Hey, I'm doing you a favor here," Tanner reminds her.

"Yes, you are. Like I did you a favor last weekend when—"

"Okay, okay." He puts his hands up as if he's surrendering.

I step closer to them and ask, "What happened last weekend?"

Tonya smirks at me. "I'll let him tell the story. Excuse me, I have to be in court in thirty minutes."

Moments later, the front door jerks open and bangs shut, and just like that, Tonya is gone.

"She's a lawyer?" I ask.

"Uh-huh. White-collar crime." He releases a breath he's been holding in. "She's also Satan. You might want to say a prayer for Gavin."

"Gavin?"

He scowls. "Her fiancé. He has no idea what he's getting into."

Tanner strolls over to the center of the living room with his thumbs hooked through the belt loops of his jeans. He looks defeated, and I'm about to excuse myself from this dystopian household, when out of the corner of my eye, I catch motion and turn to see Janey standing in the hallway, peering at me.

"Adventure?" she asks in a voice barely above a whisper.

"That's what I said. Your uncle Tanner and I are taking you someplace special. It's—"

"We are?" Tanner's expression morphs into one of near panic.

***

Ten minutes later, I pull the Tahoe to a stop next to the first window at a McDonald's drive-through to pay for Janey's chicken nuggets Happy Meal. Tanner is riding shotgun and Janey is in the middle of the backseat, where she has begun to chatter nonstop. First, she tells me all about school this year, going into elaborate detail about her friends and her teacher. She's kind of cute. Tanner apparently doesn't think so. He looks like he has a toothache. Then, Janey begins to list her favorite cartoon characters and TV shows while Tanner begins to shake his head in growing dismay.

"Is this the adventure?" Tanner asks when I hand a bag of food and a drink back to Janey.

"Nope," I reply. "We're going to Fairfield."

"First time I heard a trip to Fairfield described as an adventure," he quips.

I shoot him a mischievous smile. "You'll see."

With the GPS feeding us directions, we arrive in Fairfield in under an hour, and I take the Chadbourne Road exit. It looks like we're heading into an industrial area. I don't know if my plan qualifies as an adventure, but it'll be a surprise.

Janey is swiveling her head around from side to side, as puzzled by what we're doing as Tanner is. After a couple more turns, both Janey and Tanner see the sign that explains everything.

"Jelly Belly!" Janey shrieks.

Yes, it's the Jelly Belly Candy Company, makers of the best jelly beans on the planet. "We're taking the factory tour," I say. "Nobody goes home until we each have new cavities forming on our teeth."

Surprisingly, I find a good parking space steps from the front door. As I turn off the ignition, Janey speaks, her voice trembling slightly. "West?"

"Mmmm?"

"This is a handicap space," she says.

"No problem." Flipping open the arm rest between Tanner's seat and mine, I snatch a handicap parking placard Peter managed to appropriate and hold it up. "Presto. We're legal."

"But none of us is handicapped," she persists.

"This is like a ticket," I say. "If you have one of these, it's okay to park here."

Her expression screams pleading. "But what if a real handicapped person needs this space?"

"Why do you have a handicap tag?" Tanner asks.

"Does it matter?"

Tanner and Janey give me horrified stares as if I'm about to strangle someone's pet bunny.

I'm not going to win this one. Fine. Swallowing a growl of annoyance trying to claw its way out of my throat, I back out and repark in a non-handicapped spot a hundred yards away. What good is a stolen handicap sign if I can't use it? Janey beams at me. Little Miss Goody Two-shoes. I'm going to have to educate her a little.

The incident is quickly forgotten once we climb out of the car. Janey is bouncing up and down so hard she may launch herself into outer space. She slips her hand into mine, and we lead the way inside. Her skin is moist and a little sticky from the sweet-n-sour sauce she dipped her nuggets in, but I don't pull away. Instead, I give her hand a squeeze of genuine affection.

Janey is the opposite of me when I was her age. She's shy and maybe a little afraid of the world, whereas I was brash, mouthy, and precocious. Maybe I can teach her to have a little more confidence in herself.

Once we get inside, the sight is visually arresting. Giant jelly beans and balloons hang from the ceiling, and an explosion of bright colors hits my eyes: red, yellow, blue, and green. The crowds are light this afternoon, so we don't have long to wait to start the tour.

"We get hats," I tell them with a grin after consulting with our tour guide. "Here, let me put on yours, Janey."

Each of us is required to wear these goofy white paper hats with the Jelly Belly logo, supposedly for sanitary reasons. The tour begins with a member of the factory staff taking a picture of the three of us with Mr. Jelly Belly, a copy of which we apparently get to buy at the end of the tour. It's a little cheesy, but Janey is over-the-moon excited.

Our tour guide leads us onto a glass-enclosed overlook, which gives us a nice view of the factory floor down below. Along the way we pass by a neat exhibit of jelly bean portrait art of dead celebrities. I have to admit, it's kind of cool watching the robots at work and seeing bin after bin filled with different colored jelly beans. Even Tanner seems mildly intrigued.

Along the way, we get to try out different samples, but Tanner declines. Apparently he's not a jelly bean guy. Janey, on the other hand, greedily sucks down every one she can pinch between her fingers. At the end of the tour, we receive more free samples, and I opt to buy her a medium-size copy of our photo.

"Here, go to the gift shop and buy some cool stuff," I suggest to Janey. I offer her a ten-spot.

She gestures for me to lean down so she can whisper something. "You come too," she says in a tiny voice. Her bashfulness, which has been missing most of this outing, has returned. Of course, during the tour, she held my hand, squeezing tight the entire time. Okay, I'll chaperone her.

Tanner, on the other hand, begs off and wanders over to sit on a bench and scroll through his phone while we head into the store to shop. He looks bored, but cute at the same time. I feel his eyes on me as I guide Janey into the store. There are so many different jelly bean flavors to choose from, it's a little dazzling. Eventually, Janey and I pick three flavors each. She also asks to buy a package of chocolate-covered raisins for her mother, which is fine by me, but at checkout I learn that the raisins only come in a ten-pound box. The Cardwells are going to be eating a lot of raisins over the next month.

"Here, I'll carry the bags," I offer after we check out.

"I got watermelon, strawberry daiquiri, and peanut butter flavors," Janey excitedly tells Tanner.

"Mmmm," he replies. "Wouldn't I love to have all three of those sloshing around in my stomach. What about you, West?"

"Cinnamon, A&W Cream Soda, and toasted marshmallow."

"What a combo," he murmurs. Then he leads me away a few steps and says, "She must have twenty pounds of sugar in those sacks." He gestures over at the shopping bags sitting next to Janey. "You heard Tonya. No junk food."

"These are *gourmet* jelly beans," I reply. "Don't you dare call them junk." All the same, it probably wouldn't go over well with Tonya if Janey got sick tonight and threw up.

Tanner frowns in amazement and dismay as Janey takes a heaping handful of red jelly beans and dumps them in her mouth.

"Janey, slow down," I say and glance at my watch. "Yikes. We're going to be late. Time to hit the road, guys."

***

Barely ten minutes into the drive back, a small snore from the backseat alerts us: Janey has fallen asleep. She's leaning sideways against the car door, still clutching her bag of strawberry daiquiri jelly beans. Jeez, maybe there's real alcohol in those things after all. We drive in silence for several minutes before Tanner speaks.

"You got Janey eating out of your hand," Tanner whispers, careful not to wake her. "I think she wants to adopt you as her second mother."

"She's a darling. I don't know why you were so anxious about spending time with her."

He chuckles. "You weren't around for Easter, or Christmas, or Thanksgiving. Let's just say Janey puts on quite a show."

"She wants attention. It's normal."

He casts a glance back at Janey to see if she's still asleep. She is.

"So, that wasn't as bad as I expected. You've got a way with kids."

"Tell you what, why don't we take Janey on a follow-up adventure tomorrow?" I say. "We'll make it a full day."

Now that this Tonya person is part of the game, I need to get on her good side, and what better way to do that than to take her daughter on an outing? Well, assuming I can get her to trust me. See, if Tonya was a computer operating system, free childcare would be the hacker's backdoor. Tanner, however, looks seasick at the prospect of spending an entire day with Janey.

"What kind of adventure?" he hazards.

"I don't know yet. Still working on it."

"I have an idea," he says. "Bring a bathing suit tomorrow."

Tanner steals several sidelong glances over at me on the drive back, but neither of us says much. I can tell he's curious about me, which is a good thing. Out of the corner of my eye, I catch him staring at my breasts.

"What?" I raise an eyebrow at him in challenge.

He turns quickly away, but his ears bloom red. "So, it's you and your mom?" he asks.

I nod.

"What about your dad?"

This is a question I can answer truthfully. "Dead. Died when I was five. I don't remember him much. It's been Mom and me most of my life. Well, my cousins too. Dad was part of a huge family."

Janey is still asleep when we arrive back at Tanner's house, but she wakes up with a yawn the instant we come to a stop in the driveway.

And guess who's waiting on the porch for us when we pull into Tanner's driveway? Leah. As if this is a distress signal, Janey begins to cry.

"Shhhh," I coo at her. "I have to go home now, but I'll see you tomorrow, I promise. Tanner's got something really fun planned for us. Be ready with your bathing suit."

This works. Janey goes quiet and her eyes widen. "Really?"

"Absolutely. What time tomorrow?" I ask.

"Ten o'clock."

"I'll be here."

By now, Leah has reached Tanner and Janey, her expression confused and angry at the same time.

"She was helping me babysit," Tanner tries to explain.

Leah speaks to Tanner, but she never takes her eyes off me. "I'll be inside in a second. I want to talk to SI bathing suit model alone for a moment."

Tanner grimaces and shrugs apologetically. I wave him away. Once Tanner and Janey disappear inside, Leah places her hands on her hips. This must be her attack formation.

"Listen, I don't know what your game is," she says, "but leave Tanner out of it."

"Game?"

"That thing with the blood the other day? It was a little obvious."

So, Leah isn't your ordinary clueless mark. I'm going to have to be careful around her. "Tanner invited me out for breakfast, and I was repaying the favor by helping babysit Janey."

The scowl that spreads across her face says she doesn't believe me. "Whatever you're doing," she continues, "leave him alone. He's honest to a fault and, well, a little naïve about things. Don't take that away from him."

It's a struggle not to gape at her. Her words prick me. She doesn't know anything, but she suspects a lot. In another life, in another place, she and I could be friends. She turns to walk back toward the house.

"Leah," I shout at her retreating form, "Tanner and I are taking Janey swimming tomorrow. Why don't you come too?"

She doesn't smile, but she seems to relax. After exhaling deeply, she says, "Yeah, maybe I will."

CHAPTER FIFTEEN

I text Mom and tell her I'll be late for dinner, to go ahead without me, but when I arrive at the vineyard, dinner has yet to be served. The smell of great cooking hits me as soon as I climb out of the vehicle. The aroma intensifies when I step through the front door and see the fancy dining room table set with a white linen tablecloth and fine china. Since Mom doesn't cook, this must be Peter, and whatever he's cooking, the pungent odor is sending my stomach into impatient, hungry convulsions. Peter greets me when I enter the kitchen.

"Nicely done, Niece," he says, kissing me on the forehead. "We're celebrating tonight. We'll have a late dinner in an hour. Run off and relax and leave the work to us." He turns away to take plates out of the cupboard.

"Celebrating? We're in some seriously deep *rahat* here," I reply, lapsing into Romanian to curse.

"Not at all, Niece. You took out the competition and got us the intel we need to know what we're up against."

"So, Mom is dancing a happy dance?"

"Diana was initially displeased. But she agrees we can still win this game. However, we're going to need you more than ever."

I shake my head vigorously. "You brought me in for Tanner. Him I can handle. I never signed up for Tonya."

"We'll come up with a script. In the meantime, relax. You did great."

***

In the spacious living room, I collapse at one end of a long, overstuffed couch, armed with my Kindle. On the side table sits a pile of mail for the Kostinens, except the top piece is already opened and it's addressed to Peter Banica. What the heck is this? I don't recognize the address for Peter on the letter: it must be a mail drop somewhere nearby. The really puzzling thing is *Banica*. Why is he using his real name? On an impulse, I snatch the envelope and fish out the letter. It's from an organization in New York called Her Justice. The message is brief:

Peter, thank you for your recent contribution of $10,000. Your continued support is greatly appreciated. PS: Maria is doing fabulous. She would like to thank you in person one day—Emily

Peter is making charitable contributions? Shut the front door. This must be part of some new scheme he's working. With a shrug, I toss the letter back on the table and begin reading *The Portrait of a Lady* by Henry James. Yes, finally, I'm reading James.

The truth is I'm obsessed with nineteenth-century books. This is when the greatest women writers came into their own. Plus, the stories have amazing plots, hugely detailed worlds, and strong people.

***

A couple hours later we're eating dinner. Mom and Peter are in a great mood, each trying to one-up each other with stories about some of their best exploits. Many of the stories I've heard before, but some are new, like when Dad and Peter sold fifty fake tickets to Super Bowl XXIX and used the proceeds to watch the game from a posh stadium suite.

"West," Mom says, as dinner is winding down, "starting today, you're officially my full partner. From now on, we split everything fifty-fifty."

"Here, here," Peter answers. He offers a toast and we clink wineglasses.

With one gulp, I kill the last of my wine and set down the glass. I'm elated. This is what I've always wanted—to be Mom's equal. This is sweet validation. I'm officially *good enough*. If grifting were an Olympic sport, I'm a solid medal contender.

Atlanta set me back, but I think I'm back to where I was before the wheels came off last year. "So, what's the game plan now?" I ask.

Peter takes a giant swig of his wine and sloshes it around his mouth as if he's gargling a capful of Listerine.

"I'm going to call Hal tomorrow and take his temperature," he answers. "I'm also going to sweeten the pot a little by dropping the price by two hundred fifty grand. Maybe that will coax him to jump down off the fence. In the meantime, keep working on his son. We still need him."

"Tanner and I are taking Tonya's daughter, Janey, out for the day," I say. "I think he likes hanging out with me. He's beginning to hit on me a little."

Peter smiles, his grin so broad I can see both rows of teeth. "Obviously, he's smitten with you. You're a little scary, Niece."

Scary? Is that a complinsult?

"Remember your training," Mom says.

Yes, Mother. My training is all about manipulation. It doesn't matter whether I want someone to hate me or like me, the basic principles are the same. The key is don't be obvious and don't be phony. Those are game killers.

When dinner ends, I head downstairs to the basement. My room has a canopied, king-size bed and a bathroom with a ginormous whirlpool tub where I'm planning on spending the next two hours soaking and reading.

No sooner have I filled the tub, stripped off my clothes, and lowered myself to a sitting position in the steamy hot water, when my phone rings. Expecting Tanner, I grab the phone off the tub ledge and answer in a cheery voice.

"Hey. Perfect timing. I was—"

"Hey back," a female voice says. I recognize her instantly. Leah. Leaf blighter. An audible groan escapes my lips as she says, "I got your number from Tanner's phone."

"Oh. So, you would be calling me why?"

"Curious."

"Ask me a question, I'll tell you no lies." I laugh inwardly at this because this is a game I play well. The line between truth and lie is so fine and malleable, I can effortlessly hopscotch my way on either side as the situation warrants.

"I'll tell *you* a story first. When I was in eighth grade, I caught pneumonia. Tanner brought me my homework each day and sat by my bed. He read to me for hours and held my hand when I was too sick to speak. That's when I fell in love with him. I've waited a long time for him to come around. Just when he is, you appear out of nowhere like a hurricane."

I'm going to be honest with her. Taking a page out of my grifter handbook, I say, "Leah, you know what your problem is? You're easy. He takes you for granted. You should walk away. Let him come to you, and when he does, make him work for it. Be a freaking challenge."

"Thanks." The word comes out flat and devoid of emotion. "Now for my question. I Googled you. Nothing. No Facebook page. No Twitter. No anything."

"Is there a question in there somewhere?"

"Who are you really?"

"My name is Westlyn Rowen. Really."

"Yeah, that's what Tanner said. You know, Westlyn is a *very* unusual name. I tried searching just for it. Nothing. Well, there was a news story from last year out of Georgia."

I know exactly what she's going to say next. My teeth clench together.

"A teenage girl named Westlyn received a special commendation from the Atlanta chief of police. You—"

I cut her off. "Contrary to Google, Leah, there are lots of Westlyns in the world. You found the wrong one."

"Really?"

"You've met me," I snap. "Do I seem like the kind of person who would earn praise from a cop?" I shouldn't have said that.

"That's exactly what I'm trying to figure out."

CHAPTER SIXTEEN

Atlanta
One year ago

"Vanilla bean frap," I told the Starbucks barista. "Grande."

Filled with the sounds of dozens of conversations and scraping chairs, the place was packed with the lunch-hour crowd. Several customers roamed among the tables searching for a place to sit. They didn't seem to notice the table in the back: occupied but had a single empty chair. Once I picked up my order, I threaded my way through the throng until I stood next to the table.

The lady sitting there was dressed in off-white, absorbed in the images on her phone. Her thumb rhythmically stroked the screen to swipe through the pics. Mom pretending not to know me. I rolled my eyes. It wasn't like we were doing espionage here, but whatever.

"Mind if I sit here?" I asked.

"No, help yourself," she said, barely glancing up at me.

I sat, careful not to spill my drink, and tugged out my phone from my back pocket. For several minutes neither of us spoke as I flipped through my emails and played along with Mom's I-never-met-this-person-before-in-my-life act.

"So what's the status?" Mom asked nonchalantly as if querying about the weather. She pitched her voice low so no one could eavesdrop. Like anyone would bother.

I locked gazes with her for a moment. "It's taking longer than expected."

"I guess," Mom replied sarcastically. "You've been imbedded for four weeks. We need to wrap this up and move on."

"I need more time." Mom let out an impatient sigh. "We're sitting on a frigging gold mine," I say. "I need more time to sort through it all."

"Let's go with what you have and split."

"Why? We have the perfect setup here. There's no need to rush. I'm finding stuff every day. Why settle for half a loaf when we can have it all?"

"Because something could go wrong," she hissed. "This isn't our forte. We don't do long cons, remember?"

"Gimme another week or two. It'll be worth it. There's an entire safe I haven't had access to yet. Nothing is going to go wrong, okay?"

Mom glared at me. Part of her impatience was she was bored silly. I knew this. While I was dutifully working all day at the three Js finding the best pieces for us to appropriate, she was stuck in a hotel room, doing mostly nothing but eating and shopping. Poor thing.

"Why don't you take a vacation? Go to Florida for a week. When you come back, I'll be ready to go."

"And leave you here by yourself?"

"I'm fine. They think I'm their long-lost granddaughter. They treat me like royalty. Heck, I'm actually paying their bills for them. They'd donate a kidney for me if I asked."

"Sounds like you're beginning to like it there way too much. They're marks. Don't forget it."

"Duh."

"Remember to keep it professional," she said. "You're not there to be their friend."

I didn't realize it at the time, but Mom was right. Being friends doesn't work when it comes to marks. Mom and I were predators, and Jem and Josi were prey. The lion doesn't play with the lamb during the day and then hunt it at night.

"You could really use a vacation," I said with a teasing smile.

She huffed a brief, dismissive laugh. "I'm not taking a goddammed vacation, so stop asking."

I nodded with a tired exhale. What to do? La di da, la di da.

Mom's impatience was driving me nuts. She sent me at least two or three coded texts a day and insisted I check in with her at least once every morning. I was getting tired of sending emails from the bathroom.

"Then go see a movie or something and let me do my job," I whispered. "Stop breathing down my neck."

"This all better be worth it, West."

Rather than answer, I swiped through several screens on my phone to pull up a picture, which I texted. When her phone dinged, she took her eyes off me to study my message. She gasped at the picture of a necklace with a monster pear-shaped diamond.

"Nice," she said, almost purring like a cat. The edges of her lips lifted in a hint of a smile.

"Nice? Mom, it's fuc—"

"Watch your mouth."

I shrugged and went on, "I grade the color a D with FL clarity. That necklace would retail for *at least* three hundred thousand. And this is just the tip of the iceberg."

Mom nodded in appreciation. The value of a diamond is all about the four Cs: cut, color, clarity, and carat. The highest color grade is D, meaning the stone is absolutely colorless. Really rare. FL clarity, on the other hand, means the diamond is flawless: no blemishes or inclusions. Less than one percent of all pieces grade FL. To find a nice-size diamond with D color *and* FL clarity is beyond extremely rare.

"Okay, okay," she said, sounding reluctant. "Send me pictures of the other stuff you've got. I'm going to start shopping the necklace around to some of our buyers."

I nodded and took a long slurp from my drink. Then I stood and stuffed my phone back in my pocket. "I gotta go," I said. "I have to pick up lunch for Jem and Josi. They'll be wondering what's taking me so long."

Mom rose from her chair.

"*Urmați soare*, West."

"*Mă duc unde duce.*" I turned away and walked out of the shop without a glance back.

CHAPTER SEVENTEEN

I'm up at six again, yawning through my shower, which makes me think of turkeys, who are supposedly so stupid, they'll drown by looking up in a rainstorm. Probably an urban myth, but evocative all the same.

So am I a stupid turkey? Some days I think I might be.

I decide to wear a plain, pink tank top with bright blue pleated shorts. In my gym bag, I have a red swim dress. I'm wearing pink because it's Janey's favorite color. Why do I want to wear what Janey likes? Because I want to ingratiate myself with her and Tonya. I want to worm my way into their trust. This is what grifters do. We're like termites secretly eating away at the insides of your house. Before you even know we're here, your house is toast.

With a bowl of fresh fruit and a mug of coffee in front of me, I take a seat in the kitchen to eat and read. I'm still reading *Portrait of a Lady* on my Kindle, but I only get through a few pages before I'm interrupted.

"West."

With her arms crossed, Mom stands in the kitchen entrance, leaning against the wall. I glance quickly at my watch while sliding my Kindle onto my lap. Seven o'clock. This is a little bizarre. Mom doesn't do early morning.

"What's up? You're sleepwalking, right?" I joke.

"I'm working with Peter to set up a game for us. Don't make any plans for later this week."

I shrug. "Sure. What about the current game?"

"You'll have to handle both." Her voice is frosty, almost rude. Is she mad at me? No. She's probably still ticked off at Peter. "We need to top off our cash reserves," she says, "particularly since you bought all those stupid coins."

"Mom, read my lips—it *worked*."

"Damn lucky."

I exhale heavily with impatience. "I don't believe in luck, and you don't either."

Mom rubs her forehead as if she has a headache, and then she massages the back of her neck. I can't read her emotions. What is bothering her?

"You're moving too fast," she says. "Slow down. You're not all the way back yet."

I reply with as much indifference as I can muster. "I better go. I'll probably be back late again."

"Remember." She pauses almost as if for dramatic effect. "The only people we can trust are each other."

I nod, but I'm a little weirded out. Mom and I have been a team for so long, it's strange to hear her talk like I'm about to leave her or something.

***

After yesterday, when I arrive at Tanner's house at 9:30 am, I'm not sure what to expect. What I don't anticipate is Janey, the human missile. I step out of Peter's Tahoe onto the Cardwell driveway, carefully cradling my latte so it doesn't spill, but no sooner do my feet touch the ground than the front door bursts open and Janey races out dressed in a purple onesie bathing suit. I drop to my knees, set my paper coffee cup on the ground, and suck Janey into a tight hug as she launches herself into me.

"West," she cries out.

"I missed you," I whisper in her ear.

Strangely, I actually did a little. So, yeah, what's with that?

Janey leads me into the house and then promptly races down the hallway to get her backpack. While she's gone, attorney Tonya saunters in, her ebony hair put up in a formal office bun. Her do doesn't quite go with the green apron she's wearing or the spatula she's holding… to say nothing of the wad of chewing gum her jaws are attacking.

Judging from her smile, she seems genuinely glad to see me. A good sign. Her smile widens as she offers me her hand to shake. I take it.

"So, you're Wonder Woman," she says. "Janey won't shut up about you. I'm Tonya. We didn't get a chance to officially meet yesterday."

"Your daughter is pretty amazing."

Tonya lifts an eyebrow in an "are you effing serious" expression, but before she can say anything, Tanner bounds down the stairs in a black t-shirt and his usual khaki cargo shorts. He gives me an appraising glance and nods a couple of times, as if to say I pass inspection. Then his eyes drift over to his sister.

"Tonya, you look like white trash."

She gives him her middle finger and turns to me as if to whisper a secret, but she talks loud enough for Tanner to hear. "He's a real dick, you know. Trust me, you can do better."

Tanner rolls his eyes at her. She gives me a knowing wink, which tells me all I need to know for now. I sense she's getting close to asking me to be a member of Team Tonya. Coo-ell. I have to find a way to get her alone so I can begin my real work of nudging her toward buying a vineyard.

"Well," Tanner says, his voice filled with weary resignation, "let's get this show on the road. We've got a whole day of fun in front of us." He puts air quotes around "fun."

"Where's your bathing suit?" I ask.

He pats both of his hips demonstrably. "I'm wearing them underneath."

"What about Leah? Where is she?"

Janey, who's returned with her backpack, sticks out her tongue at Tanner. I guess it's true what Tanner told me: Leah and Janey don't like each other.

"She's not coming," he replies. He doesn't want to talk about it, so I swallow the question I was about to ask.

***

We arrive at a huge waterpark in Sacramento a little before eleven. Janey's barely able to contain her excitement. It's another blazing hot day, and the cloying smell of chlorine hangs like a limp dishrag over everything. I volunteer to pay for everyone's admission, which comes to almost a hundred dollars. You have to spend money to make money.

Once inside the park, I rent a couple large lockers, and after changing, we dump all of our stuff inside. My swim dress has a 1950s look: the suit is red with white polka dots and could almost be mistaken for lingerie—a teddy or something.

Tanner's trunks are plain, aqua blue, and hang down below his knees, a baggy fit on his lean, tall body. Unlike Janey and me, he has a pretty decent tan. My skin is PPP—pasty, pale, and pathetic. I know from experience: no matter how much time I spend in the sun this summer, I will never achieve anything more than a slight tan at best. At worst, I'll burn until my skin is the color of kimchi.

Janey is bouncing on the balls of her feet as if she's warming up before a track and field event. A nightmarish vision of her charging into the crowds and becoming lost blossoms in my mind. Tonya would hate my guts if I lost Janey in this mob.

I tap her on the shoulder, "J, stick close to me, okay? We need to sunscreen you. It's supposed to get into the mid-nineties this afternoon."

After a generous squirt of SPF 50 on my hand, I spread it on Janey's shoulders, arms, and face. Dutifully, she closes her eyelids as I work the stuff in around her eyes and nose.

"You want me to do you?" Tanner asks me.

"Janey can help me," I reply coyly. I remember Mom's admonition—don't be too easy.

"Where do you want to go first?" I ask Janey once we're all slathered up.

"Water slides."

As she yanks on my arm, nearly pulling my shoulder out of its socket, Tanner whispers a warning in my ear.

"She may not be tall enough for the height limits."

"We'll see about that."

Our first stop is a huge tube slide. Tanner is right. There is a forty-eight-inch minimum height requirement, and Janey is going to come up barely an inch short. This will embarrass and devastate her. Since Tanner and I plan to be with her on the slides anyway, she'll be fine, so can we cut her some slack here? I mean, I'm all for safety, but it's one lousy inch.

The attendant dude at the entrance to the ride is scrupulously checking all the smaller kids. I can read his face like a page from one of my novels. *Bleak House* maybe. He won't cut Janey a break no matter how close to the line she is.

I lean down and whisper in her ear. "When they measure you, lean forward on the balls of your feet. That should give you an extra inch."

"That's against the rules."

"We're not breaking them. We're only bending them a little."

Her eyes widen in surprise, but she dutifully does as I suggest. It works. The top of her head is exactly level with the minimum height line. The attendant gives her a bored wave of his hand, signaling her through. Tanner saw what Janey did, but he's not staring at her: he's staring at me.

"Did you tell her to do that?" he asks, careful Janey doesn't overhear.

I shrug as we head up the stairs to the top of the slide. "It's okay. It's only an ish rule."

"A what?" he whispers.

"An ish rule. Forty-eight – *ish*. Close calls get rounded up. That's how I see it anyway."

"An ish rule," he repeats. "You're a little crazy. You know that, right?"

"Crazy works."

At the top of the stairs, Janey, Tanner, and I line up to go down together on a single, misshapen inner tube with handles on the sides. I'm in front, then Janey, and then Tanner. Once we're in place and about to shove off, Janey gives me a panicked expression. She's getting cold feet at the sight of how high up we are.

"It helps if you scream," I tell her. "Here we go."

As soon as we start, Janey and I begin shrieking. Our momentum picks up as we shoot down the twisting white tube, our speed increasing each time we come out of a turn. Janey's screaming gets louder and so does mine. When we finally explode out of the tube and into the catch pool at the bottom, both of us are laughing hysterically.

"I think you ruptured one of my eardrums," Tanner tells us.

"Let's do it again," Janey says.

She is tireless when it comes to the slides, so Tanner and I spend the next couple hours with her zinging down various forms of water sluices. She quickly becomes quite adept at cheating her way past the height requirement.

I allow myself to think wistfully of what it might be like if she was family. I could teach her some of the simple games I learned when I was her age. It would be fun to train her.

Eventually, Janey agrees to take a lunch break. The three of us troop over toward a picnic area. The black asphalt surface of the path we're on radiates heat, broiling my skin as we walk under the sun between shady spots. On the way there, we pass a gift shop.

"I want a souvenir." Janey points to a surf shop.

"Here." I hand her a twenty from my small, waterproof purse I have in a zippered pocket inside the skirt of my swimsuit.

"Come with me," she pleads. She's still too shy to interact with a store clerk.

"After all those rides, you're the bravest eight-year-old girl I know," I tell her with an encouraging squeeze of her shoulder.

She still hesitates.

"You can do this," I whisper.

Finally, she nods and heads toward the store, her fists clenched as if she's off to confront the school bully.

As soon as she's gone, I collapse on a bench in the shade a few yards away. By the time Tanner returns from the bathroom, Janey comes back with a pair of cheap sunglasses, her expression one of alarm. Her lower lip is trembling. She's obviously upset. Wordlessly, she dumps a handful of change onto my outstretched palm.

"Expensive sunglasses," I remark.

"She said I only gave her a ten." Janey's voice cracks. "I'm sorry."

"I'll go talk to the person," Tanner offers.

This isn't my issue. I shouldn't give a crap, but I do. Janey is fighting to muster the confidence to buy something all on her own, and this miserable experience may set her back who knows how far.

I'm pissed.

Notice to the world: You mess with Janey, you mess with me, and you mess with me, and I'm going to yank your liver out through your left nostril and jam it down your throat. Figuratively speaking, of course.

"Nope," I tell Tanner. "Sit this one out. I got it. Give me a couple ones and a ten."

I hold out my hand. Tanner frowns at me, but nevertheless forks over a wad of bills. I'm surprised at the anger I feel over someone ripping off a child. Now, I'm in the process of trying to rip her off.

Hypocrisy? I prefer irony.

Inside the store, I grab a plastic thing of Tic Tacs for a buck fourteen, before strolling up to the counter where a young college-aged girl is staffing the register. She has "Robin" on her name tag. She's modestly attractive, but nothing special. She has a smug smirk on her face, and I hate her instantly for screwing Janey over. Maybe it was an accident or misunderstanding, but I doubt it. One look at her pouty, puffy lips and any thought of having a reasonable conversation with her is gone. With my bitch switch officially flipped, I begin the game.

"Hi, Robin." I lay my Tic Tacs on the counter with a ten-dollar bill alongside it. "Just this. I had a chili dog with onions earlier, and holy god does my breath stink." I flash a broad grin at her.

"I hear you," Robin replies. "My boyfriend had a jalapeno burger last week." She fans away the echo of the bad odor. "I wouldn't let him get within ten feet of me until he brushed his teeth."

As she slides eight dollars and eighty cents change toward me, I say, "I'll probably be back in twenty minutes for something for the heartburn too. It must be cool working here, huh?"

"Hell *no*," she replies with a put-out snort. "The customers are so freaking rude, it's unbelievable."

I take the eight ones, but I place two more on top of them, careful to make sure Robin sees me do this. "The problem with this bathing suit is I have no place to stuff a bunch of bills." I lean forward conspiratorially and whisper, "Of course, I could stuff them in with my boobs. Might fill me out better." I lean back, sighing heavily. "No, I'd need a far bigger wad than this to do any good. Here, can you take these ones and give me back a ten instead?"

Robin smiles at my self-effacing joke about my supposedly meager cleavage and compliantly pushes a ten across the counter at me, while I hold the ones in my hand. I take the ten in one hand as I set down my pile of ones on the counter with the other, swiftly replacing a one with the ten she just gave me.

In the grand scheme of things, this is a minor sleight-of-hand gimmick, but it fools nine out of ten people. For me, it's child's play. This is baby stuff compared to what I normally do.

"Rude? Really?" I question.

When someone is engaging you in conversation, most everyone looks at the person's face. Bad move. Never, ever take your eyes off the money, which is what marks do. It's why they're marks.

She nods. "You should have seen this one lady yesterday. Kristin was ringing her up, and the lady went all-out menopausal bitch on her when the towel she wanted wasn't on sale. She threw her gum at her."

"Jesus." I gasp. "People can be such entitled assholes. Let me guess, it's the mothers who are the worse, right? Followed closely by their bratty rug rats."

"Oh, hell yes," Robin says.

While we're having this exchange, I push the pile of bills toward her. The key with the shortchange game I'm playing is distraction. You have to force the mark to do several things all at once: handle a purchase, make complicated change, and talk and answer questions.

Robin sucks at multitasking because she doesn't notice what I did to her. Of course, I'm pretty darn good at this game—I can pat myself on the back here—I've been playing it since I was not much older than Janey. You never make much money off it, but my cousins and I used to play this for hours as we bounced around Orlando stores. God, we were such juvenile delinquents.

"Wait, you gave me nine ones and a ten," Robin says, confusion rippling across her face.

"Jeez, the chili must have gone to my brain," I laugh and slap the palm of my hand to my forehead. "Now I can't even count." I slide another one-dollar bill over to her. "Here, this will top it up. Just give me a twenty."

She smiles politely at me and hands me a crisp, new twenty-dollar bill. The clatter of a piece of fragile merchandise falling and shattering on the floor causes Robin to jerk her eyes toward the far end of the store. The moron. The pile of my ten and ones is still sitting on the counter. I deftly yank the ten back from under the pile. Marks are such freaking idiots.

"Give 'em hell," I tell a distracted Robin. I grab my Tic Tacs and leave. Once outside, I hand the twenty and ten to Tanner.

"Here's your ten, Janey's missing ten, plus a bonus ten," I say. "And, drum roll please, some cinnamon spice Tic Tacs."

Tanner stares at me, too stunned to ask questions. He has this what-the-hell-just-happened face, and it makes me smile.

"How?" he asks.

"I have a special thing when it comes to evil store clerks with thimble-size brains."

Janey tugs on my arm, so I lean down for her to speak quietly in my ear. "What did you do?" she asks me in a barely audible voice.

"I'll always have your back. Okay?"

"Okay."

"So, how about a late lunch?" I say. "I heard about this really great jalapeno burger I know you're going to love, Tanner."

***

After lunch, we spend most of the afternoon in the giant wave pool. Janey rides out the waves by floating on an inner tube while Tanner and I stand next to her. Eventually, I get my rhythm down and manage to ride out the really big waves, but not before swallowing enough chlorine water that I'll probably sweat blue for a week.

Then a huge wave slams into me, causing me to lose my grip on Janey and her inner tube, and suddenly I'm totally preoccupied with finding ways to not breathe in water and die. When I surface, spastically flapping my limbs, someone wraps an arm around my waist and drags me to shallower water, his other arm clenching my chest.

On the one hand, I want to thank this person for saving me from possible drowning. On the other, my savior momentarily clasps one of his palms over my left boob. Coughing and sputtering, I twist away from this groper guy with fists clenched, prepared to punch the perv in the nose.

It's Tanner.

"Sorry," he says. "I was trying to help."

My anger dissolves immediately and I sputter, "Where's Janey?"

He points at a laughing girl bobbing up and down in the water on a tube, who waves vigorously at us with a giant grin. Apparently, she finds my drowning panic amusing.

"Let's try this again," I say, slogging through the water toward Janey. I grasp hold of her tube to keep her close when another wave approaches.

This time, I jump over the crest, assisted by Tanner, who places his hands on my waist and lifts me up. We do this for several waves, with him careful to let go of me after each wave passes, but after fifteen minutes of this, he keeps his hands on me.

Once a wave passes, I slump back against his chest, soaking up the warmth of his arms around me. Although his chest is as hard as a granite wall, with my back against him and his hands splayed across my belly, I feel like I'm wrapped in a warm cocoon. His chin rests lightly on top of my head, and I wish the stupid waves would stop coming so we can stand here like this for the rest of the afternoon.

So here's the deal. I have *never* had a boy put his hands on me like this. For a moment my self-control wavers and begins to dissolve like a sandcastle in the face of the incoming surf. I know this is all part of the game, but I like the feel of his hands.

When I'm in the middle of hustling a mark, I pride myself on how detached and clinical I am about what I'm doing. I'll laugh, cry, get angry, or whatever the script calls for, but inside I'm as cold and calculating as a robot.

Not today.

Encased in Tanner's arms, swaying slightly with the swells, I'm completely distracted by the fluttering in my stomach and the buzz of energy, which seems to be flowing between us.

This isn't normal for me, not even close to normal. Each time a wave approaches, I wait expectantly for his hands to tighten on my waist before lifting me up. I have this fantasy of us falling to the ground in the shallows and kissing in a *From Here to Eternity* moment.

"Let's float down the river," Janey calls out.

With a measure of regret, I let her drag us out of the water. I wish he and I could spend the rest of the afternoon here. The feel of his hands on me and his body pressed against mine has totally distracted me. Like Oliver in the workhouse—*please, sir, I want some more.*

A flash of panic flares up inside. I can't do this to myself again. I wiggle free of Tanner's hold, determined to get my emotions under control.

The remainder of our time at the park, we spend floating down the Calypso Cooler Lazy River. Janey and I are in inner tubes and Tanner's holding each of our hands and walking between us. I close my eyes and enjoy the heat of the sun warming my face, but my mind focuses on the tingling sensation of my fingers interlaced with his.

I have this under control. This is all an act.

In an effort to keep my head in the game, I review how we're going to disappear with all of Tanner's family's money. But I can't concentrate. Instead, my thoughts lazily drift along like the water, wondering what it would be like to be a typical seventeen-year-old girl whose free time isn't always focused on planning the next felony.

Nobody says anything during our float down the river. I don't think any of us want this to end. If only the river could flow on forever, but it doesn't. After a couple of laps, as if by silent, mutual agreement, we clamber out of the water dragging the tubes behind us. I'm hoping Tanner will take my hand again, but he doesn't. Instead, he hoists Janey on his shoulders and we head for the exit.

Like yesterday, Janey falls asleep almost as soon as I back out of our parking space. Tanner and I drive for nearly a half hour in silence. I can tell something's bothering him, but I'm not going to pry. When you're working a mark, best to let them lead. The art of manipulation relies on finesse. In grifting, the Holy Grail is for a mark to go where you want him to go, all the while thinking he's the one who wants to go there.

"Leah and I got into a fight last night," he announces out of the blue. "That's why she didn't come today." I resist the temptation to reply. "She's jealous of you," he tells me something I already know.

"Well, you and I know there's nothing for her to be jealous about. Do you want me to talk to her?"

"Nah." He drags his fingers through his hair, looking like a trapped animal. "She thinks you're after something."

In gaining trust, rule number one: don't dance around the nine-hundred-pound gorilla in the room. Confront it head on. If you show the slightest whiff of evasion or hint of dissembling, you're toast…burnt, black toast.

"She thinks I'm after your money?" A short, derisive laugh bursts out of me. Of course, this is exactly what I'm after. "What? I'm some kind of seventeen-year-old gold digger?"

"No," he objects. "She's just jealous. She's saying crazy stuff. Forget I said anything."

"Listen, Tan. I'll put my cards on the table. I like you. A lot. But it's not worth losing your friendship with Leah. I'll butt out. You two should patch things up."

Gaining trust rule number two: never hesitate to fall on a grenade or take the bullet meant for another. This always works. Somewhere in the back of my brain, the mournful cry of a lone violin plays... it's kind of mocking me.

"No," Tanner responds. "You are kind of amazing."

"Ditto. I'm sorry if I seem a little needy." Self-deprecation, used in moderation, is also good. "I don't have a lot of friends."

This is painfully accurate. Most of the year, I'm on the road with Mom, living out of hotels. Us and my Kindle. I have nobody. I text and email my cousins from time to time, but it's different. They're not with us. They can't go shopping or eat out. Unlike Leah—the whiny little lapdog—I don't have a stable life. She gets to have friends like Tanner. I don't.

"I don't want to cause anything weird between you two," I say. If I was Pinocchio, I could punch the radio buttons with the end of my lying nose.

He grins at this for some reason. "Hey, I still owe you an afternoon in Stockton. How about tomorrow?" He leans toward me with his voice lowered and says, "No Janey."

"What do you want to do?"

He grins mischievously. "This is my surprise, and I'll pick you up at your place."

***

After dropping the gang off at their house, as I'm driving back to the vineyard, I'm caught up in a series of silly fantasies about Tanner and me. We go to school together. Friday night dates. The prom. Kissing...and other stuff. Halfway back, I shake my head to clear my brain of these idiotic thoughts and crank up the radio.

I've almost got my mind back to normal when my phone rings. It can't be Tanner. He already texted he would be calling later tonight. It's unlikely to be Mom. I called her earlier to tell her I was on my way back. Peter? Janey maybe?

I glance down at the phone screen. No name, only a number. But I recognize the number. My phone is Bluetooth-linked with Peter's car, so I push the speaker button and begin talking.

"Leah, so *very* nice to hear from you again." Not.

"The pleasure is mine."

From the robotic tone of her voice, she's muttering "not" to herself too. "More Google searches?" I chide.

"Tanner told you we got into a fight." It's a statement, not question. "I tried to apologize, but he won't speak to me."

Her voice stumbles ever so slightly on the word "speak." I sense this has never happened before. I don't exactly feel sorry for her, but this is sort of my fault. In my line of work, there is always collateral damage, but I try to minimize it. Hey, I'm not some soulless puppy kicker.

"He's a guy." I cough out a laugh. "Bake him some brownies and tell him he's got a really hot bod." I'm trying to lighten the mood a little. "He'll follow you around like a loyal pet after that."

"Tanner's not like that. He said he's not the one I needed to apologize to."

"Listen, girlfriend. For what it's worth, I told him I didn't want to be the cause of anything between you two, and I don't."

"I'm going to talk straight, okay?"

I clenched my jaw and give my phone the middle soldier salute. I don't have time for this guacamole. "I had no basis for making accusations against you. I'm sorry for that."

"Apology accepted." Can we hang up now?

"Having said that," she continues, "you're up to something. I don't exactly know what, but I can tell. All I ask is that at the end of the day, no harm comes to Tanner. Promise?"

"If I was really up to something, as you put it, my promise would be pretty worthless."

"Good point, except I have a feeling about you. I think you're a person who would honor her word."

Well, I'm a little intrigued here. "You think I'd be honest with you, L?"

"Yes, I do."

"Shit happens," I reply.

"A slippery answer." Several moments of silence hangs between us. Then she speaks again. "Something tells me I really don't want you as an enemy."

"No, you don't."

CHAPTER EIGHTEEN

"We seem to be doing fine with Tanner Cardwell," Peter observes at breakfast on Wednesday morning while sitting across the table from me, scraping butter onto his toast. "What's our angle with this Tonya person?"

"I'm trying to befriend her." I reach for the strawberry preserves. "But even if I succeed, that's not necessarily going to make her fall in love with this place."

"I suppose I could take a page from your book and try to romance her," Peter says, totally in jest. "But I'm out of practice with women."

Mom sits across from me, cradling a cup of coffee, and wrinkles her nose in displeasure. Then she chuckles softly.

"Uh, no," I reply. "We're not so desperate yet that you have to switch teams, Uncle."

He makes a mock gesture of wiping his brow in exaggerated relief. Peter has never made it a secret that he's gay.

"The best angle we got right now," I continue, "is for me to get her daughter, Janey, hyped up over this place and hope some of it rubs off on her mother. It'll have to do until we can come up with something better."

Mom grabs the last piece of toast and smears strawberry preserves on it. Watching her eat is entertaining, if baffling. She puts ten thousand calories of food on her plate, but only pecks at it. Sure enough, she nibbles one corner off the toast and drops it on top of the other piece of toast she only took two bites from. The only part of the meal she finishes is her cup of coffee.

"So when is he coming to pick you up?" she asks.

"Eleven."

"All right," she says with a resigned exhale, "I think we can safely conclude that Tanner Cardwell is falling for you. Good job." She gazes at me, waiting for me to return her stare. When I do, she continues, "Do the minimum necessary to keep him interested. Don't get involved with this boy. Keep it professional this time."

I'm never going to live down Atlanta. Not entirely. "Mom. I get it."

"All I'm saying is be careful." She holds up her hands in a defensive gesture. "I was a teenager once, you know."

"It's powerful, but I think I can fight off the urge to make babies."

Mom glares at me, but Peter lets loose with several belly laughs.

***

When Tanner arrives an hour later, I meet him outside on the driveway. I told my mother it was best if he didn't have to come inside and trade forced, awkward small talk with her. She agreed but shook her finger at me anyway. She didn't say anything, but she didn't need to. Her message was clear—watch yourself.

She's been really weird the last few days. She hovers over me as if I'm Anakin Skywalker about to defect to the dark side of the force. Ah, sorry, but aren't we already on the dark side?

"Hey, you look great," Tanner tells me as I climb into his car.

I hope so. I mean, after breakfast, Mom spent most of the morning painting my face. Then she twisted my hair into a single French braid. Tanner texted me earlier to wear jeans, which makes me wonder what he has in mind, since it's supposed to reach ninety-eight today.

Along with my ripped, high-ankle skinny jeans, I'm wearing a cream, crocheted tank top that doesn't quite cover my belly.

I study Tanner once we're under way. He's wearing well-worn jeans with holes in the knees and a tight-fitting charcoal t-shirt. He's got a rangy body, but his biceps are ripped-tastic, and, if I'm being honest, quite yummy looking. The while-lettered logo on the front of his shirt causes me to choke on a laugh.

"That's Way Too Much Bacon!"
-Said No Person Ever

"What?" he asks.

"I like your shirt," I reply around a round of giggles.

He smirks. "I like *your* shirt…what little there is."

"Shut up, jerk."

"Hey, I'm not complaining. But you're going to be cold. Good thing I have my jacket in the trunk."

Both our arms are barely touching on the seat rest between us. My hand brushes his and he quickly slides his fingers between mine, causing my pulse to speed up and my stupid cheeks to warm. I stare at his lips. Why can't we fast-forward to the part where he kisses me?

"So, what should be my next book to read?" he asks.

"You should make sure you have the mega-classics covered first. That means mastering all the man-dudes. How are you with Shakespeare?"

He glances over at me and smiles. "Him, I'm good with."

"Okay. What about Dostoevsky?"

"I've read *Brothers*, *Crime*, and *Notes*."

My head bobs appreciatively. Nice. "Me too. And Dickens?"

"*Great Expectations*." He notices my frown and shrugs. "Is that a 'you're a weeny' face I see?"

"You should at least read *David Copperfield*, maybe *Bleak House* as well."

Withdrawing his hand from mine, he twists it into the shape of a pistol, presses it against his temple, and pulls the trigger.

"Those are long-ass books. I tried to read *Bleak House*, but it was uber boring."

"Agreed, at least the first part. If you can hang in there, though, it becomes a great read. Try *David Copperfield*, then. It's entertaining from the get-go."

I love *Great Expectations*. Tan is the first person I've ever met whom I could discuss it with, so I ask, "Who was your favorite character in *Great E*, other than Pip?"

His cheeks puff out as he releases an audible exhale. "It's got to be Joe. He loves Pip and endures everything for him, including Pip. If literary characters could be elevated to sainthood, he'd be in on the first ballot."

"Not a bad choice."

"What about you?"

"You'll never guess."

"Miss Havisham," he tosses out.

"Please. I spent the whole book wanting to slap her."

"Estella?" he offers.

"Complete freaking airhead. No, my favorite is Magwitch."

"What? He's a scumbag criminal."

"Yes, but he has the biggest heart of anyone. He devotes his life to seeing that Pip is well taken care of. He rose above his sin."

"Yeah, and Iago was a tragically misunderstood fount of benevolence."

He *does* know Shakespeare. I finally meet a really great guy and he's my mark. I kind of want this boy, which is even more impossible than a Capulet falling for a Montague...and look how that one ended.

I have no idea what Tanner's plans are for this afternoon, and he stubbornly refuses to give me any clue, saying it must remain a surprise. Once we reach the outskirts of Stockton, he heads north on I-5 before exiting into a parking lot in front of a building with giant blue letters that spell Ice Arena.

Ice-skating? "Ah, why'd we drive ninety miles to go ice-skating?" Ice-skating is not a big Florida sport. It's right up there with the luge and curling.

"This is a great rink, and we're close to my house."

The way he tells me this, I'm thinking he's way too attached to this town. Mentally, I hang my head. Getting him to see the wisdom of buying the vineyard is going to be a bigger uphill battle than I thought. "I've never skated before in my life." If I try, I'll look like a human windmill.

He grins at my apprehension. "I figured as much. It's easy. I'll show you."

He's a big fat lying liar.

Once I pull my ass onto the giant ice surface in rented skates wearing Tanner's jean jacket, I gaze around the place. It looks like we're inside an enormous airplane hangar, but there's little time to study my surroundings. I'm forced to grasp the sideboards of the rink in a death grip, as my feet constantly threaten to slide out from under me at any second. I shuttle forward.

This isn't fun at all.

Meanwhile, Tanner deserts me, saying he wants to take a couple of warm-up laps. He races around the rink, gracefully flipping around at one point and skating backward. By the time he's finished his laps, I've managed to inch my way down the ice thirty yards from where I entered. Again, where's the fun in this? I know waterboarding is illegal, but what about torture-by-ice skating? Right now, I'd confess everything to get off this slippery surface of impending death.

"I'm going to steady you," he says. "Let go of the boards for a second. I've got you." He has one arm around my waist while I clutch his shoulder the way a drowning man might clamp onto a life preserver. Locked together like this, I'm forced to glide along with him on the ice at a speed far faster than I care to go.

"Too fast."

"Let me do the skating," he replies. "Keep your legs stiff and enjoy the ride."

As soon as he says this, my skate rockets forward, sending me down to the ice on my butt. He doesn't let go of me, so the collision is mild, so mild, I'm able to bust out laughing at how supremely uncoordinated I must appear.

"Let's try it again," he says.

After a half hour of practice, I'm finally getting the hang of this, although I stay close to the boards and I'm skating slightly above the speed of a lumbering hippopotamus. I manage a full circuit of the rink without falling when Tanner comes up behind me and places his hands on my waist, like he did when we rode the four-wheeler. I'm not sure what he's doing, but it helps steady me and gives me confidence to skate a little faster.

With his arms around my waist, I kind of want to flip him around so that we fall and land on top of each other, but there are parents and children watching. Finally, I'm having a tiny bit of fun. The big downside is the rink is crowded. Most of the newbie skaters like me, and those who believe slow is best, stay on the outer edge of the ice surface near the boards while the better skaters rocket around inside us. A group of four teenage guys are really aggressive, skating superfast while they weave in and out among us laggards.

"Take my hand," Tanner says. "I'll help you go a little faster."

"I don't want to go any faster."

Still, I let him interlace his fingers with mine, enjoying the warmth of his touch. Like me, his hand is also moist, but he's probably damp from the exertion of keeping me upright rather than nervousness.

After another full circuit of the rink holding hands, he lets me go and takes off for a fast lap, gesturing for me to keep going. I still have a few hiccups with my stride and frequently need to grab at the boards to steady myself, but I'm definitely getting better.

When his hands grip my waist again, the surprise causes me to lose my balance, but he quickly steadies me, and my arms stop helicoptering. "You almost made me fall."

His answer is to kiss the back of my head, which startles me, and once again my arms start flailing in a desperate attempt to maintain my balance. He's chuckling, and I want to turn around, but I can't skate backward. To try would be certain death.

After releasing me, he dashes ahead a few yards and comes to a stop, leaning against the boards with a mischievous smile on his face. I angle toward him. I'm going to lean against him, put my arms around him, and kiss him. This is totally impulsive, and Mom would totally hyperventilate if she saw me do it, but I don't care.

I've wanted to do this since the wave pool. While kissing Tanner isn't in the script, I'm thinking it's part of the game. I'm gaining trust. So what if I enjoy this?

Grifting with benefits, baby.

When I'm within a few yards of him, a red sweatshirt flashes into view. I have a fraction of an instant to register one of those aggressive boys is bearing down on me, but I don't have enough time to react. The dude barrels into me like a freight train, sending me flying forward headfirst. Tanner and a girl I don't know both lunge at me and grab me under the arms, preventing me from face planting on the ice.

"*West*," Tanner yells. "You okay?"

I manage to nod, and he releases me, letting stranger girl help me over to the boards. Tanner skates over to jaw with the boy who crashed into me. I can't make out the words, but from the body language, it appears as if Tanner is challenging the guy to a fight. They give each other rude shoves before separating. The bully's friends egg him on, which is how I learn that his name is Trent.

The fight never happens, and Trent skates over to rejoin his penis-head friends. In that instant I decide to take the kid down. Normally I'm not into revenge, but this guy has pushed my buttons.

The collision did little more than leave me shaken and angry, but it casts a pall over the rest of the outing. Tanner senses I'm not having fun anymore, but I persuade him I want to hang in there a little longer.

Actually, I'm keeping track of Trent. I'll leave when he does. Fortunately, the tool runs down someone else a few minutes later and the rink manager tosses him and his gang out. Rather than being indignant, the guy seems almost proud of being expelled.

"I'm ready to go," I tell Tanner.

Once I've changed into my tennis shoes, Tanner takes off to return our rental skates. Meanwhile, Trent rises to leave from a bench against the far wall. Hustling, I fast walk toward him, taking care to look casual. His eyes widen slightly as I approach, possibly afraid I'm going to slap him or something.

Not a chance, Trent. I'm going to do worse.

"Sorry I got in your way," I tell him, extending my hand to shake. I smile, blink a few times, and bite my lip, trying to look like I'm being shy and flirty.

Bing. It works.

He takes my hand and grins back at me. "Fate," he says. "Our bodies were meant to come together."

Oh God. I want to throw up, but I force myself to emit a simpering giggle. Then I step closer and place my hand on his shoulder. This is where Trent makes his first big mistake—letting me invade his personal space and get close to him.

"Your shirt," I say in a surprised voice while reaching up to touch his collarbone area. "Did I do this?"

He twists his head around to see what I'm talking about. My other hand brushes against his chest.

"Let me wipe off the dirt," I say.

This is Trent's second big mistake—letting me put my hands on him.

What I'm about to do is all about distraction, getting him to direct his attention where I want it and not where I don't want it. He's not really paying attention to anything but my touch and my face. He's sure as hell not listening to what I say. I mean, how does he get dirt on himself by falling on the ice?

His gaze locks on mine. I don't have to read minds to know he's thinking about sex.

Hold that thought, dude.

My left hand slips down to his back pocket, pinches the corner of his wallet, and slips it up and out. My body shields the transaction from view. His friends stare stupidly at me while I seemingly glom onto Trent. I palm the wallet into my front pocket.

He reaches a hand up to touch my hair. I let him. His eyes and his entire mind and body are laser focused on my face. So my hand floats over to his other back pocket and slides his phone out.

Now that I'm done shopping, I step back and will my face to flush red from faux excitement. This is one of my talents. I can blush on command.

In the space of fifty or so seconds, I filched his wallet and cell. He has no clue what I did.

Pickpocketing is an art most people misunderstand, thinking it's some clumsy act of sneaking up on someone from behind, bumping into them maybe, and then snatching their wallet. Sure, maybe bumbling amateurs follow this approach, but it doesn't have a high success rate.

No, pickpocketing is all about managing attention, although dexterity is key. You don't sneak up on someone: you engage them in a controlled encounter. You look them in the eyes. You talk to them. You touch them.

Really, body theft is more like magic than stealing, and I've been doing it since middle school.

"See you here tomorrow?" I whisper to Trent, grinning slyly at him.

"Sure."

I turn away and head over to Tanner, who has just finished turning in our skates.

On our way out of the building, I pause at the front desk and then slap the wallet and phone down on the counter. It was reckless to jack Trent like this. The puzzled clerk opens her mouth to ask a question, but I cut her off.

"Found 'em under one of the benches."

She gives me a bored nod. Tanner, on the other hand, gapes at me, knowing I didn't come anywhere near a bench while having no idea whose stuff I handed over. His gaze locks on me as I turn toward the front doors.

"How did you—" Tanner starts to ask.

"How did I what?" I bat my eyes innocently at him a couple of times.

"Never mind. What do you say we stop by my house for a few minutes?"

"And I thought ice skating was the pinnacle of my day."

"Smart-ass. I need to change. Then I'm taking you out to a late lunch."

"Food works."

***

When we get to his home, the place is empty. A note for Tanner is affixed to the refrigerator by a Cookie Monster magnet and says Tonya and Janey are at a nearby park and Tanner's father is shopping. I take out my phone and discover I have a text from Peter with a video attached. This is strange. Why would he send me a video? Unfortunately, my cell reception sucks and the video won't load.

"What's your Wi-Fi password?" I ask Tanner.

He straightens from searching the refrigerator and his eyes narrow in thought. "No idea. All my stuff connects automatically. You can use our computer, though. It's in the den. Username 'TC18.' Password 'Rubicon.'"

He's giving me access to the family computer? I'm the last person on the planet he should be doing this for. But using their computer is too golden an opportunity to pass up.

"Okay." I pitch my voice to sound indifferent and not betray the sudden buzz of excitement thrumming inside my head.

"I'm going to change my clothes," he says, before bounding up the stairs.

As soon as he's out of sight, I race to the den in a near dead run and make my way to a desk in the corner of the room with a computer monitor on top. A couple clicks of the mouse bring the screen to life. When prompted, my fingers fly over the keyboard, typing in the password Tanner shouldn't have given me. Next I open the Outlook contacts and search for the word "trust."

Boom. I get three hits, including "TT Family Trust." This must be the trust Tanner's grandfather set up for him and Tonya.

I study the contact info for the TT Family Trust in preview and stumble into a goldmine. Listed in the notes field are the name of a bank, account, and routing numbers, usernames, passwords...everything, including answers to secret questions.

Jack-freaking-pot.

After opening a new browser window, I quickly locate the bank's homepage and log in with utter ease. An instant later, I'm staring at a bank account with millions and millions of dollars. Just to test things, I arrange for a bitcoin payment of $100 to the account I use for my Riesling University hustle, which isn't easily traceable to me.

It works.

Sweet Easter Peeps.

This has all taken less than three minutes. After grabbing a piece of paper from inside the desk, I hastily write down all the access information, fold the paper, and slide it into my front pocket.

Who needs this stupid vineyard scam? With this bank account information, I could drain this entire account and move the money offshore and out of reach before dinner. We don't need to sell them a phony vineyard to get their money. Mom and I could blow town tomorrow and hit the road again.

Except I don't want to hit the road. I'm not ready yet.

"No," I say softly to the computer screen. Then I erase any trace of my brief incursion, click the browser window shut, and log off the computer. "I can always come back and do this later if I want to."

Now, what was that video Peter sent me? A few taps on my phone, and it starts playing. In it, Mom climbs onto the Honda FourTrax idling in the front yard. I'm guessing Peter talked her into this. She guns the engine, clearly not knowing what she's doing, and the ATV lurches forward and crashes into the side of our rental car. Mom gets off and tosses her helmet at Peter, who is laughing his insides out.

I start to giggle.

I can't wait to get back to tease her.

CHAPTER NINETEEN

Atlanta
One year ago

"What is that luscious smell?" Jem asked.

After shutting the oven door, I turned to face her while armed with pink pot-holder gloves. Dressed in sweats with a frilly apron tied on in front, along with mussed hair and flour-dusted cheeks, I looked like a mash-up of Betty Crocker and a Messy Bessy.

"Lemon cake," I replied.

"Oh goodness, Josi's favorite." She clasped her hands in pleased surprise. Jem came into the kitchen a while ago to check on my attempt at cooking, fussing with the placement of the toaster on the counter and trying not to look like she was hovering. The kitchen was her domain and she wasn't comfortable with me using it.

"Jem, I'm not going to burn down the house."

"Of course not." She nervously opened and closed a couple cabinet doors for no reason.

"Would you feel safer if I handed you the fire extinguisher to hold on to?"

She leaned against the refrigerator, trying to look casual and relaxed. "Don't mind me. This kitchen is old and finicky. Like me, I guess." She laughed, but it sounded forced.

"I'm going to make the icing now...if you think the coast is clear."

"Buttercream?"

"That's the plan." I took a couple steps closer and patted her hand. "I'm using a stable set of ingredients. They hardly ever spontaneously combust. You can relax."

She gave my shoulder a squeeze and mercifully left the kitchen to visit with Josi. I began assembling the ingredients for the icing: eggs, butter, sugar, and a couple more fresh lemons.

Today was Josi's birthday. I was making her favorite food for dinner and baking a scratch birthday cake. I did okay in a kitchen if it wasn't anything too complex. The cake was probably too much for me, but I found a how-to video on YouTube that made it seem childishly easy.

When dinner time arrived, Jem and Josi sat at the dining room table jabbering at each other like squawking magpies. They were arguing over some fine point of their family history. All I heard was the part about a great-uncle Joe running off with his first cousin Becky when he was eighteen and she was fifteen.

"Joe was a real bastard," Josi said. "I still remember the scandal it caused."

"No, it was Rebecca's mother," Jem insisted. "She let that child run wild from the day she took her first steps."

"What do you think, Jenn?" Josi asked me, as I brought over a platter of chicken-fried steak to join the bowls of mashed potatoes, gravy, and collard greens I'd carried out earlier.

"Sorry?"

"Joe and Becky," Josi said, sounding annoyed I wasn't keeping up with the discussion.

Sounded like incest to me, but what did I know about local "customs"? "Didn't they have a son?" I asked, tongue in cheek. "You know, that banjo player in *Deliverance*."

"Who?" Josi nearly bellowed.

"Nothing," I muttered. "So, who's hungry?"

Dinner was a total disaster. The sides were passable, but the steak was as tough and hard as weathered roof shingles. I didn't tenderize it enough. No one ate any of it since they couldn't even cut it. Maybe I could sell it to the army to use as armor plating for tanks.

"What do you say we order some delivery?" I finally asked, eager to put them out of their misery.

Josi pushed her plate away with a relieved expression. "KFC?"

"Here, here." Jem surrendered to the enemy and put down her fork. "How about original recipe?"

"Done," I added.

"Don't worry about dinner." Jem put a hand on my arm as I started to rise. "It's the thought that counts."

Cold consolation. It's what you tell a person who buys your great-aunt a box of See's candy only to find out she's diabetic.

While I waited for the Uber Eats driver to show, I retreated to my special office—the bathroom—and sat on my special chair—the toilet—to respond to the text Mom sent me moments ago.

Mom: *Are you done yet?*

Me: *Would I have Crisco on my face and flour in my bra if I was done?*

Mom: *What?*

Me: *NVM*

Mom: *ARE YOU DONE YET????*

Me: *NOOOOOOO!!!!!!... but close*

Mom: *[middle finger emoji]*

Me: *[Munch's The Scream emoji]*

I deleted our text exchange and stuffed my phone in my back pocket. I lied to Mom. I was done. I'd finished days ago, but I wasn't ready to leave. In fact, I had this strange yearning to stay here. The idea was stupid, of course. Jem and Josi weren't family, but this place felt like home. How strange was that?

I shook my head to knock the sentimental claptrap out of my brain and get my head back in the game. On my way out of the bathroom, I paused at the mirror before returning to the dinner table.

Long day in the kitchen. I looked like crap. I smelled like crap. I felt like crap.

And some people do this every frigging day?

***

Later in the evening, after cake and ice cream, we gathered in the Js' tiny living room for the finale to Josi's birthday evening. It was her night, so she got to choose what she wanted to do. We played rummy for almost two hours while their old record player spun through a stack of ancient LPs: Sinatra, Frankie Laine, Bing, Vic Damone, and more.

"Put on some Johnny Ray," Josi said, as the card game broke up.

"Or some Cardi B?" I offered. "Maybe a little Rihanna?"

Jem ignored me and dug out an album with the cover art nearly worn off. Soon the crooning voice of a guy I never heard of belted out a song about broken hearts and a good cry. Josi closed her eyes and moved her head to the rhythm, a lost smile on her face.

"I remember dancing at the Paradise Room to this song," Josi reminisced. "Ernie Tucker, dressed in his army uniform."

"Ernie Tucker?" Jem sounded horrified.

"He was shipping out for Korea on Monday," Josi said. "He wanted a last night on the town. I was only fifteen, but he smuggled me into the club."

"Wow, Miss J." I grinned, "I didn't know you were such a wild child."

"I'd give anything to have back five minutes of that night," she said wistfully.

I rose from my seat and Jem lifted an eyebrow at me. I nodded back at her and she picked up the phonograph needle to replay the song as I stepped close to Josi.

"Can I have this dance?" I asked.

Josi's eyes sparkled as she took me in her arms. We held each other while shuffling slowly across the rug to the lilting tune, gradually making a circuit of the faded living room rug.

Almost a half hour crawled by as we slow-danced through several songs before we came to a stop. I gave her a hug and kissed her cheek.

One of us had to blink rapidly to keep from crying, and it wasn't Josi.

CHAPTER TWENTY

"Whatever possessed you to go ice skating?" Mom asks the next day on our way into San Francisco for her mysterious new game.

"It was his surprise. He was taking me on a date." Acknowledging Tanner and I went out on a date triggers a brief thrill-flip in my belly. As my mother would wish, I ignore it and gaze around, not recognizing the road we're on. "So what's the gig today?"

Mom told me we would be working a game, but she didn't give me any details. When Tanner dropped me off last night, I tried to talk to her, but she and Peter were halfway through a pitcher of martinis and trading off-color jokes in Romanian. When Mom gets sloshed, a mean streak rises to the surface, so I stopped asking her about it.

If she didn't want to give me a download, it's cool. This probably means it's a game we've played bunches of times before, so I don't really need to prepare for it. Good.

"You'll find out soon enough," she replies. "Now, when are you going to see him again?"

"In a couple days. Today he and Janey are visiting their cousins in Fresno. They won't be back until tomorrow afternoon."

"Perfect," she says. "What's your next move with him?"

Yes, my next move. Time to lay my cards on the table. "I'm going to invite Janey to a sleepover at the vineyard. A slumber party."

A puzzled expression spreads across her face.

"I'm betting Tanner will come along," I hasten to add. "You and Peter should stay out of sight as much as possible."

"Be careful." She shakes her scolding finger. "Keep it professional with this kid."

I give her my patented dramatic eye roll, the one I reserve specially for her when she's treating me like a little girl. "Mom, I know what I'm doing. If I'm going to close out this game, I need him to desire me a little. So back off and trust me here. Okay? It's not like we're going to make it on the kitchen floor."

Her eyebrows arch up almost to her hairline.

"Relax. We'll use the couch."

"West—"

"Kidding. Loosen up a little."

She snorts a reluctant laugh. "You're like super-strong wasabi. You give me apocalyptic heartburn." She exhales heavily as if having to remind me this is disappointing and tiring at the same time. "Okay, now for today. I packed you an overnight bag and brought the red rug."

I bury my head in my hands and slowly shake my head. I hate the red wig. "Mom, not that one. I look like a slut version of Lindsay Lohan in that thing."

"It makes you look a little older. We need to pass you off as a graduate student."

"Fine." I huff. "Let me guess. We're running the sublet game?"

"Exactly. I used an identity that Peter gave me to rent us an apartment on Airbnb. It's near the UC Berkeley campus."

***

It's after four in the afternoon by the time we find the one-bedroom apartment on Shattuck Avenue, retrieve the keys, and haul our bags inside. The place is clean and elegant, with hardwood floors, but it's a little on the small side. I toss my bag on the overstuffed, honey-colored leather couch. Although Mom rented this place for two nights, we'll only be staying here tonight. By dinnertime tomorrow, we should be back in Petaluma.

"I have to get some copies of the key made," Mom says. "I'll be back in an hour. Find us some good food. No pizza."

After she leaves, I locate a stack of delivery menus on the kitchen counter, most well-worn and stained. I decide to go with the bright orange menu for Delhi Diner. For me, I order their shrimp saag, and for Mom, I get the lamb vindaloo. I also get a double order of plain naan. Mom returns forty-five minutes later, shortly after the food arrives, wearing a frazzled expression, looking as if someone tried to mug her.

We eat mostly in silence while Mom places call after call on her cell. She's finalizing our schedule for tomorrow and has hardly touched her food. Finally, she places her phone on the table, jots down some last-minute notes on a pad of paper and slides it over to me.

"Okay, here's the list," she says. "We've got appointments with these six people. I've spaced them out in forty-five-minute intervals. You've got to show them around and give them your spiel quickly. Don't be a chatty Patty. We don't have time."

"What are the terms again?"

She shoots me a disapproving scowl.

"I'm just double-checking," I hastily add.

"The sublet is for the summer. Rent for three months paid in advance. For the price we're charging, no one should argue. If they do, tell them to take it or leave it."

Mom goes to bed early, urging me to turn in as well, since our first mark is showing up at seven thirty in the freaking morning. I volunteer to sack out on the couch, giving her the bedroom, but I'm not tired yet. I make my way over to a wooden floor-to-ceiling bookcase, which takes up most of the back living room wall. The books are mostly textbooks, although I spot some novels. I'm guessing the person we're renting this place from is maybe a doctoral student.

Going to college is something I will never do, although I desperately wish I could. I remember the inspirational quote: It's never too late to be what you might have been. People usually attribute it to George Eliot. I like it, but George Eliot never said it. I've read everything she's written, and it ain't her style.

But I digress. Besides, whoever said those words was dead wrong in my case. It's definitely too late for me to ever be anything other than my mother's daughter. That said, I can't help yearning for a chance at a normal life: school, a nine-to-five job maybe. If only to see what it's like.

When I first started working full-time with Mom, I was thrilled. It's exotic. We traveled around the country, stayed in nice hotels, made lots of money, and Mom and I became close. Possibly a little too close. Plus, playing the games was exciting, even when we lost.

But after years of this, it's become a grind. Mom talks about us retiring someday, which is kind of ironic, since retirement is the word we use for getting caught and sent to prison.

Oh God, I need my brain to shut up so I can get some sleep.

At twelve forty-one in the morning, my thoughts are still racing. The more I tell myself I have to fall asleep, the more my idiot mind rebels. Finally, I pick up my phone on a total impulse and punch the speed dial number. Oh sweet Mary, what am I doing?

"West?" Tanner says, his voice betraying his total surprise. "What's up?"

"Yeah. I can't sleep. I was thinking if I called you and asked you what you were doing, it would be so boring, I might drop right off."

"Misfire," he replies. "I'm lying on a couch bed in a sick-ass living room listening to Imagine Dragons on my iPhone. If it helps, the mattress is covered with sand and Frito crumbs. Or it could be Doritos. Not really sure."

"Roughing it, huh?"

He sighs. "The things you do for family. So, what are you doing?"

"I'm lying on top of my blankets—it's really hot here—and I'm staring out a window at the small sliver of moon in the night sky."

"Cool, so what are you wearing?"

"Excuse me?"

"C'mon. Bring me into the scene."

I can't help laughing. "You first. What are you wearing, Tarzan?"

"Underwear. That's it. Which is why the abrasive Dorito crumbs on my bare back are beginning to piss me off."

I smile at my phone. "Boxer or brief?"

"Boxer."

"Solid or pattern?"

"Solid. It's a funky, washed-out green hue, sort of like the color of the mold you see on the corners of bread you kept in the back of the bread drawer way too long."

"So, it looks like your junk is suffering from gangrene?"

He snorts. "My turn. What are *you* wearing?"

"A camisole."

"That's it?"

"Well, I do have on panties, of course."

"Solid or pattern?"

"Powder blue. They're basic cotton grannies, so dial down any perv questions, okay?"

"Not a thong, then?"

"God *no*."

We both laugh, and then several seconds of silence pass as neither of us says anything. Finally, I speak.

"I really needed a distraction tonight. Thanks."

"Anytime."

"Good night."

"Later, West."

As sleep finally overtakes me, I should be thinking about the role I need to play tomorrow, but my mind is fixated on images of Tanner lying around in green boxers and nothing else.

CHAPTER TWENTY-ONE

Mom and I are up by six. We clean up what little mess we've made and make the bed. I'm wearing a simple, royal blue skirt that reaches down to midthigh and a sleeveless, button-up shirt. With Mom's help, I slide on the itchy, coppery red wig, replacing my short, brown tresses with shoulder-length hair. The only nice part of my look is that I get to wear the green contacts.

My job is to play the part of a college student, who at the last minute learns she has to leave town for an unexpected job. Thus, I'm desperate to sublet my apartment. We've played this game several times before around the country—we do an Airbnb rental of an apartment for a couple nights in a university town and purportedly sublet it out to as many people as we can get. We offer the place at an idiotically low price and our prospects are so mesmerized by getting something for close to nothing—greed by any other name— they suck it down hook, line, and sinker, and we take their bucks. Easy money. College students…best marks ever.

"Okay, I'm going to shove off," Mom says shortly after seven. "I'll be at a Starbucks a couple of blocks over. Call me if you need me."

"You're not staying?" Mom and I always work this game together.

"You don't need me." She kisses me good-bye on the cheek and says, "Follow the sun."

"I go where it leads," I reply with a hesitant smile.

Minutes after she departs, at seven thirty on the button, the doorbell rings. It's officially show time.

"Hi, I'm Katie Walker," I say, after answering the door. I'm using the name of the person we're renting this place from.

"Brent Henderson."

We exchange pleasantries as I lead him into the living room. He's in his early twenties, dressed smartly in pressed navy-blue slacks and a vanilla-colored dress shirt. He has a round face, a doughy gut, and wire-frame glasses. I envision him spending many hours a day in library carrels.

"So, this is the living room," I say, gesturing around the room. "There's Wi-Fi, of course, and besides this TV, there's one in the bedroom." I point at the forty-two-inch flat-screen TV on the wall opposite the couch.

"So what's the story?" Brent asks as I lead him into the bedroom.

"I was planning on staying over for the summer. At the last minute, I was offered an intern job in Washington, DC, with Senator Padilla's office. It was too good to pass up. But now I have to do something with my apartment."

"This is an awesome place. Your family must be rich."

"They do all right. And, yes, this place is great. It's a five-minute walk to the campus and the BART station is half a block away. It doesn't get more convenient."

He glances about the bedroom before stepping over to the queen-size bed to sit on it. Then he studies the nightstands, which are stacked with textbooks. He picks up one—Introduction to Archaeology—and pages through it.

"You had Wilkie for intro?" He holds up the textbook for me to see the cover.

And how do I answer that? The only Wilkie I know is Wilkie Collins, and I only know him because I read *The Moonstone* and *The Woman in White*, which were two of the best stories I devoured when I was fourteen. But since my Wilkie died over a hundred years ago, I may be in trouble here.

"I did." I will my voice to sound casual and not shaky. "It was one of my worst classes. I skipped a lot."

"You live alone?"

Why do you want to know? "Yeah."

"What's your story, anyway? You seem a little young."

Dude, don't be getting all up in my Kool-Aid. I decide to ignore his question. "Take your time. I'll be in the kitchen if you have any questions. Feel free to wander around and check things out."

"Sure."

In the kitchen, I prepare myself a cup of oolong tea and lean against the counter, waiting for Brent to scout out the place. He explores pretty much every corner and closet, pausing in the bathroom to turn on the water and flush the toilet. When he enters the kitchen, I move to the living room to allow him space to examine the appliances. Give him credit: the dude's pretty thorough.

"So," he says, "You're asking five thousand?"

"Yes. That's for the rest of June, July, and August, but you need to be out by August 26, when fall classes begin."

He whistles softly. "Wow, that's like half what other people would charge for a place like this."

I get this type of question a lot when we play this game, since we offer jaw-droppingly low prices, so I roll out one of several answers I use.

"Yeah, well, I'm not looking to make any money here," I say. "I have a stipend that covers about half my rent. I'm only trying to cover my out-of-pocket half, and I'm kind of desperate, to be frank."

"Well," he says with a shrug, "I'm ready to write a check now."

"That's great. You can sign a sublease once the check clears in about twenty-four hours." I pause to chew my lower lip and I shoot him a thoughtful, pained expression. "Now, I am showing this place to some other people later today. If someone else offers cash, I'll have to give it to them first. You understand."

A panicked expression spread across his face and his eyes widen. "What about a money order?"

"Same as cash," I reply. "If you can get me a money order today, the place is yours."

"Deal," he blurts out. "It'll take me a couple hours."

I give him a broad, sincere smile. "Great, come by any time after lunch. Just give me a heads-up when to expect you so I can have my landlord here with the sublease agreement."

I give him the number for the cheap, prepaid burner phone I purchased for this game. I'll toss it in the trash on the way out of town later today. Brent almost sprints out the front door.

Time to call Mom.

"We got a taker," I tell her when she picks up. "He's coming by with the cash after lunch."

"Excellent. Take a deep breath and clear your head. The next mark is due in five minutes."

For the next three hours and change, I give tours of the apartment to four other prospective subletters, all of whom are frantically eager to rent the space. Two promise to return with cash, one promises to try really hard to get cash, and the last one says all he can do is write a check. His expression is grim and fatalistic when I tell him I doubt the apartment will be available at the end of the day, but if it is, I'll call him. Cash is clean and fast, while checks are worthless since we have to go through a bank.

By the time the last appointment arrives and the doorbell rings, I'm freaking exhausted. Hey, stealing is hard work. When I open the door, two young, blonde-haired girls stand on the threshold. Neither of them can be more than a year older than me. I blink stupidly at them, momentarily too surprised to speak, before I realize that they must be identical twins.

One of the girls, the one wearing a green skirt, speaks first. "I'm Melanie and this is my sister, Maria."

Maria, who is wearing the same skirt, but in black, extends her hand. As I take the twins on a tour of the place, I discover both of them are starting at UC-Berkeley in the fall as freshmen, but they want to get a start on classes this summer under a program called the freshmen edge, and they don't want to live in a dorm.

As I lead them into the bedroom, I ask, "So, what are you two going to study?"

"We're both majoring in English literature," Melanie answers.

"Nice."

Maria wanders into the bathroom. "I love nineteenth-century women writers. My favorite is Jane Austen."

"Hmmm," I reply. "She's good, but I'd have to go with George Eliot. *Middlemarch* is the best, in my opinion."

"And they pretty much exhaust the category," Melanie notes. "I'm more interested in contemporary fiction."

"Exhaust?" Maria sounds slightly horrified. "What about the Brontë sisters?"

"Or Emily Dickinson," I add. "And we can't leave out Louisa May Alcott."

"Harriet Beecher Stowe?"

"Kate Chopin?" I say.

"All right!" Melanie raises both hands in an "I give up" gesture. "Sorry for disrespecting nineteenth-century women."

All three of us bust out laughing.

I like these girls. I wish I had friends like them. Since they're the last prospective renters of the day, I offer them tea and cookies, and we sit down at the kitchen dinette to talk terms, except we don't. Instead, we blab like girls talking about boys, but instead we discuss American literature.

To an outsider, it would sound kind of silly to hear us interrupting each other and talking over one another, each of us excitedly trying to voice our opinions on different authors and stories. I have this sudden urge to have a sleepover with Maria and Melanie, where we stay up all night arguing over the deeper meaning of *Little Women* or *Anne of Green Gables*, while eating fried chicken and doughnuts, and maybe listening to Ariana Grande. But all good things must come to an end.

Reluctantly, I turn the discussion in the direction of bucks. This is where I talk them into handing over their money.

"So, here's the deal, Katie," Melanie says. I can tell she's rehearsed this speech. "We can put up a third of the total rent now, but the other two thirds we won't have until the end of June. Mom is taking out a second mortgage to make up for what financial aid isn't covering, but the loan won't close for three weeks. But we can write you a postdated check."

My job is to bargain hard for the full $5,000, but if I can't get it, I get as much as I can. I'm a pretty good judge of character, and now that I've had a chance to talk with Melanie and Marie for the last half hour, I'd know if they were lying. They aren't.

"Well, here's my deal," I reply. "I've got a guy who's bringing over the full five thousand in cash after he gets off work at four. But he seems like a real dick. I like you two so much better. How about this, if you can get me your one-third rent in cash before he gets here, I'll give the place to you."

"Cash?" Maria says with a gulp.

I nod. "I'm afraid so. I'd take a cashier's check or money order."

In the end, the girls promise to try, but I can tell from their downcast faces that they don't see any hope in coming up with the cash this afternoon.

It's better this way. I didn't really want to steal their money. I like them. Once they're gone, I report in to Mom, who's practically dancing with delight over the results of my morning's scam-a-thon.

After Mom and I have a late lunch in the apartment—takeout barbeque—we prepare for the last part of the game: the part where we actually swipe money from our marks. Brent and three other confirmed renters call as soon as we're done eating, and I space them out a half-hour apart. Enough time for them to meet my landlord—Mom—sign the fake sublease, hand over their $5,000, and take back a set of keys. We're going to wait around to see if anyone else comes through, but in the meantime, we'll pack up and move our stuff out to the car. Once the game ends, we need to be able to clear out fast and furious.

By midafternoon, Brent and three others have handed over their cash to us and signed subleases, each with jubilant, if not triumphant, expressions on their face when we hand them a set of keys. I invite them to check out the lock to make sure their keys fit, which each of them does. Seeing the key successfully turn the front doorknob seems to confirm to them that the sublet is completely legitimate.

Alas, in three days when they attempt to move in, the real Katie Walker is going to be past angry with us, to say nothing of Brent and his fellow subletters. I'm sure cursing and threats will be involved.

Once the last mark leaves, we decide to wait until three-thirty before abandoning ship, although it's highly unlikely anyone is going to step up with cash at this point. While we wait, Mom hands me furniture polish wipes. People tend to get pissed off when we steal their money, and they usually call the cops. We can't avoid security cameras, witnesses, and other evidence we sometimes have to leave behind, but we're not going to make it easy for them. So, one thing we do when we can is to wipe a place down to remove our fingerprints. If we leave a fingerprint behind in a game, it can link us to other stuff we've done in the past. This would be a bad thing.

When the appointed time arrives, after we've sanitized the apartment, Mom heads out the door to start up the car, leaving me behind to lock up and turn out the lights. Unexpectedly, my burner phone rings.

"Hello," I say.

"Katie," Melanie answers, bubbling with excitement. "We have it. We had to max out a couple of credit cards, but we were able to get a Western Union money order for two thousand dollars." She can't hide the excitement in her voice. I can hear Maria squealing in the background.

The normal routine at this point would be to arrange a quick rendezvous with them, so they could hand over their money to me. Our game here is to take whatever we can get from whomever we can get it, and if it's only $2,000, so be it. I should start spewing happy, lying words, like "the place is yours," and "I'm so glad to rent to you," and "you're going to have the time of your life here this summer." But I can't find it in me to say any of those things.

Shit, I mutter to myself. My stomach clenches. I don't want to steal their money. I like them.

What I want to do is scold Melanie for being so naïve. How can she fall for this? Okay, first of all, anytime some stranger insists on being paid thousands of dollars in cash immediately, you need to run, not walk, away from the transaction. Period. End of story. Second, if it sounds too good to be true, trust me, it *always* is. I mean, really. Why would any sane person rent out an apartment for less than half its true market value?

The training drilled into me since I was like six, says, "Take their stupid money." My rebellious heart says, "Cut 'em a break."

My mind wanders to Josi. Forbidden territory. I messed up with her. I've spent the last year trying to redeem myself and get back on track with Mom, but time and again Josi's haunting smile derails my efforts to return to business as usual.

"I'm so sorry," I say. "Brent showed up with the cash twenty minutes ago. I would've stalled him, but I didn't think there was any chance of you pulling it off."

They're extremely disappointed when I end the call. They'll never know how close they came to being scammed. I did them a big fat favor.

I should feel sick to my stomach.

This is Atlanta happening all over again.

CHAPTER TWENTY-TWO

Atlanta
One year ago

I flipped shut my laptop and slumped into the antique wooden desk chair, exhausted. Although it was only half past nine, I rarely made it to later than ten o'clock these last few weeks. Working at the three Js took up every minute of every waking hour. When I wasn't in the shop or in the backroom slogging through inventory, I parked my butt online, hopping from auction site to auction site.

Low-end stuff I listed on different online auction sites. Midrange pieces I put up on a site Mom and I often used to pawn off stuff our normal buyers didn't want. High-end items I held back, either logging them on my hit list or saving them to sell in the shop.

"Why not sell it all in the store out front?" Jem had asked me when I first outlined what I proposed to do while sipping tea in their living room.

"It's a waste of time and space to bother with the small stuff," I explained. "Leave that junk to the mall stores. We don't get enough of the low-end foot traffic to make it worthwhile and we never will. So, I think you should focus your brick-and-mortar operation on big-ticket items only. Make the store a must-see destination for the elite buyers. That's where the margins are really big and fat."

The sisters agreed, and we were moving merchandise like free steak dinners for a starving mob. At the current rate, I would catch them up on their mortgage by the end of next week…if I was still here.

I scanned the walls of the small bedroom where I was staying, which used to belong to the mysterious Jenn. I knew nothing about this girl, except she left a hole in the sisters' hearts the size of

Chicago. The walls still held boy band posters of NSYNC and the Backstreet Boys, as well as a framed *Back to the Future* poster. I didn't think much of Jenn's music tastes, but the image of Marty McFly did tickle my brain with fond memories of staying up all night binge-watching the entire trilogy with my cousins when I was ten years old.

Then I leaned forward to take hold of the eight-by-ten framed photo sitting on the desk, which I had studied many times. In the photo, a young girl no older than me stood outside in a park somewhere wearing a rather garish tangerine orange prom dress with a huge smile on her face and an alluring sparkle in her eyes. The picture was old, and a thin layer of dust covered the glass and frame. I didn't know her, but I felt as if I did.

"Jenn the night of her senior prom," a voice behind me said.

I swiveled around to find Jem standing in the doorway, arms crossed over her chest. She was wearing a calico print flannel nightgown, which was probably the pinnacle of fashionable sleepwear during the Civil War.

"She's beautiful," I said.

"She was." Jem sighed. "It's the last picture we have of her."

Even though I didn't look at all like Jenn, Josi was convinced I was her. Go figure. Jem played along with Josi, but she knew my real name was West. For her sister's sake, she called me Jenn, but when we were alone, she dropped the charade.

"Where is she?" I asked.

Jem shrugged. "We don't know. She disappeared and we haven't heard a word from her since. Over the years, I tried to locate her, but never could."

"You think something happened to her?"

Jem shrugged again. "I'd like to think she would have reached out to us at some point if she was okay, but we parted on such bitter terms, who knows?"

All I knew about Jenn was that she was Josi's granddaughter, and her name was supposed to be on the sign out front: Jewelry by Josi, Jem, and Jenn. I didn't need to know anything more about her. She wasn't relevant to my mission. Still, I was curious. Josi loved her and, indirectly, me.

"Why did she leave?"

Jem entered and sat on the edge of the bed, her hands clasped together on her lap. Worry lines on her forehead deepened as a wave of sadness overtook her.

"She became involved with a boy she met during her sophomore year at college. Josi and I had serious objections to the young man. We argued and fought constantly with her about it for weeks, until we finally had a horrible row downstairs in the dining room. Terrible things were said. She walked out the door and never came back."

"I'm so sorry," I said softly.

"So am I. We had an ideal of who she should be, and when she didn't want to be forced into our mold, we couldn't accept it." She shook her head and let out a shuddering breath. "We're two old fools who threw away the best thing in our lives for pride and prejudice."

CHAPTER TWENTY-THREE

"We make an awesome team," Mom says on the drive back to the vineyard as we pass by Sausalito. "You have an uncanny ability to get people to trust you."

"Runs in the family."

She gives me a skeptical glance. "No, you're far ahead of where I was at seventeen. You've got real swagger. And with your face, you are *lethal*."

This elicits a frown. Lethal isn't exactly a compliment that makes my chest swell with pride. The way she emphasizes the word makes me sound like I'm some kind of emotionless terminator cyborg.

"I don't know if I want to do this the rest of my life."

She shoots me a sideways glance with one eyebrow arched. "You think I want to do this the rest of *my* life?"

"So what's our plan?"

She chews the inside of her cheek in thought. "I want to run my own jewelry store one day. I figure no one knows the business better than we do."

When I don't respond for several moments, she continues, "I know you want to go off and do your own thing eventually, but you're still young. Stick with me a while longer and we'll both be set."

"I want to go to college," I say, and for the first time give voice to my secret fantasy. Never mind I have no idea how I'd pull this off.

"It wouldn't take," she answers softly.

"You think I'm too stupid to do the work?"

"Quite the opposite." She exhales slowly as if collecting her thoughts. "You wouldn't fit in, and you would be miserable. You're not like them. *We're* not like them."

Her words sting a little at first. I'm not sure where I fit in. Sure, I'm not like *them*, at least not completely, but I'm not like Mom either. She has a defensive note to her voice, so I decide to probe further.

"I was thinking this fall I might go solo for a few months, like you did when you were eighteen."

Mom's face goes stony and the muscle along her jaw tenses. She's clenching her teeth and her nostrils flare before she inhales deeply and quickly regains her composure. "We can talk about it later. Now, find me a good oldies station. I'm tired of this pop forty bullshit."

As I punch the seek button, Mom grips the steering wheel so hard her hands are almost curled into fists. This is when I realize she is never going to let go of me. Not without a fight. I have a brief vision of Mattie in *Ethan Frome*, condemned to live out a paralyzed life with Zeena.

What if I walked away? When we close out this game, I could take my share and bail. But I can't cut and run. It would be cowardly. When the time comes for me to go my own way, I'll have to face her and duke it out.

The radio station advances to the next channel and a chorus of falsetto voices erupts from the speakers.

"Stop," Mom says as the languorous tune begins.

It's the Bee Gees crooning out "How Deep Is Your Love." I know because Mom worships music from the seventies, even including—pause to gag—"Disco Duck." So, I've had to listen to this stuff for a billion hours over the years. Occasionally, I can negotiate time for my playlists, but I got a lot of The Weeknd and Megan Thee Stallion on there, and she can't stand them.

The mood in the car is quiet the remaining drive back to the vineyard. It's time for dinner when we arrive, but no one wants to cook. So I make a sandwich and retreat to my bedroom for the night. Tanner texted me he would call later, and I'm trying to continue reading *Portrait of a Lady*, but I'm too distracted to concentrate.

I want to see Tanner again as soon as possible. My mind keeps drifting back to the wave pool and his hands wrapped around me as I leaned against him. Tanner has something no other boy I've ever known has: he's smart and reads like me, and his sincerity and honesty seem to balance perfectly with my total lack of those attributes. So yeah, it's a yin and yang thing.

Shortly after ten, my phone buzzes. I instantly push Accept Call. Should I let it ring a few times and play a little hard to get? Nah. I'm dying to talk to him.

"Hey, you," I blurt out.

"Hey back. I thought we should resume last night's conversation. I need to do more… due diligence…on your attire…or lack thereof."

A soft laugh escapes me. "If you want to know what I'm wearing, you're going to have to check it out for yourself."

His voice drops into a low, conspiratorial tone. "I might have to spend the night to do that."

"Is that a request?"

He snickers. "More like a prayer."

"Funny you should say that." It takes a surge of willpower to not start giggling. "I'm going to invite Janey to a slumber party Friday night."

"Ahhh. Well, she's gonna need a chaperone, you know."

"Exactly. You should come too."

He inhales sharply before responding. "I guess I can fall on my sword. Keeping Janey safe is paramount, after all."

Tanner and I spend the next hour talking about everything from the foods we hate to the worst dates we've ever been on. It was a short conversation on my end. My date scorecard? Zero. I've been asked out quite a few times, but not by anyone I cared to spend any time with, and a few were twice my age and not honorable in their intentions.

Instead, I bombard him with stories of my misdeeds with my cousins, like the time when I was nine and three of us smuggled a baby alligator into my grandmother's house we'd caught in a nearby drainage ditch. It was going to be my pet and I planned to raise it in the downstairs bathtub. I got paddled hard for that one.

"So, no boyfriends?" he asks.

I don't have any problem answering honestly. "Nope. I've never been serious with any guy before."

I don't want to hang up, but it's midnight and both of us are yawning. Our conversation has slowed to a trickle. I should let him go. After all, we have to save something to talk about Friday night.

At the thought of him in my bedroom during the sleepover, my stomach begins to flutter with nervous excitement.

"Good night, Tan."

"'Night, West."

CHAPTER TWENTY-FOUR

It's the middle of the morning when my grouchy-faced mother slogs down the stairs wearing blue-plaid flannel pajamas and a white satin robe almost touching her ankles. This getup is her answer to the undeclared air conditioner war we've been waging since we arrived. This place is always too hot, especially downstairs where I sleep, but Mother thinks it's too cold. She could be standing in the middle of the Mojave Desert at high noon, and if the wind was blowing, she'd put on a jacket. She controls the thermostat while she's awake, but once she goes to bed, I flip the air conditioner on high, unleashing soothing blasts of arctic air from the vents.

"It's like a frigging meat locker in here," Mom grouses.

The Kostinens have a nifty espresso machine in the kitchen, so I practice my barista skills and pull a shot of espresso for her. She accepts the small cup with a grateful nod and makes her way over to the breakfast nook.

"What are you doing, Peter?" Mom asks.

"Scrambled eggs," he replies. "Care for some?"

Mom wrinkles her nose. Knowing her as well as I do, I cross the kitchen to the refrigerator and withdraw a yogurt parfait. She gives me a warm smile in exchange for it and a spoon.

I ate hours ago. "I'm going into town to get supplies and check my traps," I tell Mom and Peter.

"Are you still doing this slumber party tonight?" she asks.

"Yep."

"Tanner is coming, right?"

"They're meeting me at the Petaluma Market this afternoon."

I'm expecting Mom to make another remark about how this may not be a good idea, but instead she goes back to humming a Romanian *doina* song, one that takes me back to my earliest childhood memories. She's happy—apparently the yogurt and expresso de-grumpified her. Also, we hauled in $20,000 from our sublet game, which has all of us celebrating. She gave me $2,000 spending money from my half.

***

Driving into Petaluma, I go through my mental checklist of what I need for tonight's sleepover. This is going to be a critical night. I must make some real progress with Tanner. I'm in the "earn his trust" phase, and in this phase you're either moving forward or falling back. It's imperative for him to have an enjoyable outing at the vineyard, and to like me.

Win his heart, win the game.

My first stop is Starbucks. I armor up with a latte and a cheese-and-fruit bistro box, which is my lunch. I surf over to my Riesling University home page to check on orders. None. Not even a sarcastic email inquiry asking me if this is another internet scam. Skunked. I can't remember the last time I didn't get a single order for a college degree. What? Doesn't anybody believe in higher education anymore?

Popping a second apple slice into my mouth, my phone buzzes with an incoming text. I glance down at the screen puzzled. Leah?

Leah: Hi West. If you see Tanner today, tell him I applied for the job.

Me: ?

Why in the name of Gimli the dwarf is she texting me?

Leah: I tried to call him, but he's not picking up.

Me: What job?

Leah: Jenny's Bridal Salon. It's a long shot but…

Me: I'll put in a good word for you.

Leah: ?

I don't respond to her last text. Instead, I carry on a short conversation with Siri about finding the number for this bride store. When I call the place, a woman with a slight British accent answers, asking how she can assist. As I've done many times before, I modulate my teenage girl voice down an octave to sound older.

"I'm Madeleine Ainsworth. I'd like to make an appointment with Miss Leah Henderson to discuss my daughter's wedding."

"I'm sorry," the woman replies, "but there's no one here by that name."

"Oh dear." I make my voice sound hoity-toity and disappointed. "I'm sure I was told she recently started with you. It must've been Maxine's."

"Perhaps I can be of assistance, Ms. Ainsworth."

"No, Leah is simply the best of the best. Sorry to bother."

After I hang up, I go back to my lunch. Who knows whether my call will help Leah land the job, but I was happy to try for her. I have to be careful around her, though. She's not really my enemy, but she's not my friend either.

Fifteen minutes later, I toss the remains of my lunch in the trash and a pulsing alarm from my phone shakes me out of my thoughts and reminds me it's time to meet Tanner and Janey at the grocery store. When I turn into the parking lot in front of the Petaluma Market, they're already waiting for me out front.

"Been here long?"

"Couple of minutes," Tanner replies.

"Let's go shopping." I try to ignite some enthusiasm. It works with Janey, who begins bouncing up and down on the balls of her feet and clapping.

I let Janey buy whatever she wants. Other than getting ingredients for s'mores, I have no food agenda. In short order, Janey has piled into the cart heat-up pizzas, a six-pack of orange soda, and several different types of chips. One of them is a bag of tortilla chips with a hot chicken wing coating. At the sight of the bag, a slosh of heartburn tries to crawl up my esophagus.

"Get some doughnuts," I advise.

Janey eagerly shovels in a dozen chocolate ones and another half-dozen maple bars into a bag.

"What, no candy?" I ask.

Janey roars down the candy aisle like a zombie after human flesh, grabbing so many bags of sweets, we're outfitted for the next ten years of Halloweens.

"Slow down, Janey," Tanner urges. "We can't possibly eat all this stuff."

"We're going to be up all night," she answers.

I raise an inquiring eyebrow at him.

He shrugs. "She wants to stay up all night and watch all eight Harry Potter movies." As I open my mouth to say something along the lines of OMFG, he hastens to add, "She'll be lucky to make it through the first one."

After stacking another ton of artery-clogging junk food in the cart, we head for the checkout.

"I'll bring my car around front," Tanner says, before heading for the exit.

The clerk shoots me a pitying, condescending gaze as I start depositing our haul of non-organic, unhealthy, un-whole foods onto the belt. Her mouth straightens in dismay at the sight of a tub of Chubby Hubby ice cream. I bite my lower lip to keep from saying something snarky at her.

I hate it when grocery store clerks food-judge you.

"That'll be ninety-seven ninety-two," she says. Her gum-chewing mouth causes her lips to smack as she talks.

As I hand her five twenties, Janey worms her way past the next person in line and edges down the checkout lane to my side. She tugs on my jean shorts. The clerk is busy straightening out the bills and studying the cash drawer before making change, and I turn away to gaze down at Janey. She's holding a lollipop the size of a small dinner plate with swirls of bold colors that look like a melted box of crayons.

Janey doesn't have to speak. Her anime size eyes are asking if I'll buy this for her, except I just checked out. Miss snob clerk will probably sneer and cluck her stuck-up tongue at me if I ask her to ring up another sale. While she's pawing through the drawer for the right combination of change, I lean down toward Janey.

"Slide it up under your shirt," I whisper to her. "Then keep your arms folded across your chest."

Her eyes widen slightly, but she quickly complies.

On second thought, maybe encouraging her to shoplift isn't such a good idea. I grew up doing this sort of thing, but do I really want Janey to take after me of all people? Not really. With a sigh, I hold out my hand for Janey to hand the lollipop over to me, which she does, looking slightly relieved.

"One more item," I tell the clerk, who started counting out my change.

As expected, the lady scowls and rolls her eyes. I smile back at her and hand her a five, resisting the urge to dump the liter of orange soda I just bought down her front.

When we emerge from the store, Tanner is standing nearby next to his car, waiting to help us load the groceries. Janey holds the lollipop aloft in a grand *ta-da* gesture. Tanner's eyes widen.

"Behold a pale horse," he mutters.

"Yeah. 'Welcome to the Terrordome.'"

His brows furrow in thought. "Say what?"

"Public Enemy."

"Who?"

"I'm going to pretend you didn't ask that, weak sauce," I tell him while administering a consoling pat on his shoulder. "Okay, so give me a sec to get my car. Then follow me. I'll lead the way back to the vineyard."

"I'm riding with West." Janey's tongue is already turning weird shades of blue and red from licking the lollipop.

"Thank you, God," Tanner mutters to the sky above.

CHAPTER TWENTY-FIVE

Atlanta
One year ago

"You ready to order?" the waitress asked.

I scanned her name tag. "Two minutes, Carol." I grinned up at her. "I'm expecting a friend."

"I'll stop back," she replied with a huff of disinterest and stuffed her order pad in her apron's pocket.

As soon as she left, I spotted Mom entering the restaurant, a scowl on her face. I set up the meeting, and I could tell she didn't like my choice.

"Waffle House?" Mom slid into the booth across from me.

"I want pancakes."

I pushed a menu across the tabletop at her. She shoved it back. Apparently, she wasn't hungry. Me? Starved. It was the middle of the afternoon and I hadn't eaten since early that morning.

"Since when do you like pancakes?" she asked.

I smiled at her. "Since I started making them for my girlfriends every morning. Nice and big, slathered in heaps of melted butter and drenched in real maple syrup. Food of the gods."

"Disgusting glop of sugar," she muttered and shook her head.

"Yum," I teased.

Mom wasn't in the mood. She glowered at me as if I'd insulted her hairstyle.

Okay, *somebody* woke up on the wrong side of the bed.

When Carol came around again a few moments later, I ordered a monster stack with a side of oink. Mom rolled her eyes and ordered coffee, sugar, no cream.

"Aren't you hungry?" I asked.

"I don't *do* Waffle House," she replied coolly.

I shrugged. "Suit yourself. It was my turn to pick, so tough noogies. So what's shaking over at your hotel?"

Mom didn't smile. In fact, her mouth tightened into a straight line that meant trouble. Oh fudge, what now?

"Chen wants the diamond necklace," she said in a near whisper, glancing around to see if anyone was listening in on our conversation. "It's worth a lot more than you thought."

Carol arrived with my pancakes and Mom's coffee. My meal also came with hash browns, which I began heavily salting. My stomach growled at the banquet feast, insisting I hurry up and start eating.

"That's a good thing. So, why the sad emoji face?"

"Chen has a buyer flying into Chicago from Singapore who wants to see the piece ASAP."

"I can't do it," I said, my hand freezing with the syrup dispenser a couple inches above my plate. I shot an annoyed glare at my mother. "I have an entire other safe to go through. If I filch the necklace now, they'll know. It'll be game over and I'll have to disappear."

"If we can deliver for this buyer, we get a finder's fee on top of our usual cut."

"How much?" I asked, resuming the flow of syrup onto my stack.

"He's quoting us a hundred and fifty K."

"Wowsome. That means he must be selling it for a million and a half at least."

"More like two million," Mom said. "It's too much money to turn our backs on."

My shoulders slumped as I went over what I'd have to do to get the necklace. I saw no way to do it without blowing my cover. The fact was, I wasn't in any hurry to close the deal with the three Js. I liked the old ladies and wanted to stretch out my time with them as long as possible. Even though I always knew the day would come when I'd have to stick a knife in their back and steal their best pieces. I shouldn't have cared, but I did.

"If we pull the plug now," I said, "we're leaving a lot of money on the table. Can't we figure out a way to get Chen his piece without torpedoing the rest of the operation?"

"I don't know. Can we?"

"Let me think about it overnight. Let's meet again tomorrow morning. Early."

"How early?"

"*Mom.*"

She leaned her head back and exhaled. "Fine. But my turn to pick. No more pancakes."

I stuck out my tongue at her.

CHAPTER TWENTY-SIX

Our slumber party starts off down by Condon Pool where I've convinced Janey to try her hand at fishing. I set her up in a chair at the edge of the water, carefully instructing her on what to do if she sees the red and white bobber dip under the water.

A puzzled expression slides over her face. "It's already dipping."

"It's bouncing, not dipping," I say. "Wait until it goes fully under the water. Then set the hook."

"You mean turn this?" She points to the reel handle.

I grind my teeth. I've already explained the monumentally basic step of setting the hook fifty-nine times. It's not sinking in. At her age, I'd caught plenty of fish and could even bait my own hook. One of my earliest memories, every August, I've gone bass fishing with my cousins on Lake Hatchineha.

"Let's do *this*," I say with a patient smile. "Sit still and don't make a sound. If you feel a jerk on the pole, holler for me."

Janey settles in on a lawn chair at the water's edge with a fierce look of determination, nodding to me as if to say "Aye, aye, sir." Total silence descends around us, except for the birds and bugs. After a few minutes, Tanner gives me an approving nod.

"Damn," he whispers to me, "I should have taken her fishing a long time ago. Who knew a rod and reel work better than a gag?"

Tanner and I settle into Adirondack chairs next to each other. The late afternoon sun warms my face, and the sky is blue as turquoise with only thin wisps of clouds. What a great day.

"This is pretty awesome," Tanner says. "*You're* pretty awesome."

I reach over and pat him gently on the arm. "Tan, you've only seen the merest tip of the iceberg of my awesomeness," I tease.

Janey doesn't last long at fishing. With my help, she manages to reel in one bluegill, but the sight of it writhing on the ground with a hook in its mouth horrifies her.

"Set it free," she screeches. Once I get the hook out and toss it back into the water, she asks in a tiny voice, "Can we be done now?"

We spend the next hour sitting in our chairs, debating what Janey should be when she grows up. I hand her a pack of Oreos and she attacks them, twisting them apart, eagerly licking away the filling before dipping the cookie halves in her chocolate milk. Obviously, she's not used to such sinful decadence.

Tanner grimaces. "You seem to revel in shoveling junk food at my niece. Tonya would have a stroke, you know."

I shrug. "Life's too short to eat Brussels sprouts when you can have chocolate."

"What's for dinner?" Janey interrupts.

"After all those Oreos," I say, "I doubt you'll have an appetite for days."

She shakes her head vigorously. "How about pizza?"

"Pizza it is." Tanner leans close to me and whispers, "We *did* buy pizza, right?"

We end up not having pizza. When we get back to the house, I lead Tanner and Janey out to the enormous, flagstone patio in the back. A raised, circular fire pit, about five feet across, sits in the middle, framed by four outdoor couches that are comfortable enough to sleep on. Before disappearing upstairs for the evening, Peter got a fire going for us. Upon seeing the blaze, Janey immediately wants to roast hot dogs to go with the s'mores.

After some kitchen prep, I bring out our food and supplies and place them on a table near the pit with plastic wrap over the dogs to keep the bugs off. I'm in the middle of getting the condiments arranged when Mom strolls outside. Even though I told her to scram, I'm not altogether surprised she decided to put in an appearance. She *is* Miss Nosy Nose.

"Pleased to meet you again, Mrs. Rowan," Tanner says, offering his hand for her to shake. "Thank you for your hospitality."

"Not at all," she replies with a short laugh. "You've made quite an impression on West. She can't stop talking about you. Both of you, actually."

"Mommm," I utter through clenched teeth in a low growl only she can hear.

When we're in the middle of a game and one of us flubs a line or misses a cue, we have a subtle hand gesture we use to alert the other person to move on to the next line. It's a slight twitch of the index finger, as if you're trying to swat away a fly. It's supposed to be a lazy, slow gesture that will go unnoticed. But not today. Nope. I'm jerking my finger rapidly, all the while I keep yanking my eyes in the direction of the door to the house. Mom grins innocently.

Tanner's eyebrows scrunch up in confusion. He can tell something is going on, but he has no idea what. He glances at the two of us, confused.

"Oh, it's almost six o'clock," I announce almost loud enough to be heard the next county over. "Mom, your favorite reality show is about to start. Can't miss that, yeah? TiVo it for me, K?"

Mom raises an eyebrow in amusement before turning to go. I'll get even with her for this.

"Follow the sun, West," Mom says as she leaves.

My response is automatic. "I go where it leads."

"Follow the sun?" Tanner asks once Mom has gone. "What does that mean?"

Why not tell him the truth? It's not a huge secret, unlike the rest of my life. "It's an old family saying," I reply. "We always use it when going into the unknown."

"Yeah, but what does it *mean*?" Janey asks.

After a couple of moments of internal debate, I decide to tell them. To my knowledge, no one outside my extended family knows anything about it, but there's nothing top-secret, confidential about it.

"During World War One, my ancestors lived in the village of *Baciu* and were caught up in the fighting between the Romanian army and the Central Powers. Because of shelling, most of their village was forced to flee into the *Hoia* forest to hide."

"The what?" Janey says.

"It's a forest in Romania," I add. "It's by the town of *Cluj-Napoca*."

"*Cluj-Napoca!*" Tanner says in fake recognition. "I *love* that place. Except I've never heard of it."

I bang my fist against his shoulder in a "just shut up" punch, and my voice turns serious. What happened next is a greatly revered part of our history, of my history. "Anyway. My grandfather said they were trapped and surrounded by armies on all sides. They were scared they were all going to die."

"What happened?" Janey cuts in, her voice breathless.

"Around midnight, after the guns had gone silent for the night, a ten-year-old boy named Razvan, my great-great-grandfather, saw a small orb of light glowing in the darkness. According to the stories, it looked like a tiny sun. Anyway, he woke everyone up and told them they were supposed to follow the sun, but most of them thought he was crazy and refused."

"Why?" Janey asks.

"He wanted to lead them straight toward the enemy lines. They thought he was stupid. In the end, only thirty people followed him, most of whom were my direct ancestors."

"Did they get shot?" Janey sounds worried about whether this story has a happy ending.

"No," I reply. "They followed the sun and it led them out of the forest to safety. Sadly, many of the villagers who stayed behind were massacred in the fighting the next morning."

"Bummer," Tanner says.

"Yeah, so 'Follow the sun' has been my family's anthem ever since."

Tanner nods. "That's pretty cool. The closest thing we have to a family anthem is during football season when Dad hollers, 'Someone get me another beer.'"

All of us laugh, including Janey, who nods vigorously as if to say, "It's totally true."

Around eight, dinner and dessert are over and Janey is lying on one of the couches, sound asleep, not having watched one minute of the Harry Potter movies. I retrieve a throw blanket from inside and spread it over her.

"So much for Janey's plan to stay up all night, watching movies," Tanner says.

I had been sitting alongside Janey before she fell asleep, but now I move over to sit next to Tanner on his couch, although I keep a couple feet between us. "So you're a big soccer star, right?"

He sighs as if this is one of the crosses he has to bear in life. "I'm not bad."

I give him a gentle shove. "Come on, Mr. Modest. I read online you're the team captain." He turns his palms up in a "what can I say" gesture. "You know, you don't seem like the stereotypical jock."

He arches a questioning eyebrow and says in a slightly annoyed tone, "I'm not sure I want to know what your idea of a stereotypical jock is."

"Well, I mean, you read good stuff. Classics."

He snorts out a laugh. "Whereas normal jocks read bad stuff, if they read at all, of course."

"I didn't exactly say that."

"Anything else?" he says with an amused smile.

"Also, you don't seem to be particularly arrogant."

He leans his head back to stare at the dark sky as if to say, "Please, God, stop her." Then he drops his gaze to study my face.

"My turn. Let's look at you. If you attended my school, you would *easily* be one of the hottest girls there. Yet, you so don't act like the stereotypical hot babe."

"Ah, thanks… I think."

"Well, you read. I mean, you read good stuff. Classics."

I start to giggle, sounding a little like Janey.

"And," he continues, "not only are you not particularly arrogant, you're sincerely nice to people around you. Even people you have nothing to gain from. Like Janey."

Okay, this is a low blow, even though he doesn't know it. I have everything to gain from being nice to Janey. And sincerely nice? I don't think so.

One day, Tanner is going to realize the truth about me and what I'm doing, and he'll hate my guts. He's going to remember this conversation and possibly hate himself too. My stomach twists at the thought, but I can't dwell on it.

Once we leave this place, I will permanently erase Tanner and Janey from my brain as if they disappeared off the face of the planet. I have to. As Mom has drilled into me all my life, you're either a taker or you're taken. There is no middle ground.

"Words to string me along by," I reply. Time to switch topics. "Hey, let's trade. You tell me the dumbest thing you've done recently, and I'll tell you mine."

He has a smug smile on his face. "Mine's easy. Happened last fall. We were playing a rival school. I tried to head the ball away, but I misplayed it." He thumps himself in the chest. "Own goal."

"What's an own goal?"

He stares as if he can't believe I asked such a question. "Haven't you ever played soccer?"

"Are you serious? You have to be able to run and kick the ball at the same time, right? See, that whole eye-foot coordination thing is a problem. I have a gap in my genetic code where athletic skill comes from."

"Come on, you had to have played something."

"Does poker or *Animal Crossing* count?"

"Nope."

"Bombardment? Tetherball?"

"Only if you're in the fourth grade."

I sigh and confess, "Okay, those are the things I was sort of good at. I used to play flag football with my cousins, but I was always the last one picked. I couldn't run fast back then. But, hey, I'm hell at bass fishing."

"Bass fishing."

I nod. "Don't knock it. It's a bigger sport in Florida than soccer will ever be."

"And that's just sad," he says with a shake of his head. "Okay, so what's an own goal? It's when someone is so monumentally stupid, they score a goal for the other team. It's the most humiliating thing you can do in team sports." He pauses to grin at me for some reason. "Now, what's your recent dumb thing?"

I can't actually tell him the most recent incident, which happened this winter in Houston. Mom and I were in the middle of a game and my job was to "accidentally on purpose" run into her while she was examining diamond rings, knocking her to the floor. During the ensuing bedlam, Mom was supposed to slip me a ring. I ran into a woman and knocked her down all right, but it wasn't Mom. Although we laughed about it later, it took a few days for her to get over my epic fail.

I suck in a deep breath before speaking. "Mom and I were staying in a hotel in Manhattan. It's a little after midnight when I decided to go to bed. Mom's already asleep. Before turning off the lights, I made up my mind to wheel our room service cart outside.

You know how a lot of hotels have this flipper thing you can use to prop open your door? I screwed up somehow, and the door slammed shut, locking me outside in the hall without a key card."

He rolls his eyes. "Come on. That's not stupid. That's inconvenient. You—"

I raise my hands. "I was wearing only pink panties, a short tank top, and no bra."

He winces as if feeling my pain.

"So, I banged loudly on the door, but my mom was dead to the world and didn't hear me. Unfortunately, everyone else on the floor did. Heads started peeking out of doors, like little turtles poking their snouts above the water. I think one guy may have videoed me on his cell phone. Eventually, a nice security man let me back in my room. In earthquake terms, my embarrassment level was at least eight-point O on the Richter scale."

"Pink, huh?"

"You and underwear colors. You're disturbed."

"Yes I am," he says, sounding quite proud of himself.

We sit in silence for a while, both of us staring out into the darkened landscape. The stars are shining, but I don't know any constellations and was never much for gazing skyward. During the time we'd been talking, Tanner inched closer so now our bare knees are touching. I have a sudden urge to put my hand on his thigh, but that minor gesture would be a monumental departure from the script. I can't lose control, and I'm a razor's edge from doing exactly that.

Trying to take my mind off the warmth of his skin, I blurt out the first inane question that comes to mind. "Where do you want to go to college?"

"Santa Clara University."

"Really. Are you Catholic?"

He makes a thumbs-down gesture. "I'm not anything, but my dad is. I want to go there because I'll have a good shot at serious playing time on the soccer team. What about you?"

"I'm not going to college." This, sadly, is the truth. "Mom wants me to work in the family business. She's not much for higher education." My voice is a little wistful and he picks up on it.

"That doesn't sound like what you want."

"What I want doesn't really matter." Bitter much? I guess I've known this was the case since Atlanta, but this is the first time I've acknowledged it openly. "Family comes first."

"That sucks. I mean, family is great and all, but you should find your own path." He pauses, perhaps sensing that this advice scares the hell out of me. "So what book are you going to read next?"

Grateful for the subject change, I say, "I haven't read any of the novels by Henry James, so I'm reading *Portrait of a Lady*. You?"

"I haven't read any of his novels either, although we had to read the short story *The Turn of the Screw* last year. I'm trying to decide between *Lord Jim* and *Moby Dick*. No, I haven't read *Moby Dick* yet. Embarrassing. My mother would've been disappointed in me."

"You said she was a librarian?"

He nods. "She wanted me to read all the classics, so I've tried. But some are harder than others."

I stretch out my legs and lean against the cushion. "You should definitely read *Moby Dick* at some point, but I think you'd enjoy *Lord Jim* more. I mean, *Moby Dick* is this big famous book and all, but looking at the story itself, it's way overrated."

"Sounds like heresy."

We laugh. "I know," I say. "If God were an English professor, he'd be hurling thunderbolts at me right now or turning me into a pillar of salt."

It's well after midnight when I finally stand and stretch. I can hardly keep my eyes open. Tanner takes Janey in his arms and follows me downstairs to a small guest bedroom next to mine, where he gently lowers her onto a twin bed.

Even though I'm about to fall asleep standing, I don't want to go to bed yet. Neither does Tanner. We end up sitting cross-legged on the floor in the game room, rolling a basketball across the carpet back and forth to each other as we continue talking. I push him to tell me about high school, his friends, classes, teachers...even the cafeteria.

I went to high school for most of one year, but I never really fit in or made close friends. I was absent too much helping Mom. Although he views high school—with the exception of soccer—with a mixture of contempt and disgust, he smiles a lot when he talks about it, and I'm a little jealous.

He wants to hear about all the places I've been. With the exception of a trip to Montana, he's never left the state of California. Mom and I have been to most of the major cities in the country, multiple times over.

"So what are your favorite cities?" he asks.

I chew the inside of my cheek, mulling over my answer. "Well, New York. Manhattan, obviously. It's a great place."

I hesitate for a moment, remembering the last time we were there in April, when we decided we would eat every meal for three days from street vendors: pizza, pretzels, egg sandwiches, hot dogs, tacos…you name it. Manhattan holds happy memories. Usually, we don't work there. We go there a few times a year to cash in our loot and then we hang around for a few days and celebrate.

"But I'm going to also say Miami. Mom and I have had a lot of fun there too." Yes we have. Some of our biggest hauls have happened in Miami.

"And your least?"

I don't have to think long to answer. "Denver." I wrinkle my nose in disgust. "We went in the winter, and the freezing temps kind of soured me on the place."

True, it was below zero when we were there, but that wasn't the problem. A game went bad on us at a downtown jewelry store. Two security guards chased me out of the store and down the street. My wig flew off while I was running, and I tossed the diamond bracelets I snatched over my shoulder, hoping it would distract them from continuing pursuit. One of the guards stopped, but the other kept coming, and, man, was he fast. I sprinted for two blocks before dashing into the Colorado Convention Center to the sound of approaching sirens. I managed to lose the guy by going up a down escalator and out an emergency door. Then I charged onto a chartered bus parked nearby, where I crouched down between two rows of seats.

I had to stay on that damn bus for three hours, and when it departed, it took me and a group of old ladies all the way to Omaha. I spent hours in a Greyhound bus station before Mom arrived at six the next morning to pick me up. I was fourteen at the time, and I can still remember sitting on that bus, trembling with fear.

No sir. Never going back to Denver.

We stop rolling the basketball and move to sit on the large black leather couch along one wall. Tanner is in the middle of a story about how he broke his thumb playing baseball when I lean my head back and close my eyes for a moment. Before I can open them again, I'm swallowed up by sleep.

***

When I wake up some time in the middle of the night with cramps in my neck, I'm still on the couch, with my head tilted back and my mouth hanging open, baring my tonsils to the world. Tanner is slumped over next to me with his head on the armrest.

Oops.

I forgot to show him the guest room where he's supposed to sleep. He doesn't even have a blanket.

After a quick trip to the bathroom, I grab a throw blanket from a closet in my room and move to spread it over him. As I prepare to withdraw, his hand shoots out and gently grasps my wrist, tugging me down beside him.

I've already gained his trust. I don't need to do this. But I don't resist.

What exactly *are* we doing?

He spoons me from behind while arranging the blanket so it covers us. As we're swaddled in this cocoon of warmth, my stomach begins to flutter, and my pulse is pounding like bongo drums. The earthy, sweaty smell of him is distracting, but then his breath stirs my hair, and when he puts his hand on my hip, I want to turn to face him. But if I do that, I'm a little scared about what will happen next.

The Lana Del Ray song about having a war tearing up your head pops into my brain. Yep, that's what's happening all right. I lie here waiting to see what Tanner is going to do…and I do want him to do *something*. After several minutes, he begins to snore lightly.

Well, that's anticlimactic. The war in my head peters out.

All quiet on the western front.

I should go to my bedroom, but I don't.

I know, I know. I'm supposed to scam him, not sleep with him.

Yet, here I am.

CHAPTER TWENTY-SEVEN

I feel a hand around my foot jerking on it, and it startles me awake. After several rapid blinks, my surroundings come into focus. Tanner is still spooned around me, snoring, and his hand remains on my hip, but it has drifted halfway under my jean shorts. His other arm is draped across my chest.

Another tug on my foot.

I glance down straight into my mother's face. The icy glare she shoots me is cold enough to lower the temperature in the room and cause my breath to fog.

She points a finger up at the ceiling and mouths "Now." Mom is certifiably p-oed. This isn't going to end well…for me anyway.

Careful not to wake him, I disentangle myself, letting his hand slide out from under the waistband of my shorts. Once upstairs, Mom closes the downstairs door and pivots to face me with hands on hips.

Ugh.

"I told you not to…" Clearly she meant to add some words after "to," but she chooses to clench her teeth instead.

"Nothing happened, not even a kiss," I say with a weary sigh. "See, I'm in my clothes."

"You're becoming attached again." She tries to whisper, but her voice comes out loud and husky. "He is your…"

Yeah, he's my mark. I get it.

"I *know*." The words come out with a hiss. "I've got this under control. I'm doing what I need to do. Trust me. We're ready to move to phase three. Okay?"

"I thought you learned your lesson. I think you're losing your edge."

"Arrgggh." I shake my head in frustration.

Mom's eyes narrow, but she doesn't immediately respond. I can tell she's turning something over in her mind. This isn't a good sign.

"Keep your day open," she says. "We're running drills. You need to refocus your mind."

Drills. Wonderful. I'd rather eat a Spam sandwich with headcheese.

When I was younger, Mom used drills to train me, and I actually enjoyed them. Now, she uses them more as a disciplinary regimen when I mess up, or if she thinks I gave a sloppy performance during a game.

"Can I at least feed them breakfast before shooing them off?"

Without waiting for a response, I turn to head back downstairs to my room and change my clothes. When I reach the top of the stairs, she answers.

"Sure, feed them." Then she points a finger at me like she's leveling a gun and practically hollers, *"No more canoodling."*

"Shhh. Not so loud."

***

An hour later, Janey and Tanner wander upstairs, and Mom has disappeared upstairs after slamming her bedroom door. I'm almost done making breakfast, and I give Janey a forced smile. She yawns and stares down at the array of plates on the table in the breakfast nook.

"What are these?" she asks, pointing at the main serving dish.

"They're Romanian," I answer. "Romanian pancakes. We call them *clătite*. They're like French crepes."

"What do you do with them?" She glances around the table, evidently searching for syrup and butter.

"You pick one of the fillings I set out and spoon it on. Then you roll it up and eat it."

Janey and Tanner take a seat at the breakfast table, and then Janey experiments with a couple crepes before settling on what she calls the perfect filling combination—peanut butter and jelly. Tanner frowns at the spread while dragging his fingers through his couch hair.

"You got jalapenos?"

I raise a jar I scrounged up and left sitting on the counter next to me. Then I grin. I knew he would ask for them.

"Impressive," he says with a whistle before taking the jar.

Tanner slathers his *clătite* with cream cheese, blueberries, and a generous mound of jalapenos. Both Janey and I hold our breath to see if he will really eat this monstrosity. He does, and then smiles contentedly.

"That's just sick, T." With a shudder at Tanner taking another bite, I spoon my usual—raspberry preserves—onto mine and take a bite.

"So, these are seriously good." After eating a half dozen, Tanner towels off his hands with a napkin. "You Romanian?"

I have to pause to swallow my last bite before answering. "Through and through. Although I wasn't born in Romania. My great-grandparents immigrated to Florida right after the First World War."

"Can you speak Romanian?" Janey asks.

"*Esti o fata draguta*. That means you're a pretty girl."

She claps her hands excitedly. "Say something else."

"*Unchiul tău este de și el frumos*." I smile over at Tanner, who lifts one eyebrow as if he suspects I may have insulted him. "That means your uncle is also handsome."

"You got that right," Tanner says.

"What's the word for moron?" Janey asks

"Uh, I'd go with *imbecil*."

Janey glances over at Tanner. "You own it."

I snicker at him and he blushes.

"I could ask about the word for 'annoying brat,' but that would be beneath me," Tanner replies. "Speaking of words, what about your name? Westlyn doesn't sound Romanian."

I nod. "It's not at all. My mom and dad were traveling through Tennessee when she went into labor with me. Dad flagged down a cop, and I was born on the side of the road in Westlyn, Tennessee, outside of Knoxville. My parents thought the name of the town was pretty, and they were grateful for all the help they got from the police and EMTs, so they named me after the town. True story."

While I clean up after breakfast, Tanner and Janey gather their stuff and Janey calls her mother on Tanner's cell. I have some time to reflect on what Mom may have planned for today. This could be really bad.

"Okay, we're shoving off," Tanner announces as I put the last item in the dishwasher.

"It's your turn to sleep over at my house," Janey says. "Dad said you could."

"Well, then, how can I say no?"

"Tomorrow night would be perfect," Tanner says.

"What time should I show up?" I keep my tone level, confident, and excited, but inside I doubt Mom will let me go.

"I'll pick you up at eight-thirty. That work?"

I sigh. "Not necessary. You don't need to drive all the way here and back. I—"

"No, I want to." Then he signals "call me later" with his hand.

As soon as Tanner and Janey speed off down our access road, Mom waves for me to follow her out to the car. I'm curious where we're going, but I know better than to ask. She won't tell me, and we'll only end up arguing.

***

Soon, we're on the 101 going south, zipping through the small communities along the way. When Mom doesn't take the Richmond Bridge exit, I know we're heading into San Francisco. Traffic isn't too bad. After crossing the Golden Gate Bridge, it takes only twenty minutes for Mom to bring the car to a stop at Golden Gate Park. I've been here before, but not recently. Since it's a beautiful day with blue skies and lots of sun, it's no surprise the place is packed. Without saying a word, Mom wiggles her finger for me to follow, and she marches off almost at a jog.

I follow her along an asphalt pathway, past a carousel packed with kids, toward a play area with a wooden sign in front that says Koret Children's Quarter Playground. A small army of young marks-to-be mobs the climbing equipment, while a long line has formed to use the enormous concrete slides.

This place looks so cool. I wish I had come here as a kid.

Mom stops inside the play area and begins scanning the crowd, as if she's searching for someone specific. Again, I know better than to ask, so I stand alongside her with my arms crossed, trying to stanch the rising tide of annoyance and impatience welling up inside.

"There," Mom finally says. "The woman in the gray yoga pants and fluorescent green top."

I peer over in the direction Mom is pointing. It takes me several seconds, but I locate the woman. She's sitting on a bench, with a young child pestering her. The little guy is pleading with her to do something, and he looks like he's about to have a meltdown. "The one with the kid?"

"The same," Mom confirms. "The drill is for you to get her wallet without her knowing."

"Really? What is this supposed to prove?"

"It's a skills test. If you've still got your A-game, you can do this easy."

"We have better things to do with our time. We're taking a stupid risk here. What if I get caught? The whole house of cards could come tumbling down."

"Then don't get caught."

"Sir, yes, sir," I reply, giving her a mock salute. She's being a real dickhead.

Mom's face immediately reddens, and she pulls her hand back as if she's going to slap me.

Dogs, I may have gone too far. She's galactically angry, so I raise my hands in surrender. As much as I may argue with her, in the end I always do what she says. I'm a complete wuss when it comes to her.

"I'll be watching from over there." She points to a distant picnic table. Then she stalks away. I flip her off and then top off the gesture by sticking out my tongue.

With anger bubbling inside, I make my way over to the woman, wracking my brains about how best to do this. When I draw close to her, the little boy begins to cry and stomp his feet. He's about Janey's age, I'm guessing, which is a little old to be acting like a two-year-old.

Boys.

"I want money for a popsicle," the kid whines.

"No more popsicles, Nathan," the mom says in response.

This little domestic drama gives me an idea. I head for the bench where the mom is sitting. There's about three feet of space available on the end. I point at it.

"You mind if I sit for a few minutes?" I ask her.

"Help yourself," she answers with a welcoming smile.

I want to make some inane small talk to gain a tiny bit of her trust, so I say, "I love this park. I bring my little brother here all the time."

My *nonexistent* little brother, I don't bother to clarify. Her keys are clipped to the strap of her purse, and the keychain sports the unmistakable logo of the University of Notre Dame—the intertwined letters N and D.

"We come here every week," she replies. "Hi, I'm Ann."

"West." We shake hands, and then I point at her keychain. "My mother went to Notre Dame. I'm applying next year."

She beams at me. Check the box—trust established.

"You absolutely have to go," she says. "It was the most fabulous four years of my life."

Wow, to hear her gush, she should be on the Notre Dame admissions payroll. I force myself to smile at her ill-behaved, spoiled brat of a son. "He's a cute little boy."

Almost as if on cue, Nathan begins to wail at the top of his lungs over the injustice of life. Ann and I both start laughing.

"Hey, what's wrong, Nathan?" I ask him. "You're so much handsomer when you're smiling."

At the sound of his name coming out of my mouth, he instantly goes quiet, apparently stunned to hear a strange girl address him. His mouth falls open and he stares at me, but his surprise is giving way to curiosity. Ann is about to say something, but her phone rings.

"Oh, thanks for calling me back, Susan," Ann says. "Can you swap Tuesday for Wednesday next week?"

Bingo. This is my shot.

"Hey, Nathan," I whisper to the kid, careful so his mother can't hear. "You want to earn ten bucks?"

He nods and comes over to sit next to me. I slide a ten-dollar bill out of my pocket and surreptitiously push it into his hand. He greedily clenches his fat little fist around it.

"Count to twenty," I tell him, "and when you get there, I want you to do something for me." I whisper simple instructions in his ear, and with a smile, he nods and silently counts.

I'm counting along too, but he must be going faster than me, because I only make it to fifteen before he bursts into action.

Nathan leaps off the bench as if shot out of a catapult and takes off running in an all-out sprint for the distant carousel. Ann drops her phone while making a frantic grab for him, but she misses him by a yard.

"*Nathan. Get back here.*" After he covers another twenty yards, she hollers even louder, "*Nathan.*"

Then, as I suspected would happen, she looks over at me with a "Please, help me" expression.

"Go," I yell. "I'll watch your stuff."

With that, Ann takes off at a dead run. She's faster than Nathan, but no way is she going to catch up with him before he makes it all the way to the carousel. I let her run for fifty or sixty yards before I calmly lift her brown leather purse off the ground and withdraw a red Coach wallet. Nice. With a glance around to make sure no one saw anything, I return the purse to the ground, calmly stand, and walk over to Mom.

When I hand her the wallet to examine, she says, "Not bad. Distracting her with her own bratty kid. I'll have to remember that one."

She hands the wallet back to me, unopened. We take a slight detour back to the car so as to avoid running into Ann or Nathan. Once we get there, I stop and heft the wallet in my hand.

"I'm going to have it returned to her now," I say.

Why generate a police report with a description of me over a measly wallet? And it's certainly not worth making the woman go through hell for a small amount of money. I'm about to flag down one of the kids playing nearby and offer him a twenty to return the wallet for me, but Mom yanks the thing out of my hand. The icy glare she shoots me makes me go rigid.

"You want to return it?" she asks softly. "Fine."

She unzips the wallet and removes a thin wad of bills, an Amex card, and the woman's driver's license. Then she zips it shut and hands it back to me.

"Now you can return it."

"Why are you doing this? There's not enough money to care about, and we don't lift plastic, remember? Why do this to her? This isn't who we are."

"This is *exactly* who we are," Mom thunders back at me. "She is a mark. This is what we do to marks. Remember?"

"You said this was a skills test. I demonstrated my skill. Game over, now give me back her stuff." My eyes widen and I point behind her as my mouth drops open. It's humanly impossible for a person to resist looking back over their shoulder to where I'm frantically pointing. Mom is no exception, and the instant she does, I snatch the cards and money she's holding.

"Too slow," I say with a smirk when she turns to glare at me.

Her answer is to grab me by the biceps, her fingernails biting into me so hard, a flare of pain shoots up my arms, causing me to wince. She yanks hard, and her talon-like grip is too strong for me to pull free.

"I thought you understood after last year," Mom says, her voice hard like cold iron. "That boy is not one of us. He comes from a different world, a world you're not a part of and never will be. If he knew what you are, you would *disgust* him."

As I thought, this exercise wasn't about testing my skill. It was about Tanner. She's punishing me. My anger explodes. "You're such a total *bitch*."

Mom and I have fought plenty over the years. I've even lobbed a few "I hate you" grenades at her, although not since I was possibly eleven. But I have never called her a curse word before.

She makes a wild attempt to snatch back the cards and money I took, but she misses. Then I mouth off too far, using her own words against her.

"*You* disgust *me*." I drizzle a heaping dose of loathing sauce over my words.

Mom slaps me hard across my cheek. The force of the blow causes me to stumble sideways a step, but I keep hold of the wallet. My left ear is ringing. Tears instantly flood my eyes, and the hot, stinging pain brings back memories. It burns. I know this sensation. I've been hit in the face before. In Atlanta. Several seconds pass while each of us stares at the other in utter shock.

"West, I'm sorry," Mom blurts out.

I shake my head and back away. "I'll find my own way home."

Without another word, I walk away, tears streaming down my face. And then I think, *Home? What home?*

"West, don't," Mom yells. "We can fix this."

No, we can't.

I start running.

I don't look back.

CHAPTER TWENTY-EIGHT

Atlanta
One year ago

"I can't be implicated," I told Mom while cradling a cup of chai tea.

The small plate in front of me held the wrapper remains of the blueberry muffin I wolfed down a few minutes earlier. Mom stilled sawed back and forth with her knife, carefully cutting her Danish into bite-size morsels. Who uses a knife and fork on pastry? My mother. She detests eating anything with her fingers.

I gazed around the dining room of the hotel restaurant where we sat off to the side by ourselves and wondered how the Js were doing this morning without me to cook for them. I made them a breakfast quiche last night before I went to bed, but Josi is so picky sometimes I worried she'd turn her nose up at it.

"You sure you don't want to try the buffet?" Mom asked, chewing thoughtfully.

"No. For the ten thousandth time, I'm not that hungry."

"You sure?"

"Will you stop trying to shove my face in the feed trough already?"

She held up one hand. "Okay. No need to be snippy."

"I'm not snippy." The words came out almost as a growl.

"You're snippy."

I gazed up at the overhead lights in frustration and shook my head. It was pointless to argue with Mom once she made her mind up about something. This morning she was convinced I wasn't eating enough.

"Back to the matter at hand," I said. "We have to pinch the necklace without me being involved."

"How? How do we take it without casting suspicion on you?" She paused to dab at her mouth with her napkin. "If they discover it's missing, it's not like there's anyone else around to blame."

"Exactly. So the blame has to fall somewhere else. That way I can stay on and finish the job, and Chen gets his necklace. Win-win."

"How exactly do you propose to do that?"

I leaned forward on my elbows so that we were nearly nose-to-nose. Time to spill the beans about my idea. "One of our appraiser friends," I said in hushed tones. "We ship out the necklace and some other stuff to be appraised."

"And?"

"Somewhere in the process, we have the real pieces swapped for high-quality fakes. When the pieces come back from the appraiser, I put them back in the safe. Eventually, someone will figure it out, but we'll be long gone by then and who cares?"

"That's crazy."

"It buys me time."

"Too complicated," Mom said, waving her hand to dismiss the idea. Then she methodically sawed off another piece of Danish and jabbed it in her mouth. "You should grab the piece and then we blow town and vanish like we always do."

"But I'm not done yet," I countered. "If we yank the plug now, we're walking away from the biggest haul of our lives. I need a few more weeks to pull it all together."

I lied to myself about needing more time. Truth, I could've finished up in a matter of hours whenever I wanted to, but I wasn't ready. I wanted to hang around for the fundraiser next month I signed us up for. The three Js bought tickets to a dinner and silent auction for the new burn unit at St. Alban's Hospital. In addition to the dinner, we donated jewelry, and we joined up with some other dealers in town to volunteer *Antiques Roadshow*-type appraisals. I would be doing the appraisals for us, which gave me an excited buzz, since I was at least thirty years younger than any of the other appraisers. As for Josi, she was as ecstatic as a ten-year-old counting down the days to Christmas.

Of course, I couldn't tell Mom any of this. She would blow a gasket.

"Let's keep things simple," she said. "How about you mail it all off to be appraised but send the package to a drop box we set up instead. While you finish up, I'll fence the junk with Chen. By the time anyone is the wiser, we're gone with the wind."

"That won't work. Jem will call the appraiser to check it's been received. I know her. Maybe you buy me two days, three at the most. I need more."

"West, you've got to be joking. Fake stones? Where are we going to get them? And how would we swap them, anyway? Infiltrate the appraiser's mailroom?" She paused, nodded, and jabbed her fork at me. "You get mega bonus points for creative thinking, though. I'm proud of you."

I anticipated this sticking point, so I smiled and said, "Leonte. He can do it."

"Leonte?"

"Yes."

"But—"

"He's perfect. We'll offer him five percent." Leonte Condurache was fifty years old, bald, and weighed over three hundred pounds. More importantly, he had a thing for Mom. The frosting on the cake? Leonte had done this exact con before.

"Not sure we can trust him," she said.

"Mom, he'd swim laps in San Francisco Bay in the nude if *you* ask him." I fought off a giggle at the image of a naked Leonte floundering away in the ocean. "The guy will do anything for you."

"Yeah, he might." She paused and pursed her lips. "But five percent?"

I sighed. Mom was cheap. If something cost a dollar, she'd haggle for an hour to get it for ninety-five cents.

"It's a good investment. We'll make it back twenty times over."

To be honest, the most attractive part of my idea was not only that it bought me time, but that it meant the blame would never fall on me.

Eventually, the pieces would be uncovered as forgeries, sure, but when that happened, angry eyes would fall on the appraiser we sent them to. The Js would never know I betrayed them.

Mom couldn't care less about blame, and it shouldn't've mattered to me, but it did.

It really did.

CHAPTER TWENTY-NINE

Moving briskly, I walk out of Golden Gate Park and into Haight-Ashbury, ignoring the bazillion panhandlers trying to attract my attention. I left my stupid purse in Mom's stupid car, and all I have in my pockets is my stupid cell phone and twenty-four stupid dollars. Argh!

I flip through Ann's cards and money as I walk. She has about two hundred bucks. I stuff the wad of bills in my front pocket and examine the plastic she carried. The lady has 'em all, including two Visa cards and a debit card. She'll call those in immediately, so they'll be worthless within the hour. The next card in the stack is for Bloomingdale's. Perfect. I'll keep it. I'm betting Ann doesn't call this one in, if she even remembers she has it. I hold on to a few cards, but toss the rest in the next trashcan I pass.

A cab is approaching, and I finger whistle the way Grandfather taught me, while waving my other hand. The cabbie pulls over.

"Bloomies," I tell the guy.

Since I have no clothes other than what I'm wearing, I have to buy myself a new wardrobe to get me through the next couple days. I won't be going back to the vineyard—not until this game is over. And when it is over, I'm not sure where I'll be going.

As we head out of the Haight onto Market Street, I paw through the rest of the poor lady's wallet. At the sight of a gray Zipcar card, I pause and flip it over. On the back of the card, Ann has written her website username and password in blue sharpie ink. She's a freaking idiot for writing a password on the back of a card, but some people just don't think.

I'd expected the card to be worthless, but with this information, I'll have full access to her account and can rent a car. Solves my transportation problem. Mom and I use Zipcars all the time. I even have their app on my phone, so this will be easy.

Two minutes before we reach Bloomies, I finish using Ann's card to reserve a Honda Civic located in a garage at Fifth and Mission, a stone's throw away from the store. I stood up and protected that poor lady from my mother, but who's going to protect her from me? I try to blame this on Mom: she's forcing me into a position where I have to steal from the woman to survive. But who am I kidding? Mom's right. This is exactly who I am.

The apple doesn't fall far from the tree.

An hour later, I'm halfway across the Bay Bridge heading into Oakland, two bags of my purchases neatly lined up on the backseat of the Civic. Traffic is heavy, and the Honda slows to a crawl, but this gives me time to text a message to Mother.

Me: *I'm going to finish this game. Then we talk.*
Mom: *[nothing]*

Mom is dead wrong. This isn't Atlanta. I'm not getting attached to Tanner. I'm working him the way I would work any mark, but Mom doesn't see it. So she's tightening her grip on me the way a pet owner shortens the leash on their dog with a yank. The only way to make her back off and trust me again like she used to is to finish this dance with Tanner and drain him dry. Fortunately, I know exactly how to do this.

By this time tomorrow, we'll be packing our bags and leaving the great state of California rich enough for me to retire for life, even though I'm not yet old enough to vote. Yet, in the middle of this exuberance, my smile falters. I've made this bold declaration before.

"Forget the past," I say out loud. "Focus on today."

The time has come to begin the final dance with Tanner.

This is phase three, otherwise known as the smackdown. I'm going to show my mother and myself I can do my job. Tanner Cardwell was, is, and always will be my mark and nothing more.

I'm a closer. I close out games. This isn't personal, and I'm sure as Sunday not going to make out with this guy again.

I'm a professional.

After several deep, calming breaths, I decide I need to demonstrate to myself I'm in control here. That's right, I'm going to call him. When traffic stalls again at the I-880 south exit, I hit speed dial. The phone rings four times.

"I knew you'd call," he says.

I clear my throat and dredge up my serious voice. "Hello. About the sleepover tomorrow night. I—"

"You're not going to cancel, are you?"

"No, I—"

"Good." He pauses for a beat, but when I fail to speak, he plunges on. "Did you know there've been a total of four full-length films titled *West*, West?"

"Wuh-what?" I stammer, flustered by his chirpy weirdness and the abrupt change in subject. My control is slipping, and I'm losing my train of thought.

"So says IMDb," he adds.

IM what?

"Of course, there are a ton of films with West as part of the title: *Westworld*, *West Side Story*, *The Wild Wild West*, and my favorite— *West is West*. That one is kind of oracular, huh?"

"How many lines of cocaine did you snort this afternoon?"

"If I *am* high, it's not…what's that word? Pharmalogical? Pharmacolic?"

"Oh God, it's meth, isn't it?"

"Pharma?"

"*Pharmacological*," I yell into my phone.

He snaps his fingers. "That's it. It's not pharmacologically induced. There. Shit, that's the biggest word I've said all month."

"You're a moron." My voice is softer. I'm trying not to laugh.

"When are we going to sleep together again?" His voice is low and secretive. "And did your mother actually accuse us of canoodling?"

He would have to go straight for the jugular vein.

"You heard that, huh?" Now I'm laughing, but I quickly choke it off. This is called *not* being in control.

He chuckles too. "It sounds like a Top Ramen dish. Try our chicken-flavored canoodles—just add hot water, cover, and stir."

"Tanner—"

"Westlyn."

"Will you let me finish my sentence? Jeez Louise."

"Sorry. Please. The floor is yours."

I clear my throat again, trying to get back on track. Except what was I saying? Oh yeah. Sleepover. "Okay. I was wondering if I could come over tonight for Janey's slumber party, maybe even stay for a couple nights?"

Several beats of silence follow before he replies. "Is this a trick question?"

"No. I—"

"West, you can flipping move in if you want."

"I wasn't... I didn't...." Oh, the hell with this. "You still wearing green underwear, cowboy?"

Our call ends moments later after he agrees to pick me up at the Sherwood Mall near his house in one hour. I arrive early at the mall, so I have time to kill. On a lark, with nothing better to do, I dial Leah's cell. I have her number from when she called me.

"West?" she answers on the second ring. Her surprised tone practically oozes out of my phone like warm tree sap.

"Hey, girlfriend, I thought I'd check in. You good?"

"I'm actually in the middle of waiting on a customer."

I grin. "You got the job."

"I did. They think I'm this big client magnet or something."

I drop my voice. "Well, Madeleine Ainsworth is one of your staunchest fans."

"Oh my effing God, was that you?"

"We girlfriends have to stick together."

For the first time ever, Leah laughs. It's brief, almost a hiccup, but there's no mistaking it. She quickly clears her throat with a cough as if to rebuild some distance between us.

"My sources tell me you and Tanner are an item."

My initial instinct is to deny this, but this is Leah, not Mom. She's supposed to think we're romantically engaged. Tanner is supposed to think this too. Still, I waffle in answering.

"Sort of."

A genuine laugh explodes from her. "So, now you get to see the real Tanner. He's kind of a redneck, not terribly literate beyond reading the sports page, and a real ass-grabbing Neanderthal."

Her words hit me like I've been slapped again. Did she just call Tanner a Neanderthal? My hackles instantly rise. "What?" My voice climbs in obvious indignation. "I thought you were his friend?"

"Friend? He doesn't sneak into my bedroom at night for me to be his friend. But I'll ask him about it next time when he puts his hands—"

"Shut *up*." I don't want to hear any more of this.

"Well, I guess he's your problem now, *girlfriend*." Leah enunciates the last word with disdain. I bite my lip to squelch the anger building inside. This girl is so spoiled, white, and entitled. She doesn't know how good she has it. And she's flat wrong about Tanner. I'd kill to have her life.

"I don't know who you're talking about," I finally say. "But it's certainly not Tanner."

"So you're defending him now?"

"Yeah, that's right," I reply. "I am. Stay away from—"

She cuts me off. "*Stop*, West. Okay, I get it." Then she starts chuckling.

What. The. Hell.

"Good," she says in a much calmer voice. "I wasn't sure about you. I had to know."

"Know what?"

"How you really feel about him. Don't worry. I made all that stuff up. A little test."

"Excuse me?"

"I had to know if you're in love with him." She stops to let me say something, but my mouth has rusted shut like the Tin Man. "I was worried you'd hurt him, but you don't hurt someone you love. Don't screw this up, okay?"

"I never said I was in love with him."

"Actually, I think you did."

Realization dawns.

Leah just played me like a cheap guitar.

CHAPTER THIRTY

"West," Janey blurts out when Tanner and I walk through the front door of his house, "why are you here?"

"We decided you and West could start a day early," Tanner replies. "This is officially your slumber party, Janey."

"Yay!" At the sound of Janey's yell, Hal and Tonya saunter into the living room from the kitchen, and I give them a quick wave.

I'm a little self-conscious about the red mark Mom's slap left on my cheek, even though I think I did a good job covering it with the foundation I bought at Bloomies. Tanner doesn't seem to have noticed.

"You're just in time for dinner," Hal says, sounding genuinely pleased to see me. "My pot roast is the best on the planet."

"Good to see you again," Tonya adds.

After I return from washing up, Janey has me sit next to her, where she explains the rules of the dinner table: I have to be careful not to spill my drink, I have to bus my own plate, and I'm supposed to watch my reach. Totally cute.

I'm so famished I have multiple servings of everything. Most of the dinner I spend talking with Hal and Tonya about the vineyard. Tonya seems especially curious about its history. I no longer care whether Tonya likes the vineyard or not, but I can't stop myself from spinning out a story about it.

"How old is the place?" Tonya asks before spearing a carrot with her fork.

"The first structure was built in the late eighteenth century," I say, making it up on the spot. "Father Junípero Serra built a summer retreat where the current main house sits."

"Father Serra?" Janey echoes, wide-eyed. "We read about him in school."

"Yeah, but you probably didn't get the TMZ version of the real dude. He built a distillery on the property, you know. He and his drinking buddies would chill out there in August and go on some real binges."

Janey's eyebrows dip down in confusion.

"Got drunk," Tanner clarifies.

"He was famous for taking baths in barrels of whiskey," I go on. "It's where we get our word 'sloshed' from."

Tonya blinks stupidly while Hal's eyes widen with a WTF face. It takes every shred of self-control I can muster to not bust out laughing.

"Not quite the saint people make him out to be," Tanner says.

"Oh, he was a horrible lecher," I add, nodding. "The native women would run for the hills when they saw him coming."

I'm making all this stuff up, of course, but it's fun. For me, making up stories is as natural as breathing.

This is a variation of a silly pastime I used to play when I was younger, when Mom would desert me, leaving me alone in motel rooms for hours while she did her thing. I would strike up a conversation with the front desk clerk or anyone in the lobby who would talk to a little girl.

The game was to make up a backstory about myself. I would try to be as outlandish and fantastical as possible, but not so hilariously ridiculous that people would immediately realize I was lying.

Once, in Raleigh, I was Princess Di's great-niece. I signed a half dozen autographs before Mom returned and dragged me upstairs to our room while vomiting up a slew of curses at me. Another time, in Schenectady, Mom and I were in the federal witness protection program. That one was really cool.

But my favorite was the weekend we spent in St. Paul when I was twelve and pathetically skinny. In short order, I became the youngest member of the US Olympic gymnast team. Never mind that I was a tall, gangly girl with the coordination of an intoxicated ostrich.

"Ah, that's really fascinating," Tonya says. She shoots a questioning gaze my way and I give her a wink. Then she rises to take her plate to the sink, which is the signal to all of us that dinner is over.

"Let's play spoons," Janey says excitedly once we clear the table.

Tonya frowns while Tanner groans. Hal rubs his forehead as if he has a headache. Apparently, Janey wanting to play spoons is a frequent occurrence. Her shoulders sag in disappointment.

"Instead of spoons," I tell her, "I can show you some magic card tricks."

She nods eagerly.

"Get me a deck of cards."

I'm expecting Hal and Tonya to leave, but they each grab a cup of coffee and settle back in their chairs to watch the spectacle. Once Janey returns with the cards, I riffle-shuffle them several times. Then I overhand shuffle them rapidly, mostly for show. It's cool to watch. I hand the deck to Tanner.

"Check it out, Tan," I say. "Make sure the deck is thoroughly shuffled."

He fans the deck, nodding in approval at how mixed up the cards are before handing them back to me. Then I riffle-shuffle the deck one more time and place it on the table in front of me.

"Janey," I tell her, "cut the deck and place one half next to the other, so there are two piles of cards on the table."

She does, and everyone stares expectantly at me.

"I'm going to peek at the third card down in this pile." I point at the left half of the deck. "And it's going to tell me what the third card down is in the other pile."

I make a show of counting down three cards and taking a quick peek at the card, not letting anyone else see it. Then I take my hand away and point to the other pile, the one I haven't touched.

"The third card down in the other pile is the six of spades. Check it out, Janey."

She grabs the pile and paws through until she gets to the third card. She pulls it out—the six of spades. Her mouth drops open. Hal and Tanner both grin at me, while Tonya directs a questioning glance in my direction.

"How did you know?" Janey asks. "Do it again."

This is the first card trick I ever learned. My great-uncle taught it to me when I was Janey's age. He schooled me in all kinds of tricks and sleight-of-hand techniques. Mom encouraged it, saying it was good training for our business. He was teaching me new card tricks all the way up to his death when I was thirteen.

I perform the trick for Janey four more times until she's left shaking her head. She begs me to explain how I did it.

"She can't," Tanner replies. "It's against the magician's code...or something."

"Let's try a different trick," I say. After shuffling the deck several times, I fan it out, cards face down, and offer it to Janey. "Pick a card, but don't tell me what it is and be careful not to show it to me." Once she has a card, I place the deck on the table. "Put your card on top of the deck."

She does, and I riffle-shuffle the cards several more times. Then I do an overhand shuffle, which is where the sleight of hand begins. With the deck gripped in one hand, I hold it up so everyone can see the bottom card. It's the jack of diamonds.

"Is this your card?" I ask Janey, pointing to the bottom card.

"No," she answers.

"Okay, then let's take it out and put it on the table." I slide the bottom card out and place it face down. Then I pull off the top card of the deck and show it to everyone. It's the ten of clubs. "Is this your card, Janey?"

She solemnly shakes her head.

"Okay, then let's take it out too." I seem to extract the ten of clubs and place it on top of the other card. I hand the remainder of the deck to Janey. "Here, find your card."

Janey searches through the remaining fifty-card deck for a couple minutes before staring up at me in confusion.

"It's missing," Janey says.

"That's odd. What the heck happened to it?" I make a show of looking perplexed, furrowing my eyebrows and tapping my lips with my index finger. Finally, I announce, "Oh, I know where it is."

I reach for the two cards lying face down on the table and flip them over. Everyone is expecting to see the ten of clubs and the jack of diamonds, but one of the cards is the seven of spades.

I point to the seven of spades. "Is that your card?"

Janey claps her hands and nods. Hal and Tonya both laugh, while Tanner stares at me suspicious.

"How'd you do that?" Janey begs.

I have a repertoire of twenty tricks I do really well. Over the next forty-five minutes, I run through a dozen until Janey's mouth is perpetually hanging open. After each trick, she keeps asking how.

"Okay, little one," Tonya announces. "It's time for you to get ready for bed."

"Tomorrow we'll do something fun," I tell Janey.

"West, I love you," she says around a yawn.

"Ditto, girl."

Tanner and I watch TV with Tonya in the living room until after eleven, when I feign yawning and exhaustion. Tanner leads me to the overstuffed leather couch in the den, carrying a blanket and a pillow. They have a guest room, but it's currently being used as a storage room for boxes of stuff like Christmas tree lights and books.

Hal offered to clear out some space, but I volunteered to sack out on the den couch. Originally, I was going to sleep in Janey's room, since the whole reason I'm here is to have a slumber party with her, but Tonya nixed that idea, saying Janey would never go to sleep if I was in there.

"If you get cold," Tanner says in a low voice before turning out the room lights, "you can sneak up to my room."

"And what would your dad do if he caught us...canoodling?"

Tanner grins. "He'd kill me."

He blows me a kiss, and I play at catching it before he flips the light switch and the den goes dark. As soon as the door is shut, my smile dissolves, and I sit up and grab my phone off the coffee table in front of the couch.

I have some time to kill before the grand finale, so I flip through my email accounts checking the mostly useless messages, including these stupid emails from a pizza joint in Providence hawking free wings. I have never been anywhere in the state of Rhode Island, so WTF? I block it for the fifth time and scroll down further.

After playing around with my phone for an hour, I make my way across the den to the family computer, taking care not to make any noise. It takes me five minutes to login and navigate over to the website for Tanner's bank.

This is my grand plan for closing out this game. All I have to do is move the money out of the account. Since I have more computer savvy than Mom, I handle all the online bank fraud for us. Under my cousin's tutelage over the years, I can steal and launder money like a pro.

After fishing out the piece of paper from my pocket with the bank username and password, I need only a few minutes to cruise through menus and access the trust fund bank account. A quick glance at the numbers in front of me and I whistle softly at what I'm seeing. The account still has eighteen million dollars. I'll take most, but not all of it. Leave a few crumbs behind to keep the account alive.

Once the wires move and the money sits in Peter's Cayman Island bank, I'll call him and have him take it from there. He'll then move it around the globe several times until it can't be traced.

Quicker than the time it takes to order a pizza, I've set up the transaction. All that's left is to push Enter and accept the transfer instructions. Just a twitch of the finger, a slight tap, and it's all over. Peter, Mom, and I will be on airplanes jetting away from California by lunch, never to be seen again by the Cardwells or anyone else in Stockton.

It's so easy, yet so daunting.

You don't hurt someone you love. What a load of crap. Leah is a pathetic loser for trusting me. *West, I believe you are a person who would honor her word.*

I'm not that person, Leah. I'll *never* be that person.

Yet my idiot finger still hovers uncertainly over the Enter key.

Dammit.

Then a list of recent transactions catches my attention, withdrawals from the trust account in the last few days. The last deduction was two days ago—eleven thousand to a private school. This would be Janey's tuition for the fall.

Since I have taken no action for over twenty seconds, the delay causes a warning message on the screen to pop up: "*Due to inactivity you will be automatically logged out in one minute.*"

Next on the list is forty-five hundred dollars for the Ben Atkins Soccer Camp. That would be Tanner.

Thirty seconds until logout.

Nine thousand dollars to a bridal shop in San Francisco. Tonya and Gavin.

Ten seconds to logout.

Sixty-two hundred dollars to an assisted-living home for Mrs. Ellen Cardwell. His grandmother. He said she had Alzheimer's. Once I take all of the Cardwells' money, I guess she'll have to move out. But where? This one hits me like a punch to the stomach. A memory of Josi surfaces, the lost look on her face when her dementia would flare up and hijack her brain.

Josi.

I can't do this.

Ding.

I'm officially logged off. According to the stern notice that materializes, I'll have to wait ten minutes before I can log back in. I slide the mouse up, click on the X in the corner, and the window closes. Time to cover my tracks.

This is a crazy Frodo Baggins moment. I'm standing at the edge of the Cracks of Doom, but I can't bring myself to do what I came here to do. And there is no Gollum around to do it for me.

"West?"

Tanner's voice catches me by surprise, and I almost fall off the chair. I didn't hear the door open, and Tanner is standing at the entrance, studying me. Good thing I stopped when I did or he would have caught me with my fingers in his bank account cookie jar.

"God, you scared me." My heart pounds.

"I got up to get a glass of milk and heard noises. What's going on?"

"Nothing. I couldn't sleep. Thought I'd get online to distract myself."

He's not buying it. He knows from my shaky voice I'm upset, but he can't have a clue why. Illuminated by the dim light of the hallway, his expression is one of trust and sympathy. He's the perfect chump...and it makes my heart squeeze.

"Come on. Let's take a walk."

"I'm in my pajamas."

"Me too."

My pajamas consist of cobalt blue, lounge pants, and a short-sleeve top—not too scandalous, I guess.

Although there's so much I can't tell Tanner, I desperately want to talk to him.

CHAPTER THIRTY-ONE

Atlanta
One year ago

"How's it going?" Jem asked, her voice in my earbuds kept cutting out, probably because my phone was in butt-dial position and I kept bumping into things as I unloaded boxes.

"Getting set up now," I told her. "Today is move-in day. Tomorrow they open the doors." I glanced around the convention center in Nashville, noting dozens of small vendors like us getting their booths and tables arranged. The antique jewelry and watch show wasn't the biggest and the best in the country—that honor went to the one in Las Vegas—but it had a reputation as one of the nicer and more respectable ones.

"I don't know if this is worth the money we're spending," Jem said, sounding worried. Maybe calling her to check in wasn't a great idea.

"We need to start getting our name out there. We should get enough sales to cover our expenses. The important thing is making the public, and more importantly the jewelry pros, aware of our brand."

"I know, I know." I hoped so, since we'd discussed this five hundred times. Still, a tremble of uncertainty touched her voice.

For the last fifty years, the three Js did no advertising to speak of, relying solely on local word of mouth and their listing in the phone book to drive foot traffic through the store. That might've been enough back in the seventies, but it wasn't cutting it today.

"That's why we're showing some of our nicer pieces," I added. "I don't expect anyone to drop a hundred grand for the diamond and ruby tiara, but having it on display shows that we're a player."

One question Jem didn't ask, but was rattling around in my brain, was why was I doing this? Answer? Because I liked Jem and Josi, and I wanted them to succeed. I didn't want them to lose their store and likely end up in a retirement home, or worse. Yet, at the same time, I was preparing to rob them blind.

How could I cling to two utterly contradictory positions at the same time? F. Scott Fitzgerald famously said, "The test of a first-rate intelligence is the ability to hold two opposed ideas in the mind at the same time, and still retain the ability to function." Well, that was total bullshit. It wasn't the sign of intelligence, but rather the symptom of a first-class nutjob. Which was what I felt like as I prepared to display a couple of emerald brooches I intended to steal later.

From what I read online, I had what the psychologists called a classic case of cognitive dissonance—holding two mutually contradictory views, and my mind would do everything it could to reconcile them or go insane. My idiot brain was a perfect example of the meat paradox. How can people who care about animals also eat them? How indeed.

On the morning of the first day of the show, I sat behind two glass display cases we rented for my tiny booth, a bowl of logo pens we were giving away at my elbow. The first couple hours passed with lots of window shoppers who stopped to "ooh" and "aah" at our big-ticket items and chat me up about the store. Not surprisingly, no one had heard of us. I handed out a lot of our bold yellow business cards, which I designed.

Shortly before lunch, my first serious buyer stopped by. Maybe in his early forties with nicely cut brown hair and a well-trimmed beard, this guy radiated money. Several things tipped me off: a really nice suit, the Gucci sunglasses propped on his head, and the expensive rings he wore. Although I wore a pricey pantsuit and one of our better pearl necklaces around my neck, I felt underdressed next to this dude.

"Can I take a look at that one?" he asked, pointing to a Cartier woman's watch. It was one of the nicer pieces I'd brought.

"You have a good eye." I removed the watch from the velvet pillow in the display case and handed it to him. "Rose gold. The gems are diamonds. Five carats total. It's early twentieth century. Very rare."

After studying the watch for a couple minutes, he glanced up at me. He had the "how much?" look on his face.

"Thirty thousand dollars," I said.

"That's a little pricey," he said with a soft whistle.

"Oh, come on. Your little girl deserves it. What is it, graduation? It only happens once."

He blinked in surprise. "Yeah, how did you know it's for my daughter?"

Seriously? It wasn't that hard to read him. "Likely not your wife or girlfriend, so that leaves—"

"Wait, why not my wife?"

I pointed to the watch he was wearing. "That's a Patek Philippe Grand Complications. At least $130,000, retail. No way do you buy wrist bling for your wife that's *less* expensive than your own bling."

He smiled. "So that leaves—"

"Daughter...probably."

"My daughter Allie, actually." Then he studied the watch for several more moments. "I'm Paul Baylor, by the way. Miss—"

"West. As in rhymes with pest, zest, and best."

He chuckled at my lame remark. "All right, West, I'll take it. Can I get it gift wrapped?"

"Absolutely. And FYI, Allie is going to love it. I guarantee it."

He handed me an Amex Black Card. My fingers trembled slightly as I took it from him. First time I had ever seen one of these puppies in person. This Paul Baylor guy must have been a big shot celebrity or a billionaire hedge fund manager, although I'd never heard of him.

As soon as he left, I pulled out my phone to call Jem about the sale. We had just sold a piece that had been gathering dust in one of the safes since 1982. This sale alone would catch the Js up on their bills.

A few minutes after Paul Baylor disappeared into the crowd, a man dressed in a nice navy-blue suit with a red tie stopped by to study our pieces. I was going to let him look for a while before trying to engage him in conversation, but I could see he wanted to talk to me.

"See anything you like?" I asked.

"You holding down the fort for the boss?"

"Nope. Just me today."

"You have a fine assortment of cameos," he said, while gazing down at them.

"The ones on the left are nineteenth century," I said. "These three over here are from the 1790s, and that one over there was carved in Italy before the First World War. Most are set in fourteen carat gold, some in silver. All genuine."

He reached into his breast pocket and drew out his own cameo brooch. It had a right-facing profile of a woman carved in white shell against a burnt orange background. It was roughly the size of a half dollar.

The man offered it to me, and I took it. As he did, a woman came up beside him and bent over to examine some of our bracelets. I gave her an "I'll be with you in a moment" smile before turning my attention back to the guy. At first I was suspicious the two might be working together, but she was acting too nervous to be some kind of shill.

"I'm looking for something that's a close match to this," the man said. "It's for my wife."

I studied it for a few seconds. "We don't have anything exactly like this, although some come close. Sorry."

"Is it genuine?" he asked, catching me a little off guard. "Mine, that is."

"I can give you my opinion. It's not always an exact science, though."

He nodded.

The first thing I did was turn the brooch over and examine the back for concavity. Then I held it close to the bright lamp we had set up. Finally, I went over the carving with a jeweler's loupe. After a few minutes, I handed it back to him.

"It's a fake," I said. "Cheap resin made to look like carved shell."

"Are you sure?"

"Genuine shell is concave in the back and translucent. This is neither. Also, under 10x magnification you can always see carving marks on genuine ones. This has none, which means it was cast, not carved. Sorry. I hope you didn't pay a lot for it."

The man's eyebrows lowered in a disappointed and angry scowl. Then he stalked off without another word. He likely paid hundreds of dollars for a brooch that wasn't worth twenty. Everybody always wants to shoot the messenger.

"I think you ruined his day," the woman observed with a hint of a smile.

I shrugged. "I could have lied to him and maybe made a sale, but at the three Js we put a premium on honesty and integrity." I actually said that line with a straight face. More cognitive dissonance. I sloughed it off. This lady had the air of a buyer, so I was upshifting into sales mode. "Can I show you anything?"

"You look a little young to be a proprietor of a jewelry store."

I smiled. "I work there. The proprietors are two wonderful old ladies who have been in business in the same shop for almost their entire lives. We're not a fly-by-night operation."

The woman nodded as if I said what she expected to hear. She was in her late thirties, reasonably attractive, with bronze-blonde hair, and dressed in plain jeans and a simple frock top. Her expression was hard to read, so I wasn't sure if she was a serious customer or not. Then she fixed her eyes on me and the rest of my little booth, and I could see she wasn't here to buy.

"How are Jem and Josi doing?"

My mouth dropped open.

She smiled before saying, "Hi, I'm Jenn."

CHAPTER THIRTY-TWO

Tanner leads me out the front door, neither of us saying anything at first as we stroll down the path to the sidewalk. The summer night air is balmy and the concrete under my bare feet is warm. Beneath the fluorescent glow of the streetlights, a slug has slimed an iridescent path across the corner of the driveway. The air has a humid, musty smell. Although the houses around us are dark, the night is alive. Crickets and other creepy crawlers with exoskeletons chirp away. The only mammal sound to intrude is the distant, melancholy howl of a dog.

"Let's walk around the block," Tanner says.

"I'm fine."

He doesn't answer, but puts his arm around my shoulders, tugging me against him. I turn my face into his chest. He can see I'm agitated, despite my efforts to appear calm.

"It's okay," he says. "Just let it out."

We walk in silence with the only sound the slap of our bare feet on the sidewalk. He's not going to say anything until I do. What a sight we are, walking through this upper-crust suburbia in our PJs in the middle of the night. I pull back from him, instantly missing the warmth of his body.

"Have you ever...?" My voice is tentative and unsure. I can't find the words to finish my sentence.

"Twice," he answers. "She was—"

"I don't mean that," I say with a burst of laughter and hip check him. "I mean, have you ever had to do something, but when it came time to do it, you couldn't?"

We walk past several houses before he speaks.

"You ever hunted?"

I scrunch up my nose. "You mean kill animals?"

He nods. "Track them, kill them, butcher them."

"God no."

"I have an uncle who lives in Montana with my two cousins, who are a couple years younger than me. They used to visit us every now and then, and my uncle would tell these stories about the hunting trips they'd go on. He made it sound so adventurous."

A cool breeze washes across my body as if I don't have anything on. It feels wonderfully soothing. "Adventurous?"

"Anyway, I was hooked. I wanted to go tramping through the woods and stalk animals too. So, Dad made it happen. When I was thirteen, I flew into Missoula to spend a week with my uncle. He took my cousins and me on a deer hunting trip."

"What happened?"

"Well, after a crash course in shooting a rifle, I figured I was ready for anything. It turned out to be really boring. We sat for hours in this tree stand, waiting quietly for Bambi to stroll by."

Caught up in his story, I momentarily forget my problems and loop my arm through his. "Yeah, but think of all that macho male bonding going on," I offer.

He laughs weakly, but there's a tinge of regret. "The bonding didn't last long," he says. "On the day before I had to fly back, damn if a stupid deer doesn't waltz right out in the open and stand broadside to us. My uncle signaled for me to take the shot."

A groan escapes me. "Please tell me you didn't." He slides his arm back around my shoulder, squeezes, and falls silent. After we walk for another twenty yards, I have to know what happened. "Did you?"

"I sighted down the barrel. I had my finger on the trigger. But I couldn't do it. I just couldn't do it."

"I'm proud of you."

He narrows his eyes and a look of disagreement crosses his face. "The deer ran off and my uncle was firetruck furious. I felt like such a failure. It didn't help that my cousins teased me for being such a pussy. But looking back, I don't regret it one bit. When I stared down the gun sight, I didn't learn who I was, but I did learn who I wasn't. I'm no hunter."

We walked about halfway around Tanner's block while he talked. He doesn't know me...but he *totally* knows me. I want to tell him all about my life, even if he ends up despising me. I live inside this cocoon of secrets that walls me off from the rest of the world. It's a prison.

"Now, what about you?" he asks in a quiet voice. He's trying to be lowkey, but he wants answers.

"I told you. I'm destined for the family business."

"What kind of business?"

I exhale slowly, hoping to buy me an extra second to plot out an answer. "Wholesalers?" Talk about waxing poetic. "Jewelry mostly," I add. *That, and the occasional vineyard.* "The thing is, it's a tough business. It can get rough."

"What? Your mom's like part of the mafia?"

I snort a laugh. "No. Nothing like that. People will do anything to make a buck. Sometimes my mom does things that aren't very friendly." Wait, robbing people blind is unfriendly? When did that happen? "I find it hard to hurt people I care about. She doesn't see the problem, though."

"How does she do it?"

"Simple," I say with a shrug. "She makes it a point to never care about anyone. Problem solved."

"That's one way, I guess."

Sighing, I say, "I can't do that."

"Congratulations. You're normal." I wouldn't go that far, but I offer a faint smile.

We walk in silence, both of us staring down at the sidewalk. Our hands come together and our fingers interlace. In the grand scheme of things, holding hands is barely a blip on the relationship radar, but this feels like I'm about to cross a line.

Then, to my disappointment, we barely cover a few hundred yards before we've circled the block and arrive back in front of the Cardwell McMansion. I don't want our night to end, and he guides me up the walkway toward their darkened porch.

Once we reach the front door, he turns to face me, our bodies less than an inch apart. In the dim light, I can't make out his expression, but my breathing comes to a stop when he closes the last piece of space between us and our hips touch. I have a moment to notice he smells like coffee and sweat before he gently eases his lips to mine.

My eyes close. His lips are soft, warm, and moist. A zing of exhilaration explodes in my chest when his hands fall to my waist and his body snugs against me.

The kiss is brief, almost experimental, and when we separate, there's a tacky sensation between our lips. I have time to take one deep breath before our mouths crash together, except this time there's an urgency to what we're doing.

His mouth moves against mine, and when our tongues collide, insistent and searching, he eases me back until I'm pressed against the wall. My arms loop around his neck and I tangle my fingers in his short hair, pulling us together tighter. His hands shift from my hips, tracing their way up my body until his fingertips lightly brush my ribs, causing me to arch my hips even tighter against his.

The kiss goes on and on until my lips buzz with tingling numbness. After a few minutes, we break apart, but neither one of us speaks. My heart is pounding, and my insides are liquid fire.

"I think this calls for ice cream," he says a bit breathlessly.

"Okay."

Ice cream sounds good. A brief chocolate break might give my mouth a chance to recover and reload.

Once inside the kitchen, we transfer several scoops of vanilla caramel fudge into two bowls. As soon as the bowls are filled, I back Tanner up against the fridge and lean into him for another kiss. Ice cream can wait. The heat of his body against mine cannot. I drag my hands up under his shirt over his hard-muscled stomach while his fingers glide up under my top.

The ice cream is melting by the time we finally call a time-out and make our way to the table, both of us breathing heavily. His cheeks are as flushed as mine feel.

He sits first and then takes my wrist, tugging me onto his lap. A twist of my body, I straddle him, and my arms link around his neck. The touch of his skin blazes against mine, and our lips lock together like the opposite ends of two powerful magnets. His hands are in my hair, mine are in his.

This is a sex position.

I have never been in a sex position before.

Oh, I've certainly read about them. And, hey, I watched *Game of Thrones*.

Still.

My usual cool and detached inner self has fled the building, retreating in the face of a raging lava monster. I always thought the first time I had sex, I would feel awkward, maybe a little shy, maybe a little scared. I don't feel any of those emotions now. What I feel is what I imagine a person senses after they jump off a cliff—inevitability. You are no longer in control of your body. External forces have taken command and you are simply along for the ride.

Tanner's hands stamp a red-hot exclamation to my crazy thoughts as the soft touch of his fingers slides up under my pajama top. I want to lean back and yank his shirt up over his head and toss it as far away as I can, but that would mean breaking off the kiss and losing his touch. I can't do it. Not yet.

I am about to have sex with Tanner Cardwell. Sex is going to happen.

In Cold War terms, the superpowers have pushed their nuclear buttons and launched intercontinental ballistic missiles at their targets. They can't be recalled. I don't care.

Our bodies are locked together. Tanner and I have officially jumped off the cliff, and the ground is rushing toward us in a wild blur.

Bring it on.

Our freefall comes to a shuddering halt at the sound of a cough from behind me.

We both freeze.

Tanner breaks off the kiss, and I turn to see what the interruption is.

Tonya stands in the entryway, her arms crossed over her chest. I can't tell if she's amused, annoyed, or both.

How long has she been standing there?

I hop off Tanner's lap and yank down my pajama top…like appearance matters at this point.

"We're having a late-night snack," Tanner offers with a wobbly smile, pointing to the bowls of melting ice cream on the table.

"Oh, is that what you call it," Tonya replies dryly. "Ah, don't wake Janey up with your…noshing."

The raging flood of lust of thirty seconds ago recedes fast, and my normal cognitive functions are sparking back to life.

What am I doing? I'm doing exactly what Mom told me not to do, exactly what I promised I wouldn't do. I'm falling for this guy. Correction: I've *fallen* for this guy.

My mom's words drift out of the ether between my ears—*"He comes from a different world. A world you're not a part of and never will be."*

Is she right?

All I know is I promised I'd never let myself get attached to my mark ever again. Things will end badly. They always do.

"I better get some sleep," I say.

Tonya lifts an eyebrow in an "are you serious?" expression, and Tanner starts to say something as I turn away, but I ignore him and casually walk out of the kitchen. As soon as I'm out of sight, I race for the den, close the door, and lean back against it.

Deep breaths, West. Deep breaths.

A short while later, I hear him tramping up the stairs to his room.

"What are you doing?" I whisper out loud.

Choices. I'm doing choices.

In *The Matrix* terms, I can take the red pill and see how deep the rabbit hole goes, or I can choose the blue pill, go back to being my mother's daughter, and believe whatever I want to believe.

With a muttered curse, I swallow the blue pill, retrieve my phone, and punch the speed dial for Mom. I'm such a freaking coward.

At this hour, Mom is asleep and it'll take her two minutes to sit up, another thirty seconds to grope around the nightstand for her phone, and by then the call will have gone to voicemail. What will I say?

Her phone rings only once.

"West?" she says, sounding wide awake.

A mixture of regret and shame washes through me.

"Could you pick me up?"

Total silence.

"I want to come home."

CHAPTER THIRTY-THREE

From the window in the den, I watch Mom arrive in her red Maxima rental, park at the curb in front of Tanner's house, and flick off the car's lights. It's five-thirty in the morning, and inside the Cardwell manor, it's as silent as a tomb. Everyone is sound asleep. Not me.

With my flats in one hand and a bag of my clothes slung across one shoulder, I tiptoe as quietly as possible toward the front door, and I wince a couple times as my weight causes the hardwood floor to squeak. The hinges on the front door creak in protest as I open it enough to squeeze out, but no lights go on inside, so my getaway is apparently a clean one. I debated leaving a note for Tanner, but I wasn't sure who might find it, and besides, what exactly was I going to say?

Mom says nothing when I open the backseat door, fling in my bag, and then climb into the front passenger seat. She doesn't even glance over at me. She simply restarts the engine and shifts into drive. The cloudless night sky begins to glow orange and yellow with the approaching sunrise, but the streetlights are still on and the road ahead lies in shadows. We drive in silence for several minutes.

"You were right," I finally say. "I don't fit in here." I gesture vaguely at the nice, suburban homes sliding by on either side. "I didn't understand before."

"Now you know," Mom says. "Look, I'm sorry about yesterday. I shouldn't have let you push my buttons like that."

She doesn't sound sorry, and she's not apologizing for hitting me. I guess she thinks it was really my fault for provoking her. I'm not surprised. Mom doesn't admit to mistakes. Like doing so would open the floodgates and wash her life away.

"I don't know where I belong anymore."

"You belong with me," Mom says. "You need to trust me like you used to."

I'm too tired to argue, too defeated. She is right about one thing. I don't trust her like I used to. Things have been off between us for the last year. Part of me wants our life to go back to the way it was before Atlanta, but some mornings I wake up and feel like I'm not supposed to be here. It's that feeling you get when you're driving down the highway and gradually you realize you missed the turnoff a ways back. You're going the wrong way.

It's too confusing. I sense a killer headache taking over my sleep-deprived brain.

"Peter and I talked," Mom says. "We want to try a different approach to closing out the sale. We pushed you too hard. You've done enough."

"So, I'm out?"

She nods. "You're out."

I'm relieved. I don't want to be the one who hurts Tanner and his family. I'll let Mom and Peter do that. I guess I'll hide in the basement, read my Kindle, and work on forgetting all about Tanner Cardwell. I've forgotten before. I did it with Josi, didn't I?

What about the bank account information? I ask myself. *Should I turn it over to Mom?*

No. I'm not going to do that.

Why?

In a rare moment of being honest with myself, I acknowledge that I hope Mom and Peter fail miserably in conning the Cardwells out of their millions. No, it's more than that. I don't hope, I want. Here's my list:

I want Mom and Peter to fail.

I want them to leave Tanner alone.

I want to go back to the way it was, hitting jewelry counters manned by anonymous people.

I want to stick to robbing stores that have lots of insurance to cover their losses.

I don't want to know anybody's name.

I don't want to meet their family.

And I certainly don't want to fall in love with them. Love is for chumps, marks, and fools.

Is this too much to ask of the universe?

"You hungry?" Mom asks when we're on the outskirts of Stockton.

"Starved, but there's no decent food until we get to Fairfield. Trust me."

I'm right on this one in terms of restaurants, but on the east side of the Sacramento River, Mom guides the car into the parking lot in front of a rickety two-story shack with a long awning. White lettering spells out Delta Farmers Market. They are actually open at six in the morning.

Almost everything is in season, so produce bins inside the store are heaping with apples, pears, peaches, oranges, etc. Too many choices, so I wander around unsure of what to get. When I meet up with Mom at the register, I'm carrying a basket with a pound of fat, red strawberries and two baseball-size plums. She has a yellow-reddish peach and an apple. She whips out a twenty to pay the nice gentleman.

Back on the road, neither of us says anything as we eat. The strawberries are amazing, and I quickly gobble them up, tossing the green tops back in the bag.

"When you are young," Mom says out of the blue, "you think you have lots of options and all this freedom, but you don't. Not really."

Options? Freedom? She's clearly got me confused with a normal person who has a real life. "And your point is?"

"We are what we are. That means some doors are open to us and some are closed. It's a fact of life."

"How do you know you can't go through a particular door until you try?"

"You don't. But after trying enough times, you learn. *I* learned. No reason you have to go through that same painful experience."

After taking a huge bite of one of my plums and swallowing, I ask, "What are we really talking about here?"

"You let yourself develop feelings for that boy," she replies, "and it got in the way of doing your job."

"Am I not allowed to ever have feelings for a guy?"

"Come on, West," Mom says in an aggrieved voice. "That's not what I'm saying. You *will* fall in love one day, baby. I absolutely promise that. And I will be one hundred percent behind you. But he will be someone who knows and accepts what you and I do. He won't be a mark."

"Got it. Listen, I won't ever see or talk to him again, okay? I want to leave this stupid town and get back on the road."

"Nice segue. I've been thinking about exactly that. How about you go stay with Aunt Nicoleta for a while? It's earlier than usual to head to Florida, but it might do you good to take some extra time off and have fun. I've been pushing you too hard. I forget you're only seventeen."

"What about you?"

Mom shrugs. "I'll finish up here with Peter and then take care of business in Chicago. Afterward, I'll join you."

I like this idea. Escape. Turn my back on this whole effing mess and walk away.

This thought triggers a memory of a news story I watched a couple years ago when we were in Philadelphia. A five-year-old boy was playing on the tracks at a rural railroad crossing. Dozens of people drove past, saw him, and did nothing. No one bothered to stop or even call the police. The boy was autistic and had escaped from his home. A train hit him.

Is that what I'm doing?

With a couple blinks and a shake of the head, the flashback dissolves.

***

Traffic was murder, and the midmorning sun blazes angrily by the time we reach the vineyard. Already the air is becoming uncomfortably dry and hot: today is going to be another scorcher. No matter. My plan is to spend today inside packing up my stuff and preparing to blow this taco stand for good.

Mom is taking me to the San Francisco International Airport tomorrow morning and putting me on a plane to Kissimmee, Florida. I can't wait. In the meantime, I flee to my favorite leather couch downstairs. I need to close my eyes and drowse my troubles away for a few hours.

I can't.

I extract my phone from my back pocket and frown at the dead screen. I forgot to turn it on. When the phone springs to life, I stab the text icon and stare down at a string of texts from Tanner starting at seven in the morning. His messages all include a question that begins with what, where, or why. I also have several unanswered voice messages from him.

I should delete them. He has too many questions I won't be able to answer. Mom's way is probably best. She'll explain my sudden departure, telling him I had to leave abruptly in order to visit my dying paternal grandmother or something like that. Tanner will probably buy this story.

Except I can't. Fine, I'll send him one text. That's it.

Me: *Sorry. I'm not trying to ghost you. I have to sort some things out.*

Okay, that's lame...and actually I am trying to ghost him. My fingers attack the screen again.

Me: *You're really great.*

Okay, that's...gushy. And I sound like his soccer coach giving him a pep talk during the game. I should stop while I'm behind. I can't explain to him what's going on with me even if I wanted to because I don't even understand it. What does it matter anyway? By the end of tomorrow, I'll be landing at Orlando International Airport and leaving all of this behind me like I've done many times before.

Only who am I kidding? This isn't like blowing town after a big job. This is going to hurt. Again.

I have a less than a day before we leave for the airport. I decide to lie down on the sofa for a bit. Within seconds sleep engulfs me. I'm not sure how long I'm out of it.

Not long enough.

***

"*West.*" Mom hollers down the stairs, startling me awake. Her voice is like a sonic boom.

"*What?*" I'm slightly annoyed at being screamed at like a puppy not fully housetrained.

"We have a problem. Hurry."

Oh, for fudge sake.

CHAPTER THIRTY-FOUR

Atlanta
One year ago

I stood there gaping at the woman who said her name was Jenn, the long-lost granddaughter and niece of Josi and Jem. Talk about blindsided. I was so flabbergasted, I couldn't get any words out.

"Jenn?" I managed.

"Yeah, and who are you exactly?" Jenn asked, smiling pleasantly, but there was an edge to her voice.

"Uh," I stammered, "West. West Rowan. I work for the Js."

Jenn nodded. "I can see that. You seem to know what you're doing, unlike others who shall remain nameless."

Her backhanded swipe at Jem and Josi irritated me. After hiding in a hole somewhere for years and years, if she wanted to emerge and bad-mouth her relatives, she needed to tell them to their face.

"I've seen nothing to complain about," I said. "They've been unbelievably kind to me."

She shrugged. "Well, they say senility smooths out the rough edges."

They do? Her smart-ass comment pissed me off. The fact that her smile never slipped made it worse.

"They've told me nothing but good things about you," I said calmly.

"That's hard to believe." She put her hands on her hips as if preparing for an argument. I didn't want to give her the pleasure, but sometimes my mouth gets disconnected from my brain and says whatever it wants.

"Well, if you hadn't turned your back on them for twenty years, maybe you'd be up on current events."

"You don't know anything about me or what happened," she said through clenched teeth.

"You couldn't even send a lousy postcard saying you were alive? I know one thing about you: you're a fucking coward. Jem has cried herself to sleep for years over you. I need only five seconds of your mouth to know you're so not worth it."

We stared at each other in silence. She broke first, and some of the color drained from her face. I relaxed my hands, only then realizing I had balled them tightly into fists.

"I was surprised when I arrived to see the three Js listed as a vendor. My grandmother and aunt would never do this, at least not when I knew them." Her shoulders slumped, and she folded her arms across her chest. The only family resemblance I could see was Josi's blue eyes and turned-up nose.

"I spent the last hour sitting out front," she went on, gesturing with her chin at the entrance to the exhibit hall. "I kept rehearsing what I was going to say to them, a speech I think I've been working on since Bill Clinton was president. And wow, they're not even here."

"You can still deliver your speech," I said, my anger ebbing. "Jem would be thrilled to see you. Over the moon, really."

"And Josi?"

I nodded. "Sure. Her too. I think she'd recognize you on her good days."

"And her bad days?"

"On her bad days, she thinks it's nineteen seventy-six."

Jenn let out a half chuckle. "I swore I'd never speak to them again. You know, they threw me out of the house." She arched an eyebrow up to punctuate the statement. "Josi told me not to show my face again unless…."

She stopped speaking as a middle-age black man approached us, his hand on the shoulder of a boy who appeared to be a couple years younger than me. His skin color was lighter than the man's and he had blue eyes.

"You okay, babe?" the man asked Jenn.

I studied the guy for a moment, careful not to look like I was staring. He wore a wool blazer and khaki pants. His hair was thinning on top and resting on his nose were a pair of Professor Dumbledore glasses.

The teenage kid took hold of Jenn's hand.

"West, this is my husband, Julius, and my son, Samuel."

I shook hands with both of them and muttered it was a pleasure to meet them. Then I reached into the bowl to grab a pen and handed it to Samuel. It was either the pen or a $150 gold chain, the cheapest item I'd brought. I gave the kid an awkward smile. He looked baffled at this strange, random white girl.

"Why don't we grab some lunch," Jenn said to her family. "I'll meet you at the concessions. I need to talk to West for a minute."

Julius nodded and turned to leave, but not before aiming a brief warning glare at me. The message was clear. *Don't mess with my wife.*

"I'm sorry," I said after the two wandered out of earshot. "I had no business speaking out. I just—"

"You care about them," she replied. "I can see it." Jenn heaved a deep sigh. "I'm glad they have you. I wish things could have been different for us."

Well, they have me for another couple of weeks. Then they're going to wish they had never met me. Oh what a world we live in.

"It's not too late," I murmured. "No bridge is so far destroyed that it can't be rebuilt with time and effort." I read that somewhere. Always wanted to use it, and bing, I had my chance. Felt good.

"How old are you?"

I guess I could answer that. "Sixteen. Seventeen next month."

"I was nineteen when it happened. Sophomore at Boston College. I had a nice scholarship or Josi would never have let me go. She called it a damn Yankee college. She wanted me to go to Wesleyan."

"One of the seven sisters of the south." I knew this because I spent a lot of time studying women's colleges, dreaming of attending one someday. But, since I wasn't likely to ever graduate high school, my meager dream was fairly pathetic.

"That's right."

"Scholarship to BC. That's fairly awesome. I'm jealous."

"That was when the problems really began," Jenn said with a smile. "I had put up with Josi's attitudes about stuff for a long time, but she got worse."

"What happened?"

"I met Julius." She paused to exhale a long, ragged breath. "Josi didn't take it well."

"Because he's black?" I whispered.

She nodded.

"When I brought him home for Christmas to meet the only family I had, she was horrible. Rude. She humiliated him and he left. Well, she basically drove him out the door."

I couldn't see it. I had only known Josi for six weeks, and all I saw was a kind and generous woman who wanted her granddaughter back so bad that she latched on to me of all people. Yet, she wasn't altogether there. I would never know the real Josi who Jenn knew and grew up with.

"I'm sorry," I said again. "She was wrong. I think she knows that now. Jem certainly does."

"Jem," she replied with a derisive snort. "She never had the backbone to oppose Josi in anything. She should have stuck up for me, but she stood in the corner of the room like a floor lamp and let Josi yell."

"Twenty years is a long time."

"Is it?" She uncrossed her arms and let them fall to her sides. "She told me to choose—

him or her. So I did. We were married a year later. He's a gentle soul. I couldn't put him through Josi again. And then there's Samuel. I swore I'd protect him from people like her. I could never expose him to Josi."

I frowned. Okay, maybe I could understand why Jenn stayed away so long, but the Josi she remembered bore almost no resemblance to the frail, loving woman I knew. Sure, Josi had a little dementia action going on, but she was a decent, caring person today. Maybe, like me, she had two persons inside her skin warring for control, and in the end the good Josi defeated the bad Josi. I hoped that was how it went.

"She doesn't have that much longer, you know," I told Jenn. "If you can ever see a way to come down to Atlanta, you, Julius, and Samuel would be welcomed. I can promise you that."

What the hell was I doing making such a promise? I wouldn't be there to see to it. I was truly shameless. Ah well, business is business.

She smiled at me. This time it was genuine. Then she extended her hand.

I shook it.

"I'm glad you're there for them. Take care of Jem and Josi for me."

I struggled to open my mouth to promise I would, but even I couldn't go that far. I clamped my mouth shut.

It didn't matter.

Jenn turned away from me and walked off before I responded.

I waved at her retreating back and bit my lip until it bled.

CHAPTER THIRTY-FIVE

Mom stands next to me, and we both stare daggers out the living room window at Hal Cardwell's Mercedes as it comes to a stop behind Mom's car. The person who emerges, however, isn't Hal. It's Tanner, and he has an anxious, lost expression on his face. Why is he here?

"What should I tell him?" Mom asks.

"Nothing."

"Nothing? Honey, I'm pretty sure that's not going to cut it. Why don't I say you had a seizure and I had to come and get you? I don't know, maybe you have celiac disease, or lupus? That should get rid of him."

Celiac disease. Lupus. Unbelievable. Does she realize how stupid that sounds? Yeah, I'm sick all right, but this isn't anything the Mayo Clinic can fix.

"I'll talk to him," I say. "This is my mess. I'll deal with it." I can't tell him the truth about who I am, but I need to be honest with him. I owe him this much.

"Right. You should do it. What are you going to say?"

"I'll tell him I'm a cowardly idiot for starters, and wing it from there."

She frowns. "Don't say anything that might torpedo the sale. String him along for now."

Without further word, I step out onto the porch. Tanner spots me immediately and strides over almost at a run. I approach him slowly, trying not to allow his hazel eyes suck me in.

"Hi," he says after stopping a few yards in front of me. "Sorry for the obsessed stalker-like routine here, but I had to talk to you."

"Let's take a walk, cowboy."

He guides me down a dirt road leading to the middle of the vineyard toward Condon Pool. We've barely gone ten steps when he slips his hand into mine. I hesitate at first, but then thread my fingers through his and grip tight. I can smell his deodorant—menthol, I think.

"You left." His voice is clinical, as if he's reciting an emotionless fact. "And you didn't say good-bye."

At least I can tell him the truth about this. "I got scared. *You're* scary."

He quirks his head to the side as if he didn't hear me right, but then he lapses into his trademark lopsided grin. I gaze into his deep hazel eyes, trying to resist the urge to smile back.

"You're being honest," he says. "Thanks. I appreciate it."

I shrug indifferently. "Not a big deal."

"Oh, it is, actually."

At first, I'm baffled by his words. Does he suspect something about me? He can't. Why would he be here, then?

"Trust me," he continues. "I've had enough experience with truth and lies to last a lifetime."

"What are you talking about?"

He kicks the dirt as if angry with it. "When my grandfather passed away, I told you he left everything to Dad, Tonya, and me."

"Right." With my stare, I urge him to continue.

"During the last year of his life, Grandfather needed a ton of help getting around, so he hired a caretaker to spend the days with him. Angelique prepared meals, took care of his house, did the laundry, that sort of thing. Anyway, after he died, she didn't really have anywhere to go, so we took her in as *our* housekeeper. We felt sorry for her, but also we were grateful for all she did for my grandfather."

Something about the tone of his voice makes my stomach suddenly queasy about the direction the story is heading. My uber-sensitive grifter antennae begin to tingle.

"She stayed with us for a year. We gave her the guest bedroom and insisted she eat with us at meals. We treated her like part of the family. Anyway, one day she ups and leaves in the middle of the night with no explanation."

Like me, I thought.

"The next morning, Dad was served with notice of a lawsuit. Angelique was challenging my grandfather's will."

"You're kidding."

His frown deepens. "Nope. She claimed she was more than a caretaker and that my grandfather had promised her his house and half his estate. Come to find out she was in cahoots with a sleazeball plaintiffs' lawyer the whole time she'd stayed with us."

"I don't get it."

"They didn't have any proof of her claims," he explained. "Instead, they tried to create circumstantial evidence. She pointed to the way we took her into our home as evidence that she was more than hired help. She even claimed to be a surrogate mother to me." He sucked in a ragged, deep breath before going on. "Their real plan was to extract a nice settlement in order to make her go away."

"Did you?" I ask. "Settle, I mean?"

"No. We refused. We spent months in and out of courtrooms, but we won. They didn't have even one-third of what it cost us in legal fees, but at least we got that back."

"Wow." It's all I can say. Angelique is French, not Romanian; otherwise, I might think she's a distant relation.

"Yeah, so I'm a little slow to trust people," he says in a low voice. He gives my hand a squeeze as he says this, which hits me like a punch to the gut.

Mom, Peter, and I are another version of Angelique and her sleazy lawyer, except we're better trained and rarely lose. What Angelique tried to do to Tanner and his family pales beside what me and mine are going to do to them.

Shit.

Somewhere inside me an ugly knot of indecision, stress, and tension unravels.

Finally.

I thought I could walk away from Tanner Cardwell and let Mom and Peter finish out the game. I thought I could forget and not care what happens to him and Janey.

I can't.

I did that in Atlanta. I'm not doing it again.

The path I have to take is crystal clear. I have to fix this frigging mess.

Our walk brings us to the edge of Condon Pool. The green, brackish water is flat and still as glass. Releasing my grip on his hand, I step forward a few paces to the water's edge. Without hesitation, I tug the slip of paper from my front pants pocket—the one with Tanner's bank account information—and crumple it up into a small ball. With a distinctly girl throwing motion, I toss the wad of paper into the water ten feet out, where it expands and begins to sink.

"Litterbug," Tanner teases.

I close the space between us. "I won't let anyone hurt you."

"Uh, bonus points for that, but what are you talking about?"

"You don't need to worry about the Angeliques of the world," I tell him. "Not anymore. I'll take care of them."

"You're kind of weirding me out here, West."

"I'm kind of weirding *myself* out."

Before Tanner can respond, his phone buzzes. We both recognize the annoying ring tone. "Tonya," we say at the same time. After pulling his phone out of his back pocket, he has an annoyed expression on his face when he punches the screen.

"What?" He listens for several moments before sighing. "Fine. Text me a list." He pauses to listen, his brows furrowing. "When?" He leans his head back to gaze up into the sky. "This better not be a waste of time."

"What's up?" I ask when he ends the call.

"I got to go. Tonya needs me to pick up some groceries in time for dinner. Why don't you come spend the night and we can talk some more?"

He waggles his eyebrows at me. As if Tonya or his dad would believe I'm having another slumber party with Janey.

"Can't. Maybe we can do something tomorrow."

"How about the afternoon," he replies. "Dad wants Tonya and me to go with him in the morning to visit another ranch he's found."

Another ranch? At first a scowl begins to creep over my face, but then it hits me. This is the answer. Of course!

If the Cardwells buy another property, then they won't be buying the vineyard. If they don't buy the vineyard, then it's over. No harm, no foul, and no one is the wiser. Mom and I can blow town and get back to our normal routine. Tanner still has his millions and he doesn't end up hating me.

What a perfect solution.

In fact, I should help out in this little venture so I can give the Cardwell gang a nudge in the right direction. I need to get myself invited.

"A ranch, huh? I've never seen a real ranch before."

"Oh yeah? You want to come? We can go out to lunch afterward."

"Awesome," I answer with an inward smile.

Now all I have to do is convince my mother I need to hang around for a while and tag along with Tanner and his family. Maybe I'll tell her I'm too sick to fly right now.

I don't know, celiac disease maybe?

CHAPTER THIRTY-SIX

"Turn left here," Tanner says the next morning, pointing to a narrow strip of asphalt shooting off the main road. "That's it over there."

"It" is a large house surrounded by a modest, well-maintained lawn. According to the roadside sign, this is the Mercator Ranch, the mansion Hal Cardwell may want to buy. The place I'm going to make *sure* he wants to buy.

Based on my initial impressions, the Cardwells are going to like it here. The house, while not as large as the Kostinens' sprawling manor, is still impressive and must be at least five thousand square feet. With three stories and a row of gabled windows along the top, it's too fancy to be called a farmhouse, but not quite luxurious enough to be a certified mega-mansion.

Once I park Peter's SUV behind the Cardwells' Mercedes, Tanner and I hop out. Hal, Tonya, and Janey are already milling about in front of their car, waiting for us. Janey wanted to ride with me, but Tanner gave Tonya a brief shake of his head, who nodded and persuaded Janey to go with her. Tonya gave my arm a gentle squeeze when I picked up Tanner earlier, perhaps feeling guilty her late-night interruption might have been the reason why I left so abruptly.

Coming up alongside Hal, I immediately begin my sales pitch. "Hey, this place is impressive."

"It has a pool," Janey adds, her voice bubbling with excitement.

I lean down and offer her my hand for a slap five. She smacks it with a grin.

"It seems okay," Tanner says with a shrug, sounding decidedly underwhelmed.

As we walk up to the front door, I hang back a few steps and tap the Google app on my phone. Now that I know the name and location of the ranch, I need to see what I can dig up on the property. I'm looking for any tidbits of information I can use to talk them into buying this place.

A man with a bushy mustache and gray-flecked dark brown hair marches over to us from an enormous utility shed located a few hundred yards from the house. We pause to wait for him, and I slip my phone back inside my pocket. He's tall with a rangy, slender build that makes the denim jeans he's wearing appear baggy and ill-fitting.

"Hello," he says when he approaches. "I'm Ben Rainer. Head ranch hand."

We all shake hands with him as Hal introduces us.

"Doris should be here any minute," Ben says.

I give Hal a "who in the Shire is Doris" look.

"The real estate broker I talked to," Hal says in answer to my raised eyebrow.

"What all do you grow here?" Tonya asks.

"Mostly almonds and walnuts," Ben replies. Then I notice a slight swelling along his left lower jaw—snus, or whatever they call the tobacco stuff guys jam in their mouth. Yuck.

"Good profit in it," Ben continues, "but yields are down. Damn drought. If it keeps up much longer, we may have to tear out some of the trees and go back to row crops. Of course, that's if the damn wildfires don't burn us out first."

Hal's brows furrow with concern. Where's Doris? The last thing I need is the hired help blabbing the truth about the ranch's agricultural challenges.

"Drought's almost over," I say, sounding like a biblical prophet. "We got years of El Nino action ahead of us," I push on. "Whole valley will be an Amazon rain forest in a year. Two tops." Tanner's mouth starts to slide open, as if he's been struck dumb. "That's what all the top meteorologists are saying," I hasten to add.

Fortunately, further climate discussion is interrupted by a garish pink Cadillac rumbling up behind us. What do we have here? Did a vat of Pepto Bismol explode all over her car? A slightly plump woman wearing a bright yellow dress climbs out of the car. She has fire red hair. The outfit looks like an advertisement for French's mustard, but she has the telltale smile of a salesperson. Sure enough, she begins to laugh before Hal even finishes introducing himself.

"I'm Doris Kendall," she gushes. "Call me Dorrie. What a lovely family you have, Hal."

"Thank you," he says.

Tanner is about to clarify my status as girlfriend, but I kick him lightly in the shin to shut him up.

"She thinks you're my sister," he whispers to me.

"This is going to be fun," I whisper back.

Dorrie proceeds to march us into the house and lead us through room after room. I make a show of holding hands with Tanner. Dorrie's eyebrows shoot up almost to her hairline at the apparent incest. It's a struggle not to bust out laughing.

"Are these countertops real marble?" I ask when we get to the kitchen.

"Absolutely," Dorrie replies. "When the house was refurbished this year, the owners spared no expense. The stone is absolute premium grade."

"Looks like a nice stove too," I say.

Dorrie positively beams at me. "You have a good eye, young lady. It's a top-of-the-line Viking professional stove. Brand new."

I whistle appreciatively, like I know anything about stoves, drawing a puzzled expression from Tonya. I think she may be remembering my musings on Father Serra.

Meanwhile, Janey is bored after ten minutes, so Dorrie gives her the green light to play video games in the downstairs den. As we troop upstairs to see the master bedroom, I tug out my phone and resume my Google search. I find something directly on point—a nice, juicy local newspaper article on the ranch. I skim the story quickly, let out an annoyed exhale, and resist the sudden urge to smash my phone against a wall.

The article lays out the particulars about the ranch in full, gory detail. The place is stigmatized property. Four years ago, Gerald Sellars killed his family in the living room, went upstairs, and then blew his head off in the master bedroom. He used a twelve-gauge shotgun, apparently striving for the maximum splatter pattern.

Oh, for God's sake. You've got to be kidding me.

If the Cardwells find out about Gerald, I'd have a better chance selling them on chickens and pigs that produce green eggs and ham.

I wonder if Dorrie is going to say anything. I can't take the chance. I need a few minutes alone with her so I can finesse her into helping me out. Our interests are most definitely aligned.

"The master bedroom is nice," Tanner observes, drawing an agreeable nod from Dorrie. "The other bedrooms on this level are on the small side."

"They're cozy small," I say. "If the room is too big, you feel like you're sleeping in a barn. Who wants that?"

Dorrie begins nodding agreeably. I'm her new best friend. My skin begins to crawl, however, as I cast my gaze around the master bedroom, wondering where Gerald Sellars bought it. What is the new carpet and fresh paint hiding? My entire body shivers.

"Take your time and explore around," Dorrie tells us once her official tour is over. "I'll be in the living room."

Tanner heads down a hallway, no doubt expecting me to follow, but I fast-walk back to Dorrie. She's sitting on the living room couch, staring at her phone when I sidle up alongside her.

"Hello, dear," she says when she sees me. "How do you like the place?"

"I think it's great." Then I gaze around as if searching for something.

"What are you looking for?"

"So, this is the room where it happened?" I whisper conspiratorially at her.

Her face goes ashen white. From her "oh my God" expression, I can tell she wasn't planning on mentioning the house's murderous past. Good. We're on the same page.

"Excuse me?" she stammers.

"Don't worry. I know all about it. But I'm okay with it. I like this place."

"Oh," she squeaks, then adds, "you should know the house has been completely gutted and remodeled since..." Her voice trails off into silence.

"Don't mention the history to Hal and the others," I reply. "Let me handle it later. It needs to be done delicately."

"Of course."

"What about the offering price?" I ask.

Beads of nervous sweat break out on her forehead. "The owners are willing to knock fifteen percent off."

They're willing to lower the price *if* someone finds out about the house's past, she means. Someone like me. I offer my hand. She takes it. We just made a deal. She's going to lower the price and neither of us is going to say anything further about Gerald Sellars.

When I catch up with the Cardwells, they've moved outside and are gathered in a huddle in the middle of the front yard. Tanner waves me over.

"We're going to tour the rest of the property tomorrow," Hal explains as I come to stand shoulder to shoulder with Tanner. "If we're still interested."

"What do you think of the house, West?" Tonya asks.

I shrug, trying to appear indifferent. "It looks pretty posh to me. But the key thing about this place is Tanner and Janey can still attend their same schools."

"Uh, I think we'd actually be in the Lodi school district," Tanner replies.

"Surely they'd let you finish your last year at your high school," I counter. "I mean, as long as you provide your own transportation, what's the problem?"

Janey, who's said nothing during our lawn conference, says, "I want to live at the vineyard with West."

I grind my teeth in frustration at this declaration.

"Hey, don't worry about me," I tell her. "I'd visit you here all the time."

Tanner frowns, while Tonya is chewing her lower lip, looking doubtful. I'm losing them.

"Guys, you should really come back and see the rest of the place," I say. "You haven't even gotten a close look at the swimming pool. How cool would it be to have your friends over for pool parties, Janey? Hal, this—"

"West," Tonya says, "are you getting a kickback from scary red-haired lady in the piss-yellow dress?"

Tanner and Janey both start laughing. Although I want to growl, and perhaps snarl a little too, I force myself to chuckle along with them. I'm pushing too hard. One of the first rules of the trade is you can't move too fast with people. As Mom says, it's like toothpaste—once you squeeze it out of the tube, you can't put it back.

"Okay, we're done here," Hal says, rubbing his hands. "Family meeting. We order pizza. Then we make some decisions. You're welcome to join us, West."

"Nah," I reply. "This is your decision. You're the ones who need to make it."

Maybe this gesture will cancel out any sense I'm Dorrie's shill. Janey wraps her arms tight around my waist, unwilling to let me go.

"You can have her if you want," Tonya whispers in my ear. "Drop her off tomorrow sometime."

CHAPTER THIRTY-SEVEN

Atlanta
One year ago

"How do you eat so much and not gain weight?" Mom asked.

Since I just stuffed a large forkful of a banana Belgian waffle in my mouth, I couldn't answer. Instead, I shrugged and reached for my large glass of moo and swallowed a big gulp before surveying my other plates: a side of bacon, and toast with orange marmalade.

We were sitting in a booth at a restaurant not far from Mom's hotel, enjoying a midmorning breakfast. Well, I was anyway. Mom picked at her granola and fruit with a spoon as if she harbored grave suspicions about the food.

"I can't hold off Chen any longer," Mom says. "If we're going to do this appraisal thing, we need to do it now."

"Not a problem. I'll have everything packed and ready to ship by Saturday."

Mom put her spoon down and lifted her cup of coffee.

"Everything square with Leonte?" I asked.

Mom glanced around before nodding. "He's on board."

"How long will it take him? I need to give the Js a time estimate."

"He needs three weeks for the necklace. He'll have to get the cubic zirconium custom made and do the cutting himself."

"Perfect," I said.

She took another sip of her coffee and added, "How much are you putting in the package?"

"Counting the necklace, three million insured value."

"Insured?"

"Yeah, I'm only including the stuff up to their insurance cap."

"Who gives a crap whether it's insured?"

I paused with my fork halfway between my plate and mouth, exhaled slowly, and launched into my spiel. I rehearsed this a few times, but the words I settled on slid out of my brain now that the moment arrived. Mom wasn't going to like this.

So, how to start? Baby steps. Begin with baby steps. "I want to take a break," I began. "Step away for a couple months or so."

"What?"

I tried to act nonchalant, like I was only proposing to take a couple days off. "You know, a vacation."

Mom squinted at me in confusion. Her breathing shallowed. I forked another mouthful of my waffle. "What do you mean vacation?"

I swallowed and shrugged as if it was no big deal. "I like working at the store. I think I can really help them turn things around. You know, make it profitable. It's a chance to use what I know about gemstones and jewelry, and they could really use my help."

Mom's mouth hung open, and she slowly shook her head in disbelief. About the reaction I expected. "Are you fucking kidding me? You're about to steal three million dollars from them and you want to help them turn it around? Sweetie, you got balls. I'll give you that."

I jabbed my fork at her in a "wait just a cotton-picking minute" gesture. "See, that's why I'm only including the stuff covered by insurance. When the fakes are discovered, insurance will cover all their losses and they won't be out a penny. It's like selling some of their inventory to the insurance company, except we get to have it. The store monetizes a bunch of its pieces that are lying around in safes, and we get to fence it for whatever we can get for it."

"Unbelievable," Mom said.

"It's a win-win for everybody. Well, except for the insurance company."

"That is *the* most idiotic thing I've ever heard."

"Shhh," I hissed. "You don't have to yell. Geez."

Mom slumped back and tossed her hands in the air as if seeking divine intervention. She's reacting about the way I expected, which is badly. "West. Honey. God bless you, you're the most imaginative thinker I've ever met. It does you proud. But you need to get your head out of your ass."

"What?"

"Seriously? First, what do you think is going to happen when those old ladies file a three-million-dollar insurance claim? The company is not going to pay it out and say, 'Oh here you go. Have a nice Christmas.' They're going to investigate the shit out of it."

"Of course they will," I say. "But they'll zero in on Leonte. Not me. That's why we're paying him all this money."

Mom frowned and shook her head. "If they squeeze Leonte, he'll finger me. Then the cat's out of the bag."

"No problemo." I tapped my finger on the tabletop to get her attention. "Listen, if the theft is discovered, I'll get word to Leonte in plenty of time for him to pack up and disappear."

"Maybe."

"Okay, assume the worst," I said. "Interpol catches up with Leonte in Bucharest, say, and he gives me up. Fine. I'll bail like we always do. No biggie."

Mom sighed and chewed her lower lip. "For the sake of argument, let's assume you never come under suspicion. What are we really talking about here?"

Now we reached the bottom line. What was I *really* talking about? I pushed my plate with its half-eaten waffle off to one side and folded my arms on the tabletop, leaning closer to Mom. She stared back at me, and her lower lip quivered slightly, but I couldn't tell if it was from anger, worry, regret, or something else.

"What if I'm tired of doing all this shit?" I said. "What if I want out? I'm not saying I want to break up the partnership for good, but maybe I want to step away for a bit. Call it a sabbatical. With the necklace and the other pieces, I'll be setting you up for a long, long time. You won't need me. Hell, you can have my share."

Hurt flashed in her eyes, and my heart squeezed a little. I loved my mother, but I didn't particularly love myself. I wasn't asking for a lot from the universe. I just wanted to live somewhere inside the penumbra of normal. My mother led a lonely, isolated life, constantly traveling from hotel to hotel and always looking back over her shoulder to see if someone was following. I didn't want to become that person.

My mother took a deep breath and held it, nodding slowly as if she agreed with everything I said. I thought she might, kind of, understand what I was saying, possibly even sympathize with me. So, I took another run at things.

"Listen, we could both settle down," I said. "Get a place here. Maybe in time we even open our own shop. Diana and West's—"

"Shut up," she snapped. "Will you listen to yourself? What, you want a house with a picket fence, a pet dog, and a flower garden out front? Sure, why not? You can go to high school and I'll attend PTA meetings and parent-teacher conferences. And you know what? Thursdays will be meatloaf night, and on Sundays we'll go to church potlucks. In the evenings, I'll embroider doilies and you can join the campfire scouts."

"*Girl* scouts," I corrected.

"What-the-fuck-ever."

"Sorry, could you speak up. I don't think the dishwasher in the back caught all that."

Mom's hands clenched into fists and the tendons in her neck stuck out. "Do you really want to be like all those people?"

I wasn't exactly sure who she meant. "Define *those* people."

"Take a drive through the nearest suburb and what do you think you'll find?" she asked. Then she pointed out the window as if that was the direction she wanted me to head toward. "I'll tell you what you'll find. Zombies. Zombie daddies going to zombie jobs, while plastic zombie mommies take care of their zombie brain-dead kids. They all stumble through their zombie lives half asleep until they fade away and die in a zombie nursing home."

"Seriously?"

"You're not like them. *I'm* not like them. We're awake. They're not."

"I don't believe that."

She sneered at me. "You will. One day, you will."

CHAPTER THIRTY-EIGHT

"You've reached the voicemail of Teela," a woman with a phony Southern drawl screeches in my ear. "Leave me your name and number and I'll call you back."

"Dammit, Mom, where are you?"

I've left some variation of this same voice message four times. Five hours have passed since the tour of the ranch ended, and now I'm only ten minutes from the Kostinen vineyard. I spent the afternoon in Stockton, schlepping around the downtown area, waiting for Tanner to call after their family meeting.

He never did. I don't know what's going on, but I take it as a good sign that he's not contacting me. This must mean the Cardwells have decided not to buy the vineyard and Tanner can't quite bring himself to tell me yet. Perfect.

Once word gets back to Peter that the Cardwells are not buying the vineyard, we're done here. Mom and I can leave. Tanner can get on with his normal life. One casualty is that Tanner and I will never see each other again, but there is no scenario where this can turn out any other way. My heart squeezes and I feel physically ill.

Leah is right. I'm in love with the guy.

I can't keep doing this.

After leaving my fifth voice message on Mom's phone, I toss my cell onto the passenger seat. Neither Mom nor Peter is answering their phone.

What the *hell* is going on? Usually, I'm slightly amused when I hear Mom's Teela voice, but not today. I have no idea where she dredged up the name. She says Teela is a cartoon character from her youth. Whatever. Right now, Teela is pissing me off. It's not like Mom to go dark on me like this.

Then my training kicks in. If Mom disappears on me without a heads-up, I'm supposed to assume the worst. Abort whatever I'm doing and go to ground. She's drilled this into me since forever—go someplace random, hunker down, wait.

Except I don't want to. There's got to be a perfectly mundane explanation for this situation, so I stay on my present course.

I immediately begin to question my decision, though, when I come to a stop in the driveway in front of the Kostinen mansion. It's night, and every single light in the house is out, as if no one is home. Either they've been arrested or they had to flee. Either way, I shouldn't be here. This is really dumb, but I keep walking toward the front door anyway. I know, I'd make the perfect clueless victim for a teenage sex-and-slasher film.

Once I push through the front door and confront the darkened interior, I'm barely breathing, and my muscles are so tense, they're starting to cramp. Mom's car is parked out front, so she and Peter should be here, but why is the house dark? I take a couple of cautious steps into the mudroom when the lights immediately snap on and handfuls of multicolored confetti are thrown in the air, over my head.

"*Surprise*," Mom yells.

"*There* she is," Peter proudly says.

Before I can respond, Peter pops a cork off a champagne bottle and begins pouring the foamy mess into flutes.

"What is this?" I ask. "My birthday isn't for two months." And seriously, let's not do this when that day arrives.

Mom smothers me in a hug, and even Peter joins in, making it a somewhat awkward group thing.

"I knew you could do it," Peter shouts, sounding positively ecstatic.

"Uh, do what?" I ask cautiously.

Releasing me, Mom steps back and looks me in the eye, a sloppy, silly grin on her face.

"Hal called earlier," she says. "He said they're all on board now with buying the vineyard, and they're ready to go forward immediately."

Peter gives my shoulder an affectionate squeeze. "We close in four days. *Excellent* job, Niece. Whatever you did in the last twenty-four hours, it worked as slick as snot on chrome."

"Uh, that's disgusting," I reply before slugging him on the arm. He only laughs harder.

My mouth starts to slide into a scowl, but I quickly bump it up into a fake smile and pretend to celebrate our imminent triumph. Beneath the façade, an icy lump of dread is growing in my belly. I vowed to Tanner, and to myself, I wasn't going to let this happen to him.

What do I do now? I have to think.

"I'm beat," I tell Mom and Peter later in the evening, who have moved on to a second bottle of champagne. "I'm going to bed."

"It's only eight-thirty," Mom says. "What's wrong? You're white as a sheet."

Get a grip.

I can't let her see my turmoil, but hiding it is hard. Mom can read a person cold. It's what she does. It's what *I* do. Rather than fake something, I let the genuine exhaustion I feel show.

"Long day," I mutter. "Here." I offer my half-drunk glass to Peter, who takes it and gulps down the now-lukewarm bubbly in one swallow, before emitting a gross belch. Mom doesn't say anything as I head for the stairs, but I can feel her eyes on my back.

Once I reach my room, I strip out of my clothes and take a long, hot shower, hoping the water will massage away the throbbing headache I feel coming on and help me figure out what to do. After putting on my pajamas and squeezing the water out of my hair, I leave the bathroom and discover I've missed a call. Tanner. I need to talk to him.

"West," he says after only one ring. "You heard, I assume?"

"I did."

"We're coming up tomorrow. Dad has to sign something with your uncle. What do you say we slip away and find a quiet little room in that big mansion where we can be alone?"

My skin begins to tingle at the memory of him pressed against me, but the thrill fades quickly as I confront the cold reality of what is about to happen. Once the sale closes, the Cardwells will move in, unpack boxes, hang pictures, and buy new furniture. Then, one morning a couple weeks from now, the Kostinens will drive up and march into their house, weary from a long day of planes and airports. Maybe Hal and Janey will be sitting in the breakfast nook, eating dinner when a group of strangers barge in. I hope Tanner isn't around for this part. There will be yelling. Accusations will be hurled about. Eventually someone will call the police. I wonder if it will be Hal or the Kostinens. My stomach clenches at the vision of the ensuing chaos, confusion, anger, and pain.

With a shake of my head, I force the nightmare to dissolve. I can't let it happen. I *won't* let it happen.

"Coming to kick us out now that it's about to be your place?" I say, trying to sound light and airy, even though I'm panicked.

"Not a chance. Your uncle agreed to stay on as caretaker for a year. He's going to live in the guesthouse with you and your mom."

"It'll be a step down," I say, "but we'll survive."

"I think we're going to have a great senior year at Petaluma High School next year," he says. "It's going to be weird having you more or less live with me. Weird in a cool way."

If only the lies were the truth. I would kill for this to be real—living in the guesthouse, going to school each morning with Tanner, having no secrets, telling no lies. But this is a fantasy, a really great dream I don't want to wake up from, but still only a dream.

I let the fantasy play out a little further. "We can take AP English together. That would be pretty awesome."

"We will. I—"

A loud squeal comes over the speaker, the sound of someone either yelling a death scream or Janey airing her tonsils with an excited shriek.

"That's Janey. She's thrilled about the vineyard. If you can believe it, that's her happy wail."

"When will I see you?" I ask.

"We'll be there tomorrow around noon."

Hearing Janey only solidifies my resolution to protect Tanner and his family, to stop the sale of the vineyard any way I can, regardless of what I have to do. It would have been easy if the Cardwells had simply chosen to buy another place, but with the demise of the Mercator Ranch property, that ship has sailed.

I don't see any other option but to spill the beans and tell them it's all a scam. They'll hate me, of course, but they would hate me anyway even if I didn't tell them. Whether I spill to them now or they find out later after the sale closes, either way they're going to know all about me. The real problem with telling the Cardwells everything is that Mom and Peter will also know, and they will never forgive me. I have no doubt that Mom will disown me.

There has to be another way.

These thoughts are rattling around in my head like a ping-pong ball when the proverbial light bulb goes on.

Of course. I know how I can stop this. Mom and Peter never have to know about me.

Minutes later, I creep up the stairs to the second floor, trying not to make any noise. The sound of the laughing outside on the patio drifts through the screen door. They'll be drinking champagne and telling war stories for hours. I tiptoe up to Peter's bedroom, careful to avoid the squeaky floorboard at the top of the stairs, not that Mom and Peter could really hear me over their loud voices.

Peter has the contact information for the Kostinens somewhere. It has to be on his phone, but he never lets it out of his sight. But Peter has a laptop. It should be in his room. After several minutes of searching drawers, nightstands, and under clothes strewn across the floor, I find it in the bathroom of all places, sitting on a stack of towels.

Some people do their reading on the can. I guess it's Peter's preferred place to get online. Whatever.

His machine is a MacBook Pro, which I'm intimately familiar with. On the off chance he hasn't password protected his machine, I boot it up and wait for a screen of icons, but, alas, a white box appears asking me for a password.

"Maybe it's my lucky day," I mutter.

I type "?" into the box and press Enter. It's a gamble whether Peter has set up the password hint feature or not. Some people do. A new image appears on screen. Sweet. The computer asks me if I want a hint. Why yes, I believe I do, thank you very much. One word appears: brother. With a broad smile on my face, I type in my father's name, Lucian, and presto the login prompt melts away. Immediately I go straight to Peter's email account and search his inbox for "Kostinen."

It doesn't take me long to find an email with "itinerary" in the subject line. I open it and skim down to find Anders Kostinen's name and his current location: St. Tropez, France. In parenthesis next to the place name is a long phone number. I copy it down and log out of the computer, not bothering to cover my tracks. Peter's computer skills don't extend much beyond point and click.

For the next couple hours, I sit on my bed, staring at my iPhone on the bedside table, trying to build up the courage to pick it up and make the call. Shortly before eleven, Mom and Peter come upstairs. Their party has ended, and they are ready to sleep it off.

Gazing down at the world clock app on my phone, I see it's a little before eight in the morning in France. A touch too early. I'll wait until midnight to call. This gives me an hour to agonize over what I'm doing.

My new plan is a simple one. Instead of telling the Cardwells that everything is a scam, I'm going to make an anonymous call to the Kostinens and tell them instead. The plan isn't perfect. Yes, I'm counting on the Kostinens to intervene once they learn what Peter is trying to do, but Tanner will learn the whole mess too. The key, though, is that Mom and Peter won't know I was involved. There must be a thousand possible ways the Kostinens could be tipped off, and I have to be last on the possibility list.

When midnight arrives, I grab one of my burner phones and swiftly dial the number for the elder Kostinen before I have time to second-guess myself. The phone has a strange, melodic ring tone that repeats several times. No one is answering, and I'm about to hang up when the phone clicks and an elderly man's halting voice comes on the line. His Scandinavian accent is thick.

"Hello," the man says.

"Yes, I'm trying to reach Anders Kostinen."

"That is me."

This is it.

"Sir, I have a story to tell you."

CHAPTER THIRTY-NINE

Shortly before noon the next day, I drift outside to the front patio to brood and wait for Tanner and his family's arrival. This will be good-bye. Tanner and I will only have a short time together, and I can't figure out what to tell him.

To complicate things, I haven't actually told the Kostinens about selling their vineyard. Not yet. I tried to tell Old Man Kostinen about the sale of his vineyard last night, but the old fool wouldn't hear me out. He thought I was pranking him.

"Who are you?" he bellowed at one point.

"Who cares? What matters is someone is trying to sell your property while you're out of the country."

"How did you get this number?"

"Who cares?" I repeated. "I'm telling you, by the end of the week—"

Doink.

Call ended.

Jerk.

If he's really this stupid, he deserves to lose his vineyard. If only we had time to find a buyer other than the Cardwells, I'd cheerfully scam the old man and sing the "Battle Hymn of the Republic" while doing it.

I called the bastard back five times, but he never answered again. On my last attempt, I immediately got voicemail. The moron blocked me. So I left a brief voicemail about the scam, but I doubt he'll ever listen to it. Who listens to voicemails from blocked callers?

Fine. I'll call him from another phone and keep trying different phones until I get through. Eventually, I'll make that senile old wanker listen to me. It's only a matter of time.

Until then, what about Tanner? I want to prepare him for what's coming, because it's going to hit him like a tsunami. Eventually, I *will* get through to the Kostinens, I *will* make them understand. I mean, if I have to, I'll hire a plane to fly over their resort with a sky banner saying, "Anders, Stop the Steal!"

Once I give away the game, the Kostinens and the Cardwells are going to want blood when they see the magnitude of this scam. In two hot seconds, Tanner will realize I was helping my mother and uncle defraud his family. If only I could find a way to tell him before all the dirty laundry tumbles out that I changed sides.

It shouldn't matter what he thinks of me in the end, but it does. This time it does. The important thing is nothing is stolen. When I skip town, I need to know I protected him.

As I'm fumbling in my head for what should be my final lines, the Cardwell Mercedes hums up our long driveway and brakes to a stop twenty yards away. Hal is here so he can submit his offer on the property and fork over some earnest money. It's a bit of a formality since the plan is to close the sale in a few days anyway.

The entire family has come for the event. I guess Hal wants them to see the place one more time before he takes the plunge. Janey is the first one out of the car, and she charges at me like this is a football game and I'm an open-field tackling victim. She wraps her arms around my legs, knocking me sideways.

"West," Janey hollers. "We'll be like sisters."

My heart lurches. I'm going to miss the little rug rat. Tanner approaches with a broad grin and puts an arm around my waist. His touch is still electric.

"Let the two lovebirds talk," Tonya tells Janey, who smiles up at me.

Peter holds open the front door to allow Hal, Tonya, and Janey inside the house, while Tanner and I start off on another walk through the grapes, holding hands. So the time has come. It's frustrating since there's only so much I can say at this point, but I have to say *something*.

As soon as I get through to the Kostinens and bust up the sale, the Kostinens will surely call the authorities, who will want to talk to Tanner and Hal at length about Mom and me.

I can visualize the encounter now. It takes place in a dimly lit, windowless room in the basement of the police station. A burly detective with pit stains and an extra-wide tie shows Tanner security camera pictures of me from various jobs we pulled the last couple of months. Tanner admits that "Yes, she's the girl I knew." With a smirk and a snarky comment about how gullible he is, the detective proceeds to tell Tanner all about me and all the stuff Mom and I have done. My crimes will come as a slap in the face.

"Yes sirree," I imagine the detective saying, "your girlfriend is a real piece of work, son. She's the biggest liar, thief, and all-around fraudster I've come across in thirty years on the force."

"I thought she really liked me," I can hear Tanner say.

"Love. Oldest scam in the book."

I clench my eyes shut while we walk, forcing this disturbing vision to go poof. Yes, he's going to find out all about me eventually and it won't be pretty, but I'm not going to let anyone else write my narrative. I must find a way to make him see I'm not all flimflam and razzle-dazzle. It's a façade. Behind it, I'm…well, I'm just like him. Mostly. Alone a lot. A little lost. Searching. And in love.

Once we're out of sight of the house and lost in the rows of vines, Tanner wraps his arms around me, drawing us together, and our lips meet for an urgent kiss. His hands glide down to my back, giving him leverage to crush me even tighter against him. I feel a sudden urge to wrap my legs around his waist, but we'd probably lose our balance, topple over, and one of us would get concussed.

As if reading my mind, Tanner slowly lowers us to the ground, with me lying on top of him, our lips still locked together. In this part of the vineyard, strips of mown grass separate the rows of grape trellises. The rich, loamy smell of dirt mixed with fresh-cut grass drifts over us as he pulls me tighter against his body, his hands in my back pockets. Our kiss deepens.

As much as I want this to go on and on, I have to stop. The longer I stay in his arms, the harder it's going to be for me to say what I have to say. Reluctantly I break the kiss and roll off him, immediately missing the heat of his lips and the pressure of his body.

"What's wrong?" he asks.

"I have to talk to you."

Both of us are lying on our sides, facing each other, his head propped up on one arm. Pieces of grass cling to his hair, so I brush my hand over his head, fighting the temptation to lean into him for another kiss.

"Okay," he says. "So talk."

Inhaling deeply, I reach inside myself for a dose of courage, but come up dry. I have no script for what I want to say. "I'm not exactly the girl you think I am. I mean, I am, but I'm not. Does that make sense?"

He grins. "Not even a little."

"Let me back up. There are things about me you don't know."

"And there are things about me *you* don't know."

Like ripping a Band-Aid off your hairy arm, I should do this fast and quick and let it all fly out. But I can't. So I continue to run in circles. "I don't live a...normal life." My voice is halting and unsure, which is completely out of character. "Mom and I don't have a real home, and Mom doesn't have a real *job* job." Oh God, just spit it out already. "We wander around the country, stay with friends and relatives for a while, and move on."

Tanner nods at my quasi-confession, as if he's finally understanding a foreign language.

"You're homeless," he says.

Uh, that wasn't exactly where I was going, but technically true. We don't own a home.

"I don't care about that stuff," he continues. "You don't have to be ashamed about any of it with me. You should know that by now."

Frustrated, I stare down at the grass for a second. Let's try this again. Rewind and push play. "Tanner, I'm not a typical girl. I dropped out of school in the spring of my freshman year."

This seems to have an impact. Tanner's eyes widen and his mouth falls open slightly. "West, you're the smartest person I've ever met. You could teach my AP English class, and probably do twice as good a job as Mrs. Knowles."

Another misfire. I let out a heavy sigh. Let's try a different tact. "You've read *Jane Eyre*?"

He grimaces. "Required reading."

"What, you didn't like it?"

His grimace deepens. "Too chicky."

Seriously?

"Well, you remember Mr. Rochester, right?"

He nods.

"He did a lot of bad things he hid from Jane. Yet, as hideous as he was, Jane still loved him and returned to him in the end."

"So?"

"What if I'm Mr. Rochester," I say softly, "and you're Jane? Would you still come back for me in the end?"

His eyes narrow in confusion. "You're not married to a crazy guy you keep locked up in the wine cellar, are you?"

"*No*. Of course not. I was making a literary analogy."

Tanner's phone buzzes with the Tonya ring tone. He answers it, nods several times, and shoves it back in his pocket. "Time to go," he says with a shrug as he gets to his feet and offers me a hand.

Another Tonya phone interruption? Is there some higher force at work here?

"Tanner." I take his hand and stand, but I tug him back to face me when he turns to walk away. "I'm trying to tell you something."

"What? You're not like other girls, and you're hiding an insane husband in the upstairs bedroom...figuratively speaking. I got this."

He doesn't have it at all. And why would he? *I* don't even know what I'm trying to say at this point. "I—"

"West, we'll talk later. I mean, we'll be living together. We'll have all the time in the world." He laughs softly and kisses my forehead.

Actually, this is the only time we'll have. And now it's over. I force a smile and try to make it as genuine as possible. His last memory of me shouldn't be a frown face.

So much for trying to explain the real me to him. Maybe there is no real me anymore. I've worn so many disguises, told so many lies, maybe that's all I am. A pretend person. A stick figure. Well, that's depressing.

Tanner has started walking back toward the car, so I follow a few steps behind. Mom and Peter are outside on the lawn, shaking hands with Hal and Tonya, smiles all around when we arrive. Everybody thinks the deal will close in a few days and we'll all live happily ever after. They have a couple days to savor that thought before the bubble bursts. One way or another, I will get a hold of the Kostinens and end this game for good.

I tried to tell Tanner I am more than the terrible things he's going to hear, but what a failure that turned out to be. The real me is buried so deep it would take a freaking backhoe to dig me out.

Tanner slips an arm around my shoulder as we approach the gang gathered around Hal's car. Mom glances over at me for a moment, but quickly goes back to laughing at some comment Hal made. Now that we're near the end of the game, she doesn't care what I do with Tanner. All that matters is we'll be out of here in a few days with a shitload of cash.

Tanner hops into the backseat next to Janey, but pauses before tugging the door shut, wiggling his finger for me to lean in toward him.

"I'd come back for you, West. Hideous or not. Promise."

CHAPTER FORTY

Atlanta
One year ago

"I don't want to wear this," Josi huffed in annoyance.

"You have to," I said in as patient a voice as I could muster. I glanced over at Jem to back me up on this, but she merely stood statue-like in the doorway, looking slightly horrified.

"I know how to go to the damn toilet, Jenn."

"Yes," I agreed. "Your brain knows what to do, but your body doesn't always get the message."

In the week since I returned from the jewelry show in Nashville, part of my daily routine was stripping the sheets and blankets from Josi's bed and washing them. She had become about as incontinent as it was humanly possible to be. Her internal organs were like a rain gutter system for someone's roof. Liquids came in up top and flowed straight down and out at the bottom. She had zero bladder control.

I held out the adult diaper and shook it slightly to emphasize my point. "Here. Lift your right foot." I stooped to help slide on the tan, stretch panty.

"I can pull up my own damn underwear," Josi barked.

"Yes, but you fell doing it on Wednesday. Remember? I don't want you to hurt yourself."

"Fiddlesticks."

"It's okay to accept help. It's what family is for."

Did I just call us family? Yes, I did because family is what Josi and Jem have become. I told Mom I wanted to step away and spend time with them, but the truth is I don't ever want to go back to swindling people for a living. Josi and Jem have accepted me, taken me in, and offered me a chance at a fresh start. I want to grab that chance and hang on for dear life. As for Mom, I expected her to fight me on this more than she has, so maybe I misjudged her. Maybe her heart isn't as cold and ruthless as I thought.

"Fine," Josi huffed and nodded. Still, her neck flushed red with irritation, probably more at herself than me.

Once the deed was done, I helped her dress, combed her hair, and applied her favorite Forbidden Fuchsia lipstick. Minutes later, she was ready for prime time.

Coffee cup in hand, I ambled down the stairs to flip the Closed sign over to Open and unlock the front door. It was nine o'clock on a Saturday morning. My thoughts drifted back to my meeting with the real Jenn. I planned to tell Jem about it eventually, but I kept putting it off. It would break her heart all over again to find out Jenn was alive but refused to come home or even contact her. As for Josi, I'm not sure if she could handle it. Not yet, anyway.

As usual since I started working here, I planned to be at the counters in the morning before handing off the store to Jem after lunch. Almost no one ever came into the store this early, so I had a lot of the time to read my Kindle and relax. It was a nice gig. This morning, however, was different.

Today was the big day for shipping out my chosen pieces to Leonte. I was almost done with the packing, and after that, all that remained was to wait for the pickup van scheduled to stop by at noon. I was using a specialty shipping service, which would come out to the store, get the package, and handle the transportation from there. I was mailing several million dollars of jewelry, and there weren't many shipping options for items that valuable.

As the morning wound down, it was time to put the last piece in the box: the necklace. I held it up for one last inspection. The diamond on the necklace was truly dazzling. No wonder Chen would get a premium price for it. The rest of the pieces were also exquisite. The ruby brooch alone should net us at least a hundred K.

Josi came in from the back room, shuffling her feet and gripping the doorjamb for balance. She smiled as she came over to me and then gazed at the necklace dangling from its chain in my fingers.

"What have we here?" Josi pointed to the necklace. "My goodness, that is a gorgeous one. Wherever did we get it?"

I had no idea, so I shrugged and handed it to her. She brought the diamond closer for inspection. Then Jem appeared, probably wondering where Josi had escaped to.

"That was one of Father's acquisitions," Jem said. "From the Rhodes estate, if I remember correctly."

"We never sold it? It's magnificent," Josi said.

Jem shook her head. "Father wanted to keep it in the family as an heirloom for his descendants, remember?"

"That's right. We meant to give it to Jenn." Josi held it out to me.

I caught Jem's eye and bit my lip apologetically. Josi was always saying stuff like this.

My mind wandered away from jewelry to the grilled cheese sandwich I planned to have for lunch, but Josi and I never finished the handoff. At 11:15 am, according to the antique clock on the wall, the front door rattled open, and in walked a young man with unkempt black hair and a scruffy beard. He wasn't dressed impressively—faded jeans and a red Atlanta Falcons hoodie that was too big by a couple sizes.

It didn't take a genius to see he wasn't here to buy anything. It didn't take a genius to see he was trouble.

The guy surveyed the interior, not caring in the slightest that he was casing the place in plain sight of the three of us.

"Take Josi in the back," I whispered to Jem.

Jem took two steps forward, grasped Josi by the elbow, and started to lead her out. I grabbed the shipping box, intending to slip it off the counter and out of sight.

"Hold on there," the guy said. "I think we all need to talk."

I opened my mouth to ask him what he wanted when he tugged a pistol from his back waistband. He pointed the ugly black hunk of dead metal straight at me.

Wait, was this a holdup? Today of all days some random guy off the street decides to rip us off? Fortunately, our silent alarm system was still on, so I calmly inched my hand under the counter to push the hidden button that would summon the police.

"Hands where I can see them," the guy said. "In case anyone hasn't figured it out, this is a robbery." He tossed a white pillowcase at me, which I grabbed out of the air. *"Fill it up, shopgirl,"* he shouted at me. "I want everything."

Jem began to cry quietly, while Josi simply stood there with her mouth open, too stunned to speak. The shop went silent as I hesitated for a couple moments, debating whether to comply with his command. In the end I cursed under my breath and began shoving jewelry into the bag. What choice did I have? He had a gun trained on my face.

It didn't take long to dump all the jewelry lying on trays into the pillowcase. I offered the heavy sack back to him, praying he would take it and vamoose. He snatched it out of my hand but made no move to leave.

"Now give me the box."

"What box?" I said, as if the opened box of carefully packed jewelry wasn't sitting on the counter in plain view.

He raised an eyebrow and pushed the gun closer to my nose.

"Oh, this one. Here." I pushed the box toward him and backed up a couple steps, hands raised, hoping he had enough to be satisfied.

Instead, the evil jerk swung the gun to point at Josi. Then he wiggled it in a gesture for her to give him the necklace dangling from her hand. She remained paralyzed with either fear or total confusion.

"Hand *it* over," he snarled.

When she still didn't move, he closed the ground between them, stepping past me and the display case I stood behind until he was face-to-face with Josi.

"Last chance, grandma."

"*Leave her alone*," I yelled. Then, in as calm a voice as I could muster, I said to her, "Give it to him."

Josi blinked several times, as if reanimating from a coma. With shaking hands, she offered the necklace to him, and he snatched it out of her grasp.

"Please," Josi begged. "It's an heirloom. It belongs to my family."

"Not anymore," he said with a smile.

He raised his hand to pistol whip Josi, but I slid between them at the last second when I realized what he was about to do. The butt of the gun slammed into my nose, sending me stumbling back into Josi. We both crashed to the linoleum in a heap, and Josi's head hit with a sickening thud. She didn't move. She was out cold—or worse.

I staggered to my hands and knees as warm blood and snot oozed out of my smashed nose. The mess trailed down over my mouth, hot and tangy.

The man started chuckling. "Mission accomplished. *Sânge şi vânătăi.*" He spoke Romanian. This was no random guy. No way. Even more surprising was his choice of words: *sânge şi vânătăi.* It was an odd expression. Where had I heard that before? "*Curvă,*" he said, calling me a bitch and wiping his hand on his pants.

I should've stayed on my hands and knees, but I couldn't. Josi needed help, so I stumbled to my feet, even though my head was spinning. I lost it.

My fist rocketed forward and hammered him dead on the chin. His head snapped back, and he went down like a puppet with its strings suddenly cut. He wasn't expecting me to put up a real fight. Surprised me too.

The scum lay on the ground, moaning, still clutching the gun in his hand. He tried to sit up, but I kicked him as hard as I could in the temple.

Once. Twice. A third time.

He stopped moving.

I grabbed my laptop off the counter, snapped it shut, and bashed him in the face with it twice.

"This is for breaking my nose," I yelled after the first overhand smash. "And this is for Josi," I said after the second. "And how about our special, 'buy two, get one free' sale?"

I raised my arms above my head for a third blow, but it never came. Jem grabbed my wrist, and all the strength drained out of me. I didn't even try to break free. She sobbed while shaking her head in utter disbelief at the scene around us.

I hugged her, dropping the remains of my laptop to the floor. We held each other for several moments. Then I remembered Josi.

Releasing Jem, I stumbled over and knelt at Josi's side and stared down at her face. Her skin was pale and bluish around the lips. Her chest was still.

"*Jem, she's not breathing.*"

"Oh God."

Was this a CPR moment? Yes, I believe it was.

My initial instinct was to panic, but I reminded myself I could do this. I took a basic first aid course last spring in Cincinnati. We were in between jobs, I was bored, and the class was free. So WTF. Now it was time to put that training to use, except performing CPR in class on a rubber dummy was one thing; doing it on a real person, a person I cared about, was a whole different enchilada.

"Call nine-one-one," I told Jem.

Before leaning down to begin, I used the back of my hand to swipe away the blood from my face, but I ended up smearing it all over me instead.

Forget it, no time, I told myself.

After leaning her head back and clearing her airway, I began rescue breathing as I had learned in class. I lost all track of time. I was in the middle of doing chest compressions when two EMTs came up and pulled me off her. The police arrived moments later.

I knelt on the floor a few feet away, fending off a third EMT who wanted to examine my smashed face. I was fine, dammit.

Not sure how long I stayed there, barely breathing, but my world abruptly collapsed when the two EMTs working on Josi withdrew their hands from her.

"I don't have a pulse," one said. "Looks like a heart attack."

"Okay, let's move her," the other said.

"Is she…" I started to ask.

Both of them shook their head.

"*Nooooooo.*" In the middle of a giant pool of blood, I curled up in a fetal position on the store floor, and I cried and cried and cried.

CHAPTER FORTY-ONE

"You two go relax," I tell Mom and Peter once the Cardwells left. "It's my turn to make dinner later." I need to be alone and distracted with some menial task so I can stew and agonize over what I'm going to do. I've tried twice more to reach the Kostinens on different phones, but no one answers, and on the last call I was informed that the number I called was disconnected. I'll have to rummage Peter's laptop again to find a different contact number. If I could only get sixty seconds with any member of the Kostinen family, I know I could persuade them to listen.

Calm down.

This was no time to panic. The closing was still days away. I had plenty of time to try a different approach. If the Kostinens wouldn't talk to me, what about their lawyer? They had to have at least one. Nobody as rich as them could get through life without an attorney. Only I wasn't sure how to find this person.

If nothing else works, I could always call the police. The timing might be tight. I imagined it would take days for my complaint to work its way through the bureaucracy and eventually prompt somebody to get off their butt and check into the matter. Even then, I envisioned them calling the house and talking to Peter, who would send them off on a wild-goose chase. No, the police would not be a reliable solution.

Anyway, back to dinner.

"Any preferences?" I asked.

"You choose," Peter says. "We have a ton of food. Use it or lose it."

"Steaks?" I offer.

"Medium-well," Mom says.

I raise an inquiring eyebrow at Peter. "Rare. Show me the pink and let there be blood."

Ugh.

"I'm taking a shower," Mom says before charging upstairs.

As the sun slips toward the horizon, I stroll outside onto the patio and fire up the stainless-steel grill, and then mostly sleepwalk through dinner preparation. After tossing a green salad and slicing a loaf of Italian bread to make Texas toast, I heft a plate stacked with enormous porterhouse steaks outside to the grill.

Despite my efforts to talk myself off the ledge, the anxiety inside is nearly suffocating. But I push it aside by focusing on imprinting the meat with perfect, cross-hatch grill marks. In stark contrast to everything else in the world around me, the steaks come out perfect. I should take a bow—she closes *and* she grills. But I have no sense of humor left. During dinner, Peter single-handedly downs an entire bottle of 2000 Cabernet Sauvignon, declaring it the best he's ever had, while casually noting that it retails for almost a thousand dollars a bottle. Mom is mostly silent during the meal, watching me out of the corner of her eye from time to time, as if she's waiting for me to say something.

Near the end of the meal, Peter's cell clangs with his mooing cow ringtone.

"Yes." He stands and saunters out of the dining room and into the living room. My ears strain to pick up his end of the conversation, but the words are too muffled. After a hearty laugh, Peter rejoins us, stuffing his phone in his front shirt pocket.

"Well?" Mom asks.

"That was Hal," he replies. "It worked. He took the bait. We're moving up the sale date. We close tomorrow morning at nine."

Mom thrusts her fists in the air in triumph. My heart drops like a rock into my left shoe. If I'm going to stop this, I have exactly twelve hours to do it. So much for lawyers and the police. My only option is the Kostinens, but the hard reality is that they have gone dark on me, and I've all but run out of time.

"Tomorrow?" I ask nervously. "That's really fast. How? I mean, doesn't the process take more time?"

Peter shrugs. "Normally, sure. But we're not really selling the property. You do get that, right?" He grins at me.

"Yeah, but don't we need, I don't know, papers, pens, notaries, a smelly conference room, a grumpy secretary?"

Peter shook his head. "Nope. All we need is—"

"Trust," Mom said. "We need Hal's trust, and thanks to you, we've got it."

"Never delay, never hesitate," Peter adds. "You know the drill. When you have your prey in your sights, pull the trigger."

I know his philosophy. Until lately, it was mine too. Like a lion prowling the African savanna, if prey offers itself, you take it down—no wavering, no mercy, no remorse. It's survival of the fittest. The way of nature. Except, I'm not an animal and Tanner is not my next meal. Not anymore.

Mom stares at me. I can feel her eyes boring into my skull, while I struggle to smile at Peter. Meanwhile, the blood drains out of my face.

Mom's eyebrows start to rise. She's in face-reading mode and I need to slide my game face back on before she figures out I'm edging toward a nuclear meltdown.

I have to get out of here. Only I can't. Peter isn't finished yet.

"So, let's review the game plan," he says. "Everybody pack up tonight. You need to be ready to go by seven thirty. That'll give us time to wipe the house down. As soon as Hal wires the money, we hand him the keys and leave."

"How much time do you think we have?" Mom asks.

"We should have at least a week, probably more, before anybody begins to question anything."

"Good," Mom replies with a nod. "West and I will fly to Chicago and then to Kissimmee. We're going to take some time off."

"Right," Peter says. "I'll contact you in the fall when I have the next job lined up."

"The next job?" I say. What next job? This was supposed to be a one-shot deal.

Mom bites her lower lip. "I was going to talk to you about it on the plane." She aims a disapproving glare at Peter. "We've decided to team up and focus on really big jobs from now on. It's a waste of your talent to use you on the little stuff."

My talent. They're going to make me do this again and again...and again. I can't. I absolutely can't.

With that, Peter grabs a bottle of bourbon and a shot glass from the sideboard, and heads for his room.

"You look like you're about to be sick," Mom says, after Peter has left.

"I'm fine."

"Being a closer is hard," she soothes, placing a hand on my back. She gently massages one shoulder, waiting for me to speak. I remain in my seat and don't say a word, so she presses on. "You had to immerse yourself in this boy's life, and you had to open up to him in order for him to open up to you. We all get that. I've been there too."

"I'm so confused, Mom."

"You really like him, don't you?"

I nod.

"That's why this worked," she replies. "If your feelings hadn't been genuine, he wouldn't have responded and come around."

"I wish I failed."

"I know you do. You say that now, but you'll get past this. Remember, he's not one of us. Even if he hadn't been your mark, it couldn't work. There's too much about us, about you, he'd never understand or accept."

"Why do we *do* this?" My voice cracks a little. "Why can't we have regular jobs?"

She barks out a laugh and a distant, forlorn expression steals over her face. "You think I never tried?" she replies softly. "After your father died, I took you to Boise and got a job waitressing. I hardly made enough to feed us, let alone make rent. So I started running a few games on the side to bring in some extra cash, but—"

"Let me guess, you can't ride two horses at the same time."

She smiles. "You're either all in or all out. I chose to go back to what I do best. I don't make any apologies for who I am, and you shouldn't either."

She hit the nail on the head about what bugs the horse manure out of me about my life. Mom had options. She *chose* all this. I didn't. I never asked for any of it. I was never given a choice.

"What if I'd failed with Tanner?" I ask. "What would you and Peter have done?" It's a casual question. I don't think I really care what the answer is.

"Whatever we had to. Beg, plead, cajole." She shrugs. "Or worse case, *sânge și vânătăi*."

Sânge și vânătă? A shiver runs down my spine at the sound of those strange, ugly words. I've heard them before. But where? A moment later, a vivid memory blossoms in my brain of a getting punched in the nose by that loser. Those were his words.

My breath catches and our eyes meet. "What did you say?"

CHAPTER FORTY-TWO

Atlanta
One year ago

"She's going to be fine," Doctor Gregson told Mom. "I want to keep her one more night for observation. The blow to the head gave her a nasty concussion."

Mom nodded. "What about her face?"

"Her nasal bone is broken, some cartilage fracture, but no septal hematoma. She'll be black and blue for a while, but there won't be any permanent damage. No scarring."

"The idiot." Mom sighed. "Thanks, doctor."

I overheard this conversation unfold next to my hospital bed. They thought I was asleep.

Twenty-four hours had passed since the robbery, most of which I spent in a pain med haze. Lots of people came in to visit me, including police officers asking questions and wanting to take a statement. It hurt to talk, so my responses were hoarse and brief.

This was Mom's first visit.

"I'll leave you two alone," the doctor said before turning to leave.

Mom approached my bed and gave my shoulder a nudge. "You can stop pretending to be sleeping."

"I'm not an idiot," I said.

"Resisting a man pointing a gun at you? That was really stupid."

"He was going to—"

"Never mind. It's over and you're okay." She took a newspaper out from under her arm and unfolded it in dramatic fashion. "Congratulations, by the way. You're a hero." Her gaze drifted down to the paper and she began to read. "Police Chief Daniel Sykes commended seventeen-year-old Westlyn Jenn Tinsley for her bravery and courage in breaking up an attempted armed robbery of her grandmother's jewelry store."

Westlyn Jenn Tinsley. Jem must have given the police this name. Why? Whatever the reason, Josi's death must have devastated Jem. I needed to be with her and help her through this, help us both through this. Anger surged inside me at the memory of Josi crumbling to the ground.

"It was a setup," I murmured while massaging my forehead. Despite the pain meds, a dull ache throbbed behind my eyeballs.

"I know."

"Someone tipped him off."

"I know."

I tried to shake my head in disbelief, but it hurt too bad to move. "Leonte double-crossed us."

Mom came over and clasped my free hand in hers. "I talked to Leonte. It wasn't him. As best as he and I can piece it together, someone found out about the incoming shipment and leaked the information to a gang of criminals."

"What?"

Mom squeezed my hand, and I remembered the robber's ugly sneer, how he tried to hit Josi. I winced at the memory.

Josi was dead, and a tidal wave of grief surged inside. At the same time, a heavy weight of guilt pressed down on me, making it hard to breathe. I wished that I had never walked into the three Js, set in motion the entire series of events that led to this moment. I tried to protect Josi and Jem and look where it had led.

"Do you think you can walk?" Mom asked.

"Legs feel fine. It's the rest of me that hurts like a…" I let out a long exhale. Even my eyelids ached when I blinked.

"Good. Let's get you dressed. Then we need to leave, pronto."

"What? Why?"

The doctor said I needed to stay another night. I kind of agreed with him. Why would Mom want me to leave now? What was the big rush?

"Your attacker is in a room two floors above," Mom said. "He's unconscious for now, but he's going to wake up before long."

"So?"

"So the police will question him. He'll probably talk."

"Again, so?"

"It won't take the police long to trace the robbery back to information from Leonte," she said with a grim expression. "If they get to Leonte, he'll fold like a cheap lawn chair and send them my way."

"I don't see the problem. We had nothing to do with this. All we're guilty of is trying to mail some pieces out for appraisal."

Mom shook her head. "I'm not worried about the necklace, honey. What I *am* worried about is the authorities coming around and asking us a lot of questions, looking into our lives. If that happens, other stuff—lots of other stuff—is going to come tumbling out."

"You want to run?" I couldn't believe she was suggesting this. I sort of understood her concern, but not entirely. I mean, even if the police came snooping around Mom and me, it should have become pretty clear, pretty fast that we had nothing to do with this. I got the crap beat out of me, which is hardly what you would expect to happen if I was involved. It was the truth, but I of all people knew all too well the truth was rarely much of an obstacle.

She nodded. "It's best we disappear."

"If we do that, we're going to look guilty," I said.

"I know."

"*No.*" The word flew out of me with such force that I bit my lip from the pain. "I'm not running."

If I had to leave, I was going to walk out of town with my head held high, not slink away like a cockroach scurrying from the light. Not this time. Also, I wanted to talk to Jem. She was going to need someone. If not me, then who?

"West, don't get sentimental on me."

"You go ahead. I'll meet up with you later. I need to help Jem pick up the pieces."

Mom sighed and grimaced. "Not a good idea, sweetie. She might find out about you, and it will only cause more pain. Let it go. You don't belong here."

In the end we compromised. I spent the night and checked out of the hospital in good order the next morning, but I didn't see Jem. Instead, I left a message on the store voicemail while we sped north on I-75.

After making up a flimsy story for why I had to leave town, I finished my message by saying, "Jem, I...I'll see you again." I choked back a sob and added, "I'm so sorry. Please call me." Then I gulped and read out the Nashville phone number for Jenn and Julius.

Maybe Mom was right. Maybe I didn't belong here. I had done enough damage and maybe Jem was better off without me.

CHAPTER FORTY-THREE

"What did you say?" I repeat, sliding my chair back from the dining room table.

Mom looks puzzled and blinks a couple times. "Beg, plead—"

"No. You said blood and bruises."

"Yeah, so?"

Sânge şi vânătăi. Why would she say that? It's an unusual expression. I've only heard it one other time in my life.

"That's what the guy said after he hit me," I murmur in a half-whisper, almost talking to myself.

Mom turns her gaze away. She doesn't want to look me in the eyes.

"He said it because you said it to him, didn't you?" Realization suddenly dawns. "You knew the guy, didn't you?"

"What?"

"You knew him."

"I had nothing to do with what happened," she says. "*Sânge şi vânătăi* is a common enough Romanian expression among criminals. I—"

"I said 'blood and bruises.' I never said he spoke Romanian. I didn't even tell the police that."

She blinks and licks her lips nervously. "I assumed."

Assumed? Right. "You're lying."

She stares back at me, speechless. My mother is never speechless. Then she takes a deep breath and opens her mouth to speak, but I raise my hand to cut her off.

"Don't bother. I can read it all over your face."

The air seems to vanish from my lungs and I can't breathe. I can feel the blood draining from my face as the pieces all slide into place. It was my mother all along. She set up the robbery. She found some lowlife goon and told the poor kid what to do. He was following her orders.

"Let it go," she says in a terse voice. "It's water under the bridge. It doesn't matter anymore. We've all moved on."

"And what about Josi? She *died* because of your stupid robbery."

Mom gulps and pumps her hands, gesturing for me to calm down. "Listen, sweetie, it was a mistake. I never meant—"

"*I want to know why.*" My voice is shrill, and it causes her to flinch.

Her expression hardens and her voice turns cold. "You really want to do this now?"

"Oh yeah, I really want to do this now."

The edge of her mouth inches up in a sneer. "Leonte was a mistake. Your idea was stupid. He would have charged too much."

"Whereas…?"

"Whereas Marku only cost a few thousand," she answers.

"You never even talked to Leonte, did you?"

She shrugs.

"You lied and used me like I was some…some *mark*."

She shakes her head emphatically. "No. I did what was best for you, for us."

"Best?"

"I did what I had to. You were talking crazy shit. You actually wanted to stay behind with those people. They were weak and feeble and stupid. And they completely blinded you. I had to open your eyes."

"*By killing Josi? By almost killing me?*"

Josi's death did open my eyes, but not in the way Mom intended.

As I gaze at my mother sitting near me, I see clearly who she really is, and what I see disgusts me. On the outside, she's a stunningly beautiful woman, but on the inside, there's nothing, only an empty darkness where her heart used to be. Worse, I'm on my way to becoming…just. Like. Her.

"No." Her eyes flare with anger. "That wasn't the plan. You weren't supposed to fight back. Your getting hurt was an accident."

"But Josi getting hurt wasn't," I reply bitterly.

She clamps her mouth shut and glares at me. I shake my head in disbelief. "You're right. I was blinded, blinded to what you are and what you're making me into."

"I have only ever done what was best for you."

"Best for *yourself*, you mean."

This Marku thugster wasn't only about grabbing the necklace: Mom had lashed out. She wanted to hurt Josi and make things impossible for me to remain at the three Js. She would never let go of me, and she would punish anyone who got between us. All the pain and grief she causes is her way of keeping me isolated and dependent on her. I feel used and betrayed.

When did she become this spiteful, manipulative woman? Or was she always this way and I simply never opened my eyes enough to see?

"I don't even know you anymore," I murmur.

"Grow up," she answers in a jeering voice. "You have no right to judge me. You're no different than I am. We're the same, so deal with it, daughter."

Without a further word, I rise from my chair and stride toward the basement stairs. I've heard enough.

"Remember," Mom yells at my retreating back. "We're in this together."

I know what she means. I shouldn't get any ideas of talking to the police, because if I do, she'll drag me down with her.

"Not anymore."

"Where are you going to go? What do you think you're going to do? You're nothing without me."

"Honestly, I don't much care about you any longer."

CHAPTER FORTY-FOUR

It's a little before seven in the morning, two hours before the deal closes, and the sun is steadily climbing up the morning sky, promising another blisteringly hot day. It's taken me all night to come to this place since I stormed out of the house and took the rental car.

For hours I drove aimlessly around back roads under a waxing crescent moon hanging above in a cloudless night sky, wrestling with my mother's betrayal.

A little before dawn, I drove into Bodega Bay. Nothing was open, unless you counted the convenience store I passed ten miles back. No matter. I parked the car in a trailhead parking lot and hiked out to Bodega Head in the dim light to watch the sunrise dance on the surface of the ocean.

The show was worth it. Tongues of orange and red soon sparkled on the water below. On the walk out here, I hoped to find the courage to do what I had to do. No one likes pain, and my God was this going to hurt.

With a stiff sea breeze blowing back my hair, I took my phone out of my back pocket and made the call. It was six o'clock in the morning, way too early to be calling anyone, but I knew he would answer.

The call lasted less than thirty seconds. I told Tanner we had to meet and hung up before he could ask any questions. Afterward, I chucked my phone as far as I could throw it and watched it spiral down into the sea below.

No calling him back. No second thoughts. No getting cold feet.

The spot I chose for our eight o'clock meeting is only ten minutes from the vineyard. A few miles north of us on Route 121, the road takes a hard right at a place called Big Bend, and at the turn is a small, triangular park-and-ride lot. This is the place. This is where it will happen.

The lot is mostly empty when I arrive, so I have no trouble finding a spot to park, and there are no witnesses as I yank out a tissue from the middle console and dab the stinging tears from my eyes.

Life's a bitch and then you cry.

I step out of the car to wait. The scenery isn't much to look at. There's a gas station across the road with a giant oak tree beside it, and the line of hills mark the distant horizon. This view will be burned in my memory.

One day I'll look back at this spot as a big turning point for me. Good or bad. Meanwhile, I have nothing more to do but wait.

In the words of Gaius Julius Caesar, the die is cast. It's time to ford the Rubicon and march on Rome, although I go not to conquer, but to surrender.

A green Subaru hatchback enters the parking lot and comes to a stop twenty yards away. I don't recognize the car, so I ignore it and continue studying the scenery while scanning the line of cars approaching from the east. It's ten minutes past the hour. Time is running out.

Where is he? He's late. Are you kidding me?

Someone clears his throat from behind.

I whirl around and Tanner stands halfway between the green Subaru and me. His hands are jammed into the front pockets of his khaki cargo shorts. He's wearing a gray shirt with the logo: *Zombies eat brains—relax, you're safe.*

"What are you doing skulking over there?" I ask.

"Watching you. Trying to figure out what the hell is going on."

A deep exhale escapes, and my shoulders slump. The left side of Tanner's mouth hitches up slightly. He wants to smile at me, and I want to smile back. Why not? One last time.

Leah said you don't hurt someone you love. Oh yes, you do. All the stories I've read wouldn't fixate on love the way they do if it didn't come with pain and a sharp barb that stings sometimes.

"Leah told you about her Google search?" I ask. "The one that turned up a news story about a girl named Westlyn?"

"Yeah, she showed it to me. The story said the girl broke up a jewelry heist in progress."

"That was me. I stopped a robbery. A robbery that wouldn't have happened if I wasn't trying to con the store out of the same jewelry myself."

His eyes narrow. "Con?"

I nod. "We were set to clear at least two million on that job."

A storm of warring emotions play out on his face. "What? Why?"

"What am I or why steal?"

"Both."

"I steal because I'm a thief. It's what I do. Well…did."

"Why?" His eyebrows draw together as his confusion deepens.

I never dwelt on the why of things. All that ever mattered was the where, the when, and always how much. So I give him a little child's response. "I don't know. Why not?"

"What kind of answer *is* that?" He runs his hand through his hair, clearly agitated. "What are you saying? You're some kind of career shoplifter?"

As if it were that simple. "Please. Shoplifting is what stupid people do. Mom and I travel from city to city, casing jewelry stores, running cons, and stealing the pieces we want. We are… were very good at it."

"You're *good* at it," he repeats to himself. "Well, congratulations on that. But why are you telling me this? What's going on?"

I sigh, hoping he can put two and two together and spare me from spelling out all of the gory details. From the way he stares back at me, this isn't going to happen. He's not getting it. Damn his naïve trust in people, his misplaced trust in me.

Instead of the anger I so deserve, his eyes betray his hurt, and my gut twists a little.

"My name is Westlyn Banica, not Rowen. Rowen is a lie. Last month I was supposed to go to Chicago with my mother to fence some jewelry we…we *acquired*. Instead, I came here to help my uncle."

"Help with the vineyard," he says.

"Help with *selling* the vineyard."

"What do you mean?"

Is he really going to make me say every single letter of every word? This is like the *Wheel of Fortune*, and I've spotted him every vowel and he's guessed almost every consonant, but he refuses to see the sentence.

"Tanner, my uncle isn't authorized to sell the Kostinens' vineyard any more than he's authorized to sell the state of Vermont. The owners have no idea what he's doing."

He doesn't respond.

"The sale of the vineyard is a *con*." I enunciate each word slowly and with deliberation. "Aka a scam, a hustle, a fraud, a game of sucker ball. It's all a ruse designed to swindle you out of your money. If your father goes ahead with the sale this morning, you will lose everything."

He points a finger at me, about to say something, but instead he twists around, leaving me to stare at his back. I guess he's going to walk away without another word. A moment later he turns back to me and begins to slowly clench and unclench his fists.

"Well, say something, *please*."

"Why would you do that to us?" he asks.

I give him the best answer I can. "Because it was my job. Stealing is what I do."

His face crumbles. He looks like he's about to cry. I expected anger, not this. I take a step toward him. He backs away two steps, raising his hands in defense.

"Tanner—"

"Don't. Just don't."

"I—"

"Stop talking."

"Listen to me," I say. "I was brought here because my uncle thought you were holding up the sale. My job was to persuade you to go along with the deal, but I can't do it."

"Can't? You already did. Why are we even talking?"

"So you can stop it all from happening. I tried to end it, but I failed."

"Unbelievable," he mutters.

The anguish on his face makes my heart crack. I don't want to hurt him. It would be so easy to make up a lie to explain all this, a lie that wouldn't make me look like such a douchebag, but I can't do it. I'm done conning him. "Meeting you this morning was the only way I had left to halt the deal. Believe me, if there were any other way, I would have done it. Telling you like this was the last thing I ever wanted to do."

He swears and disgust flashes across his face. I expected this, but it still cuts like a knife.

"Wow, you're really good," he finally says. "I swallowed everything you fed me hook, line, and sinker." He lets out a snort. "I really thought you liked me. How *stupid* was that?"

"Not stupid. I *do* like you." Then I go completely lame. "And more."

He waves his hand dismissively. "Oh please. You can drop the act already."

"I'm not lying now."

He chokes out a laugh.

"Yes, I was supposed to gain your trust and use it against you." I sigh heavily. "I wasn't supposed to care—"

"About ruining my life? About destroying my family? Wow, you—"

"*I wasn't supposed to fall in love with you.*"

He stares at me, mouth open.

"But I did." I have to stop and swipe at my eyes. "It's stupid and reckless and…and impossible. I'm in the process of losing everything I ever cared about. But falling in love with you is also the best thing that's ever happened to me. You may forget me, and probably you should, but I am never going to forget you."

We stare at each other like two gunfighters facing each other on Main Street, each waiting for the other to draw first. Our guns stay in our holsters.

"So now what?" he asks.

"You better call your dad fast." I glance down at my watch. "You have thirty-two minutes before it's too late."

"And you? You and your mom move on to the next patsy?"

Before I came to Petaluma, the answer to that would have been "Yes, of course." But that's not the answer today.

"No," I reply. "Mom and I are done. Time to find something else to do with my life. It's like you said that night. I didn't find out who I was by coming to this town, but you helped me figure out who I wasn't. Thank you for that."

"So you just turn around and drive away?"

"Yes."

"Aren't you worried we're going to call the police?" he asks.

"You should. I would."

His eyes narrow. "You don't care about going to jail?"

"It's no more than I deserve. I need a few days to take care of some things, that's all." I don't have time to explain to him that there are things I need to fix, things I need to answer for. After that, what happens, happens.

He nods, and I manage a weak smile before striding back toward my car. There's no Hollywood ending in sight, but I never expected one. When I open my door, he calls my name. "West."

I glance back at him. "Yeah?"

"Follow the sun."

I bring two fingers up to my lips. "I go where it leads."

CHAPTER FORTY-FIVE

Atlanta
One Year Later
Jewelry by Jem & Family

"Where's Sam?" I refocus my phone for another pic. "He said he would update the website for the new items."

I reposition the antique chandelier earrings on the velvet display so the light better reflects off the pearls. Perfect. The camera clicks, and the image pops up on my screen. Got it. It's the last shot I need.

"I think he's upstairs." Jem removes a tray from one of the display cases for storage in one of our back room safes. We're closing in fifteen minutes.

"You need to grab him by the ear and drag his butt down here."

Earrings done, now for the two Patek Phillipe nineteenth-century pocket watches. These will sell fast. No longer paying any attention to Jem, I remove the beautiful platinum pieces from their holders and begin arranging them for photos. As usual when I'm concentrating, my tongue sticks out between my lips.

"Oh, let him enjoy his video game, West."

"What? We're not paying him to play *Fortnite*. He's the one who asked for a job, remember?"

Jem grimaces as if I'm asking her to snake out the plumbing. Then, a bit sheepishly, she says, "Jenn will get off work at four. Let her talk to him."

"Wuss," I mutter.

The tiny silver bells hanging above our front door tinkle as someone comes into the store. Instinctively, I grab the watches off the counter and head for the back room. Jem is officially on counter duty in the afternoons, so let her deal with this last-minute customer.

Moments later muffled voices emanate from out front, but I ignore them. I'm too busy getting my last pics, which I'll send to Sam for posting. That is if he ever puts down his PS4 controller.

I start to hum a Romanian folk song as I finish up with the camera and my mind begins to wander. Business is good. Real good.

Since I returned last year, sales have been crazy. When I showed up at Jem's front door a week after leaving Petaluma, I didn't plan to stay for long. I didn't think she would want me to. I only came to explain and do what I could to make things right. Or at least better.

I never finished the speech I rehearsed for hours during the lonely days of driving across country along I-40. Seconds into my spiel, Jem cut me off with a hug, and then she squeezed me so tight the rest of my words vanished. Turns out she knew I was a grifter—a sharpie, in her words—from the day we met, but Josi had been sitting around waiting to die until I showed up. She *let* Josi take me in.

"I don't deserve—" I started to say that morning when she asked me if I wanted to move back into my old room

"Yes you do. You brought Jenn back to me."

So I moved back in. I expected the police to come looking for me, but they never showed. Now I have a family: Jem, Jenn, Julius, and Sam. The house is crowded, loud, and out of control sometimes. We're a little dysfunctional, but what family isn't?

"West," Jem hollers from the front room, interrupting my meandering thoughts.

I can't get anything done around here if Jem keeps pestering me. "Yeah?" I snap. "Kinda busy here."

"You have a visitor."

"One sec." I'm expecting Jem to ask me to give a quickie appraisal of somebody's grandmother's brooch. We do this as a service, but I hate it. Ninety-nine percent of the time, the junk we're shown is worth little or nothing. It's kind of a waste of my time, since we don't buy from people off the street anyway—unless they're offering us a nice discount on the Hope diamond or something.

When I enter the front room, Jem steps aside and I reach down inside myself for my best customer service smile.

"Hey, West."

I freeze. I know that voice. I know those *eyes*. A year has passed since I last looked into them, but I haven't forgotten. I'll never forget. "Tanner?"

Neither of us says anything for several beats, but he gives me a shy smile. "You look good." He jams his hands into the pockets of his cargo shorts.

His black hair is longer than when I last saw him, and he has a scruffy, two-day beard growth, but otherwise he's the boy I remember. He could be wearing clown makeup and I'd know him by his hazel eyes. "What are you doing here?"

"You're a hard person to find."

He's been searching for me? I expected the police would be hunting for me. Not him. My heart slips.

"Well, this place isn't exactly at the center of the universe." I force a laugh.

He's wearing a gray t-shirt with an orange paw print in the center, right below the word "Clemson."

"College boy, huh?"

He nods. "Freshman. Up the road a little in South Carolina." He pauses, looking sheepish. "Got a soccer scholarship."

"No more own goals?"

His smile is a little distant, a little lost on echoes of shared, private conversations maybe, as he glances down at his feet. "You look like a businesswoman."

Suddenly self-conscious, I reach down to smooth out my tweed skirt and straighten the matching blazer. I still hate dresses, but as I am now one of the proprietors of this fine retail establishment, Jem made a persuasive case I needed to look professional. "How did you find me?"

"I've been looking for you for a long time," he replies.

My breath catches. So many nights I've lain awake staring at the ceiling and wondering what he was doing at that very moment. I've come so close to reaching out to him on a number of those nights: a call, a text, an email. But I convinced myself he couldn't possibly want to hear from me ever again, and here he was searching for me all that time. I didn't make it easy for him, or anyone, to find me—old habits—and yet he didn't give up.

"I guess I didn't exactly leave a forwarding address."

"No, you didn't. But I finally caught a break when I stumbled onto this goofy website with a picture of a way-too-cheery girl dressed in a bunny costume. I'd recognize your face anywhere, even with big floppy rabbit ears."

I hold back a laugh. "That was for our Easter promotion." My cheeks heat with embarrassment at the memory of climbing into the fluffy Thumper uniform. "I really need to take that picture down from our website."

He inhales deeply while scratching the back of his head. Talking to him had never felt clumsy like this.

"Uh, your mother," he says. "You—"

"Gone. Running. Probably two steps ahead of a jail cell."

"We never called the police, you know," he says. "I didn't want..." He pauses to take a deep breath. "Sorry about your mother."

"Don't be. I'm not." My teeth scrape over my lower lip, and I start to say more, but no words come out. I'm trying hard to forget about my mother, to forget about a lot of things.

Perhaps sensing the awkwardness of the situation, Jem shuffles toward the back room, no doubt trying to escape.

Not so fast.

I grip her arm and drag her back. "This is my Aunt Jem. *Found* aunt, actually. This is Tanner. We have history."

"Pleased to meet you," they say nearly simultaneously, and they shake hands.

An awkward silence threatens to swallow us up again, so I rush to fill the void. "Interested in buying something special?" I ask. "We have the finest antique jewelry in the city."

He simply stares at me as if I'm speaking a foreign language.

"Maybe a bracelet for your sweetheart?" I hazard.

Tanner starts laughing. "I guess what you're really asking is if I have a girlfriend. And, no, I don't."

I shrug as if it makes no difference to me, but it does.

"I mean, how could I? You're a hard act to follow."

More silence.

"What about you? How many boyfriends since I last saw you?"

Don't cry, you idiot. "Nada," I reply, fighting a sniffle. "I had one once back in California, but I messed things up. I'm hoping one day I can tell him how sorry I am."

"He already knows."

Jem clears her throat. This conversation is making her slightly uncomfortable.

"Why don't you invite your friend to stay for dinner," Jem says. "Tonight is your dessert night. Speaking of which, I should check on Sam in case he's back into those cookies."

Once Jem leaves, I'm not sure what to say to Tanner. "I guess you probably know all about me by now."

"Quite a bit. Came across a lot of stories online about a mother-and-daughter team… Well, you know."

I nod. "I—"

"But, hey, are you going to invite me to dinner?"

He knows about my past but doesn't want to discuss it. He knows but he still came. My heart begins to pound. My mother would never understand this, never believe this, but I do. I am *not* my mother.

"Well, my cousin Jenn does fry up a killer pork chop. You'd like her and her family."

"Yeah, and what's this dessert you're making?"

I exhale deeply.

Must he ask?

"Apple brown betty," I say in a near whisper. Not sure why I feel slightly embarrassed to tell him, but whatever.

He starts to chuckle. "I was just thinking about apple—"

"Oh shut up." I glance away, not able to meet his eyes any longer. I'm so confused.

He places a finger under my chin and gently lifts my gaze up to meet his. I expect to see his eyes clouded with pain, possibly regret, but instead, he's smiling softly at me. "I promised I'd come back for you no matter what. Remember?" For some reason his smile broadens.

He's here despite all I've done. I may not have an insane person imprisoned in the attic like Mr. Rochester, but it's close. A weight I didn't realize I was carrying lifts from my shoulders.

I've spent the last year learning to live with my past and put it behind me, but I've had to cope with an emptiness in my heart, and only now, at the sight of him, has it finally stopped hurting.

I match his hopeful smile with one of my own. "What I remember, soccer boy, are jalapenos and green boxers."

"Nothing's changed." His expression turns serious. "So what do you say, West? Do you want me to stay?"

I could give a long response or a short one. I have so many questions, like do Hal and Tonya know he's been looking for me? What about Janey? But for this one moment, they can wait. Simple is best.

"Yes."

When he doesn't immediately respond, I add, "But if—"

He places a single finger on my lips. "I'm not going anywhere."

"Why are you really here?" I murmur against it.

His voice drops to a whisper. "What is it you always say? Follow the sun?"

"Go where it leads," I whisper back.

"I think that's what I'm doing."

His lips are on mine an instant later, and I lose myself in the kiss. It seems neither of us wants this moment to end.

We won't let it.

The road to this point has been a long and painful one, an adventure, at times harrowing, and at other times exalting. I lost people along the way, some I loved and some I didn't, it turns out, but I found people too.

I found him.

And maybe, just maybe, on this long road to me...

I found myself too.

ABOUT THE AUTHOR

KD is an attorney who, while growing up, moved around a lot before settling down on a ranch outside the town of Nespelem, Washington on the Colville reservation. Today, he lives in the great state of Maryland with his standard poodle, Aloy.

KD has published numerous young adult books as well as an eclectic mix of short stories. He has won awards for his stories and gained favorable recognition for his writing. In his spare time, he enjoys road trips, hockey, and anything to do with poodles.

Connect with KD:
website: kdvanbrunt.com
FB: KDVBauthor
Twitter: @KDVanBrunt
IG: @kdvanbrunt

www.BOROUGHSPUBLISHINGGROUP.com

If you enjoyed this book, please write a review. Our authors appreciate the feedback, and it helps future readers find books they love. We welcome your comments and invite you to send them to info@boroughspublishinggroup.com.

Follow us on Facebook, Twitter and Instagram, and be sure to sign up for our newsletter for surprises and new releases from your favorite authors.

Are you an aspiring writer? Check out www.boroughspublishinggroup.com/submit and see if we can help you make your dreams come true.

Love podcasts? Enjoy ours at www.boroughspublishinggroup.com/podcast

Made in the USA
Las Vegas, NV
25 July 2022

52138167R00152